MW00682522

Barbara Langhorst

WANT

B. Langhorst

(P)

Palimpsest Press
1171 Eastlawn Ave.
Windsor, Ontario. N8S 3J1
www.palimpsestpress.ca

Book and cover design by Kate Hargreaves (CorusKate Design)
Cover photograph by Elizabeth Lies via Unsplash
Edited by Aimée Parent Dunn
Copy edited by Ginger Pharand
Author photo by Shelley Banks

Palimpsest Press would like to thank the Canada Council for the
Arts, and the Ontario Arts Council for their support of our publishing program. We also acknowledge the assistance of the Government
of Ontario through the Ontario Book Publishing Tax Credit.

 Canada Council
for the Arts
Conseil des Arts
du Canada
 ONTARIO ARTS COUNCIL
CONSEIL DES ARTS DE L'ONTARIO
 Ontario
Ontario Media Development
Corporation

Library and Archives Canada Cataloguing in Publication

Langhorst, Barbara, 1958-, author
Want / Barbara Langhorst.

Issued in print and electronic formats.
ISBN 978-1-926794-96-9 (softcover).--ISBN 978-1-926794-97-6
(EPUB).--ISBN 978-1-926794-98-3 (Kindle).--ISBN
978-1-926794-99-0
(PDF)

I. Title.

PS8623.A527W36 2018
C813'.6   C2018-903138-7
C2018-903139-5

PRINTED AND BOUND IN CANADA

for Fr. James Gray, OSB

part one

I

M Y FATHER ALWAYS SAID that crazy was a thing that didn't just happen, no, not in *our* family. Behaviour evolved, all his books told him, people never simply snapped. But when my aunt drove flat across the country toting three small children born in four short years, she gave no warning at all. She didn't call until she'd reached Lloydminster, less than three hours away, spouting some nonsense about KGB moles, the glove compartment, a plain brown envelope holding twenty thousand dollars in slippery-soft bills. But duty was duty, blood was blood, and what could we do but set a place for trouble at our own table?

I knew better than to argue when they sent me to my room. I started up the stairs as nicely as could be. When I'd made it to the shadows, I settled just out of sight, sat there fraying at the edge of the faded carpet runner, soaking up every word while my parents talked it through.

They asked themselves why Francie would leave a man who was, by her own admission, a better-than-average provider. Of course he shouldn't mistreat her when she was pregnant, though Mom said that was all the time, or flaunt his affairs with busty women, or sell RCMP secrets to the Ruskies. There were children to think of, for Pete's sake. Marriages didn't just end, I heard them say. It took two to tango. So what if that Catholic priest told Auntie to file for divorce? Priests are *men*, my mother said. She could just imagine the hold Francie had on him. I envisioned a hammerlock. Women know what they're up to. And who could live with Francie, after all?

Well, not us, not for long, in any case. My sister Emma, who is eight years older than I am, said that it was like taking LSD being around Aunt Francie, everything went *psychedelic*, and she slowed the word waaaayy doowwwnn, gyrated and danced through the halls to show me what she meant. But even I could see that, psycho or not, Aunt Francie made our family the envy of the neighbourhood. There were no fast food joints in Edmonton in 1968 except the A&W, where you stayed in your car and turned on your headlights so the waitress would roller-skate out to take your order. But Auntie had lived in Montreal. She taught Mom to make something called *pizza* using frozen bread dough and tomato paste and green peppers and pepperoni and a ball of mozzarella you could bounce like indigo rubber if you could afford the expense.

Though her food was not fast, Aunt Francie was, and she cooked like a dream. All the men said so, even my father. Her pizzas were exotic, her turkey dinners to die for, her Sunday roasts with Yorkshire pudding were better than the Plaza's. My mother and Aunt Edna were both prize-winners, we all knew that, but even they had to admit there was something sensational about their little sister. They stood in her stylish living room and tut-tutted quietly when dinner was two hours late, but Aunt Francie just quipped, "More time for cocktails," and poured another round of Crown Royal and ginger ale for the men. Her striped apron covered her black see-through blouse and pencil-slim skirt as she whisked her fancy Hollandaise sauce. She had black nylons with seams up the back and high heels on, too, even to cook in.

My mother was all dressed up, of course we all were, and Mom looked very pretty in the latest outfit she'd sewn herself. It was navy blue. She called it a boat-necked sheath and she wore it with its trim cropped jacket and the pink silk scarf she'd found at $1.49 Day last month. The colours set off her fair hair and complexion, I heard Aunt Francie say, but before long she was offering to shorten Mom's dress to show off her beautiful legs. "For God's sake, Monique. Live!" Auntie laughed in that way only she could, all rippley and oh so loud. My mother just sipped her rye, rolled her eyes, and gave me a little wink when Auntie wasn't looking. Mom was a lady; she never, ever argued in public. I knew that hemline wouldn't budge, not even an inch.

By the time Aunt Francie had been in Edmonton for two full months, the fixer upper she'd bought with all that glove-box money was already fancy. Her hallways had shiny gold wallpaper with fuzzy black velvet designs, and there was no plastic on the white tablecloth where she set out her very best china every Sunday with the real silverware she got her little kids to help her polish.

Six months later, Aunt Francie went back to her husband down east, leaving our lives topsy-turvy. I heard my mother say that her sister's life was like something out of a magazine. Aunt Edna snorted, "*True Romance* or *True Confessions*?" That didn't sound very nice. Anything true must be good! But Aunt Francie had changed us, she'd upped the ante, Dad said, and even I could feel it.

Better Homes and Gardens started to arrive once a month in the mail, and not long after Mom announced that our living room had gone out of style. She changed the deep salmon walls to a nice soothing turquoise, and we replaced the old green tweed couch. The new sofa was sleek and modern, as dark as the *Coca-Cola* we were allowed on Saturday nights while our parents had cocktails with the neighbours. I liked to look at the pictures in the new magazine, though I was ever so careful not to smudge the coloured ink. It was a nice change, I thought, though I had no idea, really. For years our only subscription had been to *TIME*, a weekly news magazine my father poured over for hours and hours, preparing himself for what my mother called "another loud brouhaha about the state of the world" with my long-suffering Danish grandfather at Sunday dinner.

Dad's parents, my French and Irish grandparents, lived far away on a farm with our Uncle Theo. Or they used to. We'd gone up there the summer before for Granny's funeral, and Dad said we'd visit there again when hell froze over. At my age, I was not expected to understand politics, though I could spell every word on Paul's Grade 9 spelling test, including "psychiatrist." I knew what "assassination" meant, too; I'd seen it over and over and over again when I was little and our TV was brand new. There was something called the Cold War, even in summer. I remember when Jack Kennedy was alive, and then he was not, so when his brother Bobby followed in his footsteps it seemed foolish to me—foolhardy, my father said. As much as we admired the Americans and felt for their loss, my father was certain that one day they would come for our water. His theories embarrassed Emma to no end but I knew he was right. I could read signs, too.

Looking back, I can see my mother's graceful stealth as she escaped his world, the twice-daily coffee breaks with the neighbourhood women, talking of fashions in clothes and paint, the hours she spent in the chiropractor's cool blue office, just waiting for an adjustment, flipping through *Cosmopolitan* and *Vogue*, all of Dad's theories lifting away, page after page after page.

The salmon paint appeared six weeks after I did, just days after the police escorted my father to Woodward's Department Store, because Paul, then nearly seven years old, had stolen a stapler. Emma made a point of telling me all the trouble I'd caused, and that our brother was strapped with the belt and sent to bed without any supper, and henceforth suffered my father's near-constant wrath, though all that discipline, I heard Mom say, never did one single snippet of good. Mom and Dad used to shake their heads and wonder why the world was a maze that Paul never learned to find his way through. They looked for help from a battalion of doctors, social workers, and priests, but always hit the same dead end. And when the police made their weekly appearances at our front door, I would slip up the stairs to my perfect pink room, away from the angry voices.

Though she never put up flocked wallpaper, my mother kept our house stylish and chic, immaculate. We lived on tenterhooks, I heard Mom tell Aunt Edna, never knowing what fine dignitary my father might invite home without warning. It had already happened once, but we had pulled it off with what she was already serving, a golden pork roast with all the fixings, whipped potatoes, rich gravy, tiny garden carrots and fresh green beans. Oh, she'd dressed the vegetables with mint jelly and almond slivers, and thawed out a raspberry pie, and our MLA, Mr. Stevens, left happy and full of compliments. But what if it was laundry-day next time, or the menu was meatloaf or shepherd's pie or fish sticks? What would we do then? A smothering fear hovered over us. I believed that must be how Kennedy had felt, pinned by the phone in the oval office, steeling himself for a call from the Kremlin to say that the nukes were armed and launch was just minutes away.

As part of keeping up appearances, my mother took down the large gold-framed still life paintings of impossibly bright flower arrangements, their showy white and pale yellow dahlias and full-blown roses in deep pinks and corals and dark tulips so purple they were almost mere shadows against the black backgrounds. They'd been here as long as I had, but were too old-fashioned, I heard her say. I remember wondering if I'd be put away, too, since Paul was living at St.

John Bosco's by then, but my father said that was turning out to be a think-tank for enterprising young criminals rather than the reform school it was supposed to be.

Though our parents were holding their breath, I was mostly happy at that time. I adored the turquoise walls that soon showcased my father's new hobby, lakescapes in blues and browns and greens, paintings of sunny river valleys in fall colours so vibrant, so pulsing, he said, that he had to keep the photos on hand for evidence. Proof was important, even I could see that. Emma and I came to view the world through his mantra: "Look at those colours. If you painted them like that, no one would ever believe you."

There was plenty to disbelieve. For most of my childhood, we hauled water and blocks of ice and canned and fresh food and badminton rackets and toilet paper and sleeping bags out to our cottage at the lake, where we passed every day of our annual July and August vacation from school. The first one we spent in the city was the summer I turned thirteen and my mother seized her chance: she and I taped and cut in and rolled wall after wall through every room on the main floor. We had just finished a quick lunch of tasty salmon sandwiches made with Miracle Whip and minced dill pickles followed by sweet tea and sugar-topped crackle-faced gingersnaps when I happened to glance out the big picture window just as Emma drove up. I watched her get out of her rusting red Volkswagen, let herself in by the front screen door and step gingerly over the paint splats on the canvas drop cloths in the living room, where we were just about to get back to work. As she entered I climbed my ladder and started to roll, showing off my usefulness. I was no lollygagger.

"That was quite the show you missed last night," I told her from my perch near the ceiling.

"That's one way to describe it," Mom smiled broadly, brushing the hair from her forehead with the back of her hand.

Emma narrowed her pretty green eyes, glanced back and forth between us. "Why? What in the world—?"

Mom and I took one look at each other and burst out laughing. To celebrate Canada Day, we always bought the supersized set of fireworks that came in a cardboard schoolhouse as big as a shoebox, despite the fact that Dad, who'd been a teacher when he was young, inevitably got a little hot under the collar at our rendition of "We have seen the glory of the burning of the school! We have tortured all the teachers and have broke the Golden Rule." But Mom always prevailed that fun was fun, and we had ours. She made sure of that, and we never doubted her, especially since it invariably rained at the lake on the July 1st long weekend. As long as I could remember, for all those years, Mom had been the one to get the show on the road. The only time we ever saw her like this, being the star performer, doing what most people still thought of as a man's job, was when she went out in the pouring rain, wearing my father's green plaid wool work jacket, a purple paisley satin scarf on her head. She would bury the long sticks of fireworks in the wet sand on the beach and nail pinwheels to the poplars by the water. Then she'd just step back inside to light one of Dad's cigarettes, take a long drag to get a slow burn, and before we knew it she'd be setting things on fire. We'd oooh and ahhhh for a full fifteen minutes while Roman candles tossed ball after ball of fire into the sky, gushing cones showered sparks over the damp canopy of trees, and the pinwheels whizzed streams of light in every direction.

This year was different. We were in the city for the long weekend. Dad and our neighbour Bill, the realtor from next door, decided it was their turn. It was high time to show the women how the thing should be done.

I looked at Mom, and started to laugh. I struck the pose of Rosie the Riveter and choked out through my teeth, "Did you know what would happen?"

Emma was cross, waiting to hear.

Mom cleared her throat, looked around to make sure Dad was not in earshot. "It seemed like an explosive situation, if you get my drift." She smiled. "Especially when they got out the beer." She started to laugh. "But like he said, what fool can't set off a box of fireworks?"

I made a "Kaboom" sound and threw my hands in the air. The ladder wobbled for a moment, and I teetered there, almost falling, laughing my head off, just remembering.

Emma was exasperated again, but that was the norm in those days. I gasped, "The WHOLE box...all at once... the very FIRST Roman candle...fell over...straight through the grass..." I had to hang onto the ladder to catch my breath.

"Straight for the schoolhouse!" Mom choked out. "Couldn't have aimed more perfectly if he'd tried!" She bent over, holding her knees.

Emma yelped, "Oh good God, not Woodcroft?" She swivelled to look out the living room window towards the public school, kitty corner to our house. It was still standing there, white and serene and vacant.

I was on fire, I was a mind-reader, I knew what she was thinking. "No, no, no—not the school...the school*house*... nine balls of fire...straight through the grass!...Dead centre...into the fireworks box...the entire collection, every single last stick...one after the other, and then...the whole thing blew...Shebang!!"

"Oh good God!" Emma's face blanched. "Was anyone hurt?"

I shook my head. "No, not a bit." But I needed her to really imagine it, the noise and the chaos. "Flares shot in all directions, sparks showered to earth. And all those kids crow-hopping around..." I was enjoying myself almost as much as I had the night before.

Emma broke down and laughed a bit, too, thinking of Dad's hubris, but she was cross with us. How could we be so irresponsible, *Mother* especially? Emma shook her finger at us. "People have their hands blown off by fireworks. What were you thinking—?"

Mom wiped her eyes. "You're right, of course, sweetheart...They—we—were lucky, very lucky." She slowly pulled herself upright, rubbed her back, winked at me, poured more paint into her tray, and filled the wall with big Ws of white.

"All's well that ends well," I quipped, wiping my eyes with the back of my hand. "We'll never see the likes of that again."

"Let's hope not," Mom said. "Some he-men!"

Emma was on her way to Westmount Mall to shop and had the grace to seem genuinely disappointed that we couldn't go with her. We wanted to pick up steam. Our hair and our hands and our rooms soon glowed with three coats of the latest sensation that was sweeping the 70s, *Bone White*. After we'd finished, Dad's paintings floated in the serene gallery that our home had become, set off by the glamorous new Danish modern walnut dining suite with matching coffee and end tables that Mom had ordered at Eaton's. Gold wall-to-wall broadloom covered the old-fashioned polish-every-Saturday hardwood floors, and suddenly, we were content.

Or so it seemed for a long, long time.

But while my mother was used to waiting for things, the craze for white walls seemed to outlast even her patience. Emma was doing her master's in psychology and living with her fiancé Geoff, despite our parents' tut-tutting. I was already absorbed in my own little world, working downtown after my second year of an art history degree, living in a rented studio apartment across the river from the university. Paul was up north, drifting, at what my father said was a safe distance. From time to time we heard of his whereabouts through the casual gossip of friends and relatives. He broke into a cabin here or there, drank beer or ate through the stores of tinned food, but aside from that, he seemed harmless enough. He had been staying with Uncle Theo, since Dad and his brother had made up at long last. This miracle occurred at their father's funeral the year before. They started talking again, though in those days Dad rarely left Edmonton and Theo seldom phoned long distance; the prices were daunting, even for us. And at about that time, for whatever reason, my father became a man that none of us knew. He retired from selling life insurance, and put in long days in his reading chair, immersed in details about the assassination of John Lennon and the eruption of Mount St. Helen's.

One Sunday, Mom announced at brunch that she wanted to smarten things up, and Dad just smiled and said, "Why not?" as if she'd said, "Pass the croissants, please." Of course, we were all too busy to help. With the threat of Dad's surprise dinner guests no longer a concern, she had no one to consider, no one to plan for but herself. Emma and I shook our heads when she told us she was going to outfit the bathroom with fuchsia towels and brass accents and a plush wall-to-wall rug of the deepest shade of violet. "She must be channelling Francie," we joked to one another, though Francie was still down East. We could just imagine that flocked velvet wallpaper going up next. Mom's energy seemed boundless; she rounded out the week by repainting the kitchen walls in *Clotted Cream* and the cabinets in a bold mid-range coral called *Flamingo*. At last she sat down in her easy chair, closed her eyes and dozed off while Dad enjoyed working himself up over *The National, Marketplace,* and *The Nature of Things*. By the time he went to wake her, she was already cold.

WHEN THE PRIEST TOLD US SHE HAD GONE to her eternal rest, I knew better. Something so sudden takes forever to settle. She was barely fifty-five, for God's sake, and for a long time we agonized. Why in the world hadn't we helped her? How could we have let her do all that alone? We asked the doctor whether strain could have brought on a stroke. We tried so hard to sort it out. We were all so sure her strong Viking blood would carry her on as her father's had, to eighty years old, at least. Aunt Edna came to comfort us, and Aunt Francie flew in from Ottawa, but we hardly noticed them, even though Francie cried noisily during the funeral and hissed ever-so-loudly, "Why are there no tissue boxes in this church? Or garbage cans?" Aunt Edna hugged Francie then, and hushed her for us, and left us to float through the rest of the service, dazed by our grief.

We knew Mom was beloved, but even to us it seemed to be a huge turnout, a sea of storm-swept faces waving and bobbing above all the black clothes, pews of people I'd never heard of amidst so many I'd met but couldn't remember. I caught myself searching the crowd for some sign from Mom. When we stood numbly beside one another in a receiving line after the Mass, I saw my Grade 4 and 5 teachers, Mrs. Sareta, with her elaborate mile-high hairdo, and Mrs. Marion, with her grey pincurls and efficient smile. They told me they had come to see how I'd turned out and I had to swallow hard just to keep from lambasting them both. Be grateful, some wry inner voice told me. And in a strange way I was; their unbelievable nerve and tasteless gawking gave me an emotion I could tether myself to, even if it was fury. Apart from that, I was only conscious that I was in church on a Wednesday, wearing the last birthday gifts my mother would ever give me—a white shawl-collared blouse with a tiny lace trim and the pink and black flared skirt she had found at the Bay—and I was utterly absent, nodding and shaking hands as pleasantly as if I were running for office.

With the end of the mourners nowhere in sight, I made my excuses to the next long-lost cousin, though, she told me, she had come all the way from High River. I walked quickly through the unlit corridor, slipping out to sit on the concrete steps behind the church. I had to look twice to recognize him; yes, it was Paul. How long had he been there, leaning against the wall, looking uncomfortable in the suit Emma had rented for him, a cigarette pinched in his left hand? Well, the fireworks were over. He glanced at me, reached inside his jacket and held the pack out in my direction. I did the numbers in my head, calculated how old he must be. Until just before the service, I hadn't seen him for...was it really nine years? I was almost twenty, so he would be twenty-six, twenty-seven come November. He didn't look so dangerous. Just worn out, like I was. I had to admit I was curious, wanted to know his side of the legend.

We started with small talk, his smoke clouding the mosquitoes away. We had just reached the topic of what he had been up to, his words still hanging in the air, a balloon bright with the promise of an explanation at last. "I saw Mom last week, I was in getting supplies for Theo, told her it'd be two years in September." Just then Emma popped her head out the door to call us for lunch, and she stayed put, waiting to make sure we didn't dawdle. Paul played the gentleman, holding the door and following his sisters into the darkened church.

Downstairs almost every oilcloth-lined table was packed full. Soon we were seated on cold folding metal chairs beside Dad and the aunts, nodding to God knew what questions, eating slippery egg salad with watery lettuce on crustless whole wheat, all of us, the perfect family, united at last. Almost. At the side, the church ladies had laid out half-a-dozen desserts, leathery apple strudel and sugary saskatoon crumble and some airy golden meringue pie along with enormous platters of Mom's favourite hermits and crumbly matrimonial cake, and some buttertart bars oozing thick syrup. I should have been in heaven.

With her. How I wanted to be with her.

THE FUNERAL DID ABSOLUTELY NOTHING to convince me that she was gone. I felt that she still had something to tell me. I saw her everywhere, on the streets and at the park and strolling down the mall. I had no doubt why people called the dead "the late departed": she could have been running a train station with her daily arrivals and sudden departures. These ran like I did, too late and too soon. I was going through the motions, making my way to Botany or finding some excuse not to go home after my class on the Baroque, when the precise constellation of my mother's features would arise on some lovely blonde on the bus at 109 Street, or on an elegant woman stepping out from behind the vegetarian cookbooks at Audreys on Jasper Avenue. A middle-aged beauty would lift her left hand, brush her hair back from her face in just that way, and my heart would bubble with ridiculous hope. But no sooner had I thrilled to her presence than she would vanish, and I'd be left beaming into the face of one more perplexed stranger, the loss ever more excruciating, tracing each nerve, over and over and over.

My family would surely have questioned my sanity had I been foolish enough to admit to these goings on, but I knew enough to hold my tongue. Mom was using these others to carry herself to me, I was sure of it. She had something to say. Sometimes I got *this close* before the spell lifted and the owner's face reassembled. But when the opposite happened, when I could no longer recognize the living, then I worried: I would think, that's a nice-looking young woman, and before I knew it, Emma or one of my friends would walk out of the stranger and hug me hello. I was terrified, but no one would listen.

"Honestly," Emma told me, "you have to calm down. Prosopagnosia does not start at nineteen, Delphine. It's psychosomatic, it's got to be, with you it's always mind over matter. Mom always said that if anyone whispered the word *leprosy*, your fingers would fall off."

As if that were the problem.

So instead I let all that confusion and loneliness nudge me right back to the faith I had let lapse as a teenager, when the luxury of sleeping until noon had become so much more of a temptation than going to church. I had a hard time remembering the elation I'd known as a child, anxiously watching the skies, hoping to see Jesus on some billowing cumulonimbus rent with light as I walked home for lunch. But though there were plenty of clouds that broke into long shafts of sunbeams, runways fit for a King, I looked and I looked, and never saw Majesty arrive.

Even when the spectacular mile-wide F5 tornado ripped through Edmonton in July, seven years after Mom's death, I completely failed to see it because I was in the kitchen, painting.

2

ALMOST THIRTY YEARS LATER, high noon, and I was just finishing up my regular half-day at the Humboldt New Horizons Art Gallery. My colleague Stan—the half-monk, the one who got away—was on a roll. "What do they think? That 'civilization,'" he jabbed quotations in the air with two fingers on each hand, "with all its injustices, ancient and new and Internet-driven, will simply glide to a halt, and some fabulous new era of 'fairness and equality' will arrive with the fanfare of trumpets?" He jabbed again.

"Something like that," I nodded, as I glanced out the tall window in the brick wall behind his desk to see if it was still raining. Folks young and old were strolling down Main Street, toting umbrellas and sporting spring jackets, relishing the unseasonable weather, apparently without a care in the world.

"Seriously, who knows what the collapse might look like? Or whether it's already happened, and we just haven't the sense God gave a goose to see?"

As he spoke it hit me that maybe we were under some kind of attack. I sat down hesitantly in the chair across from him. I'm not sure why suddenly I felt the need to speak quietly. Aside from Hugo, Stan was the closest thing I had to a spiritual advisor, now that dear Fr. Lewis was gone. No one paid the slightest attention to our wild conversations. Although he was on a rant, he seemed busy, books and papers and invoices scattered in random piles all over his desk. But when he saw me sit down, he said, "All right, Delphine. I know that look. What's up?" He folded his arms across his chest and leaned back in his chair.

I paused.

Nadine and Marie were some thirty feet away, getting ready to set up the new show, prying crates open with a crowbar, carrying work out into the gallery, clambering up and down the ladder, creating quite a racket. I had to be certain they couldn't hear; the last thing I wanted was for Marie to know about my dilemma. On the other hand, I needed advice badly—and so, before I could lose my nerve, I just bent forward, keeping my voice as low and quiet as could be, and flat-out asked, "Do you believe in spiritual warfare?"

"Absolutely," he boomed. "It's what monks do. We're—I mean they're—God's hunting party."

I cringed. Could he be any louder? What he said had nothing to do with what I meant but I knew I had to persevere. I really needed his support. His replies were often cryptic, somehow perpendicular to my questions. I tried again. "When first I met him, Fr. Lewis told me to read St. Teresa of Avila's *The Interior Castle*. She says that once you start to seek the divine you enter into the light, but then the things that hide in the darkness can see you—and attack, right?"

"Absolutely," he boomed again. Looking straight at me, he bent forward and lowered his voice a bit: "Look at the men in the abbey. Old Abbot William, so hunched over he can't lift his head, has to twist his neck…can only look up side-ways…more of a hero than any twenty-year-old athlete. And take Fr. Sven: fell on his shotgun, thirty years in that wheel-chair. The brightest spirits, the keenest powers of discern-ment… We're aware of the dark forces around us, always, and we go forth nonetheless."

"So," I hesitated, trying to speak as quietly as I could without whispering, "A spiritual attack can harm you materially—I mean, in the physical world? Disrupt your relationships?"

Anyone else would have at least raised an eyebrow at that. Stan only said, "It's what the enemy wants. Complacency and pride and envy and fear are the tools IT uses to drive us, make us miscalculate. At first, the dark forces leave you clumsy, disrupt your judgement. Later, when you perceive them…"

He turned to glance out the window. At that moment the sun was reflecting off the windows of the building next door, light bouncing back in on us. "Think of Brother Elliot at the lake…"

My head hurt. I felt the pressure in my ears pop. His last word was a gate. It didn't even occur to me not to pass through it.

The weather was unimaginably perfect that summer at the lake—our lake—the year I turned four. We were allowed to choose a pack of cereal, our own choice; it came in tiny waxed paper-lined boxes that turned into bowls for break-fast. We had bean and bacon soup or ham sandwiches or hot dogs, roasted fresh for lunch outside every day. We swam and sunbathed and picked wildflowers that wilted before we could get them home to Mom and put into tall glasses of water. Then one day in August during breakfast, I dropped my spoon, glanced under the picnic table as I picked it up. A huge wasps' nest—the size of a basketball—hung per-fectly centred under the table. The fierce leisurely circling. The frantic disbelief, my mother and brother and sister all jumping up, the squeals and confusion when I announced what I'd discovered. Emma's allergy. Twenty minutes from Athabasca, almost never a doctor at the hospital.

But if the dangerous forces made people clumsy, that's what Stan said, clumsy was the one thing we were not that morning. What in the world had saved us? We had seen a few wasps circling our jam jars and hovering over the little quarters of honey on toast I loved, never guessing the hundreds so near, and none of us stung. Any one of us could have bumped the nest with our knees at any time—.

"His awareness protected him. He was the strongest spiritual warrior. In the end the struggle…"

My mother burned the nest at midnight.

Stan was staring at me, reading my distraction. He was clearly annoyed that I wasn't paying attention, and his manner became brusque. I forced myself to listen. He shook his head, spoke slowly and more loudly than I liked, as if he were trying to impress a key concept on some particularly unpromising candidate. "The struggle will kill us all, in the end. What you have to remember is that everything, every single thing in the entire cosmos, is completely pitted against us. And at the same time, everything, absolutely everything, is protecting us, cheering us on."

But surely good was good, and evil was evil? Could all those nuns and priests I'd had as teachers be wrong? Stan was making no sense, but I nodded anyway. As I did I could see Fr. Lewis on that last winter day, himself a nest, chickadees flocking in the trees about him, floating down to light on his slender hand.

And then I was back. Stan was looking guarded, just when I most needed his help. Surely he'd forgive me, surely he'd help me, if I told him all the strange things that had happened to us. I would start with the past, sketch the pattern before I filled in recent events.

Nonetheless, what burst from my mouth was a surprise, even to me. "So that first summer when Hugo and Gina and I moved to Saskatchewan, and the horse kicked me three times, and Gina rolled the car, and lightning struck the house twice, burnt out the satellite, telephones, and modems, and there I was the second time, standing in the shower, my hand on the metal tap, when the great burst of pink light rocked the house—that was a spiritual attack, right?"

Before I had even wrapped up, I knew I had botched it. The way I had gasped it out, it sounded so bizarre, how could he not think I was exaggerating? He'd give up on me, and then what would I do?

Stan only looked down, spread his fingers on the desk near the keyboard as if he were summoning patience, or fortitude, or some other virtue I couldn't name. At last he lifted his face to me.

He looked straight into my eyes as he boomed, "Well, no. Those were coincidences. Just poor timing."

I felt myself flush. I tried again. "It had to be an attack, right? A whack of problems designed to make us put our tails between our legs and run back to Alberta? But we were brave; we stayed, stuck to the plan. The fact that I wasn't hurt shows that we were meant to be here. Fr. Lewis as much as said so."

Stan shook his head emphatically, his long grey-brown hair rippling in waves. "Capital-C Coincidence." He paused. "You've got to understand," he said, his eyes focussed on something behind me—or within himself, I couldn't tell which. "The supernatural forces I'm talking about are trying to destroy humanity."

That kind of crazy was too much, even for me, even when I needed reassurance. I would have to figure things out for myself. As I rose to go back to work, I noticed a yellow-jacket buzz by from behind me, light on the coffee table to the left of Stan's desk, and rim the bowl of sugar, slowly.

3

WHERE WOULD A WASP COME FROM at this time of year? I must be seeing things. It was definitely time to go home now. It had rained on and off for a week, despite the fact that it was only March, a month too early for the snow to go. Last Sunday afternoon, of course, once the weekend was ending, the sun had come out and the land had started to dry off nicely, the fresh wind rattling last fall's dead leaves as they clung to the trees. Yesterday March had gone out like a lion—but it had been sleet and thunder and lightning instead of the usual two feet of snow.

I had tried, in my anxious way, to listen with all the gravity that the topic deserved and that Stan had earned, but what I really wanted now was to revel in the anticipation, no, the utter delight for what I had scheduled for the upcoming weekend: three days of complete, absolute relaxation. I knew Stan was just being Stan; he was always worked up. But I couldn't shake off that tug of dread. Maybe something important was about to happen. I told myself it was more likely that my pal Marie, who was looking suspiciously pleased with herself that morning, had crammed my old car with Styrofoam packing peanuts or fake flowers or dead chickens.

I hurried, sure I was imagining things. I gathered my work, stowed it hastily in my bag, and was making my way across the broad gleaming old maple floor when I heard it.

I could have sworn that someone right behind me clearly said, "Take papers."

I rarely heard voices like that, not these days, anyway. But as I pulled my keys from my jacket pocket, I heard it again. Calm words, stern, resolute. Insistent. "Take papers."

What in the world? I had my papers. Still, I knew it was never wise to ignore my intuition. At last I gave in and re-crossed the gallery, propped the tricky top steel door of the filing cabinet up on my shoulder, and rifled through the files of historical articles, photos, and clippings from magazines. I ran my thumb through the thick bundles of surveys and draft reports that Marie and I had compiled, two years worth of work. Surely I couldn't be expected to carry all that paper home? Between the stacks, a full-page newspaper feature about Fr. Lewis caught my eye. What was that doing there? I pulled it out, looked with real longing at the photo, set it by my bag to read over later, and kept looking through the file cabinet. At last I felt a jolt of recognition: this must be what I was looking for, a file bloated with kitchen photos and floor plans labelled with Marie's cryptic flourish of thick black pen: Kitch Reno 4 Del 03. But when I shoved the hanger in and stepped away to look over my prize by the light of the west window, the cabinet door fell shut with a BANG! so loud it rocked the building.

Everything slipped into slow mo, rolling and rolling and rolling. I forced myself to turn back to the gallery. Bulbous bright shapes floated by, neon colours, turquoise and lime green and vibrant orange. I couldn't think, and I couldn't not think. After what seemed like a long time, my eyes cleared and my thoughts settled back into sync. I glanced as casually as I could around the room, just to see if the others had noticed the racket I'd made, but they all looked the same as they had minutes before: Jim was on the phone in his office, and Marie and Nadine were seated in the corner, talking quietly, heads bent over the latest reports and piles and piles of papers. Stan was peering into the screen of his computer, oblivious. I shook my head and stuffed the folder and the article into my leather satchel, the gorgeous one that our boys, Erik and Marc, had given me for my birthday last August. Relax, I breathed. Compose yourself. All shall be well. All shall be well. All manner of thing shall be well.

I made myself stride back down the long length of the bright, shared office, past the sleek Eames chairs that faced each clean-lined mid-century desk. When I reached the back again, I surprised myself by turning to call, "See you tomorrow!" The women glanced up, squinted to see me in the dark doorway, and shouted, "Drive safely!" and "Don't work too hard!" Stan, focused on his monitor, waved goodbye without even looking up. I performed my best imitation of the Duchess of Cambridge, right hand raised, swivelling at the wrist, while I pushed hard on the steel door with my other hand and slipped outside into the parking lot.

The dusty old Toyota was waiting for me, empty. No chickens, no pranks. Just the faithful chariot that had seen me through so many soothing drives.

And love to drive I did.

As I wound my way past the open fields, I heard CBC Radio's Bob-the-Night-Sky-Guy urge listeners to rise in the middle of the night to observe the total lunar eclipse that would be in full swing early Saturday morning.

"The show is different each time," he assured listeners. "The moon's colour is determined by the amount and type of pollution in the air. Before the last eclipse there were two volcanic eruptions, one in Iceland and another in Japan. And just one month ago, the Villarrica in Chile erupted.

Three thousand people forced to evacuate. Perfectly timed," he enthused.

"And there's one last detail, if you like patterns: over the last two years, all four total eclipses fall back-to-back, no partials in between, and all take place on Israel's feast days. Apocalypse seekers are thrilled by the prospect of blood moons, a sign of sacrifice, not just copper but full-on red, a thing that will only take place if conditions are absolutely right."

Right is not the word I would have chosen. But perfectly timed, no one could argue with that. I could imagine Stan saying, as he always did, "Mother Nature loves metaphors. She's a safecracker, her ear trained to the dial on the lock of our existence—and when those tumblers line up—click, click, click—"

But surely it wasn't the moon or the weather that was tugging at me with dread. The sky was a mass of scudding clouds, thick and woolly and low, shredded by sun and bright patches of blue. I was ten minutes south of town on Highway 20. The news rattled on and on, falling oil prices, layoffs in Alberta and Saskatchewan, the dollar dropping, and then the toneless chief economist of the Central Bank came on to assert, with all the enthusiasm of a bowl of pudding, that the low dollar was good: Canadian exports were sure to soar.

"What exports?" I asked him, "with the entire economy married to the oilsands?"

Of course the important man did not reply.

As I passed the landfill, the announcer said, as cheerfully as if he were telling the time: "The president stated today that although he favours a diplomatic solution in Iran, he will not hesitate to take military action, with or without the approval of Congress, should the Iranian government refuse inspections of its military or nuclear facilities."

All the morning's free-floating anxiety had shape at last. If the U.S. really did what Israel wanted, supported "the military solution," as they called it, Russia would side with Iran, and China would—

Aside from Hugo and Stan, no one ever seemed to see the danger all around us. Even my father, the man who'd kept rows and rows of bleach bottles filled with tap water in the basement for emergencies, the man who stormed through my childhood preoccupied with missile silos and the atrocious terrorism of Yasser Arafat, even he was now too busy with his Tai Chi flash mobs at the mall and lawn bowling tournaments, keeping himself fresh and fit at eighty-two years old.

"You're just like Granny," he told me. "If you don't have enough trouble to call your own, you're always ready to borrow a pinch. Never leave home without it."

Pot to kettle, I thought, *pot to kettle*.

There was no point in trying to warn Marie, either. She had no interest in hearing that the Arctic ice would be gone in three years or that there was a new outbreak of polio or measles or whooping cough, vaccinations out of date or ineffective against the new strains. She never worried about the Chinese hackers who routinely launched cyber attacks on Canadian banks and the national defense system. She'd just glance up in disbelief for a moment, as if I didn't have the brains God gave a five-year-old, and then she'd relent, flash me that brilliant smile, throw her arm around my shoulders, and say: "You two still watching the news every night? How you find time for TV, I have no idea. It's pure sensationalism!"

As I drove past the old church, the rest of the broadcast tumbled on, but it made no sense to me. Maybe it was the early spring but suddenly the car was an oven. Either I was having a hot flash or at long last I was finally descending into hell itself. I drove on, numb thoughts floating by, a convoy of ghosts.

Somehow, before I knew how I'd driven there, I was parked in front of the small grey house. I was home. Home, at last.

4

SECONDS LATER, WHEN I OPENED MY CAR DOOR, I was greeted by the sound of the mower whirring far away. He must be out working on the back forty, as we called it, the yard and gardens we'd built from scratch that first year, when we were new to Saskatchewan and newer still to acreage living, before we'd become acquainted with the endless chores that hobby-farming held for those dreaming the life pastoral. I unpacked the car, trudged up the stone path to the house, and Lucky bounded over.

Here was someone glad to greet me, anyway. When I'd scritched the black lab's ears and fussed over him for a few minutes, I managed to open the screen door and cross the threshold before he did: it was important to maintain one's position in the pack, people were always telling me that. The two of us were crowded onto the small landing, and I reached over the dog to hang up my jacket. When I slipped off my boots, my socks got wet, and Lucky and I tangled our way up the stairs to the kitchen. I tried to think of something delicious to eat to console myself. I opened the refrigerator, and found that the last piece of pecan pie was gone. Hugo must have beaten me to it. I looked for the Genoa salami I'd bought last week, but it was already greeny-grey; the slices reproached me with their dead white eyes of fat. Suddenly, I wasn't hungry. Lucky, however, was not so fussy; he tried to help himself to the cheese sticks on the lower shelf, but I pulled him back by his collar.

In a few minutes I finished some peanut butter on two pieces of raisin toast and a quick glass of instant iced tea, but I was not what anyone would have called satisfied.

The work wasn't going to do itself, so I wandered into the dining room to clear the table—Mom's table—so that I'd have room to code the latest batch of surveys. Lucky knew the drill and settled on the floor with a soft thump. Hugo had picked up the mail and, as usual, had left it a jumble on the table. I tut-tutted to myself as I sorted the mess: catalogues, mammogram notice, an envelope thick with unsolicited labels from the Red Cross, the atrociously high SaskPower bill. But before I even started, I spied it there, lying in wait beneath the letters, the thing that promised me an hour of pure, uncomplicated relief.

The latest *Homeward* magazine.

As I touched it, a chime rang out and I jumped, drawing my hand back, just for a second. But it was only the wall clock Hugo's parents had given us for a wedding present, more than three decades ago. I was so used to it that I rarely heard it, but this time it was enough to make me glance over to check the time. It was only one-thirty. I told myself a quick looksee would revive me, sustain me through the tedium of the work I needed to do. "Lose yourself in the kitchen reno issue, SIX Before & Afters," the cover called. I couldn't resist, but I forced myself to remain standing as I flipped through, pausing now and then to study an image or read a description. It was all so fresh, so utterly charming. Before I knew it, I'd pulled up a chair at the table and had started back at the beginning, reading slowly through ads and articles alike, lingering over page after page of glossy photos. Kitchens far less miserable than mine went under the saw, the hammer, the roller—and emerged elegant, refined, soothing. It was all perfectly logical. If the kitchen was the heart of the home, ours was on life support and I didn't recall signing a DNR.

Hugo and I are impulsive people, though you would never guess it from looking at Hugo. We love the strange and the quirky, and it was in one of those odd situations that we met. I was struggling to speak Swedish when a tall stranger strode into the museum where I was interning, the Liljevalchs Konsthall. He seemed to bring the single glorious day of sun we were granted that foggy October I was in Stockholm. Before long, he'd asked all manner of questions about the collection—in charming English, of course. Before many days had passed, we were chatting over the world-famous desserts at the Blå Porten, the café next door to the museum.

Humboldt, SK (population 5,000) is a far cry from Stockholm, but seven years ago, after three children and two careers together, Hugo and I moved to our acreage, a complete 180 from life in Edmonton, AB (population one million). Humboldt's little gallery hosted an ambitious line-up of coffeehouse nights featuring local bands playing golden oldies spliced with poetry readings and sing-alongs, children's studio programs in two languages, and a series of professional workshops, not to mention rotating art shows and regular gallery hours. We did outreach to small towns within a radius of 75 km, with free seminars for seniors and cost-recovery for the rest on topics ranging from stained-glass to linocuts to salt-glazed ceramics and textile arts and of course, portraits in oil. Those last were officially my area, though I was sad to say I couldn't remember the last time I had painted for pleasure. All my time was taken up with my colleague Marie on a SSHRC research project, a full grant to survey my absolu-tively favourite thing, as my daughter Gina would say, so-called "shelter rags," or home décor magazines.

I had been teasing myself with fantasies about a new kitchen for most of my time in Saskatchewan. In March, Marie told me she was tired of watching the pile of inspiration photos colluding and whispering on my desk, said she'd help me measure the kitchen when Hugo was in town swimming laps at the pool. It was her idea to open that file, the "papers" the nameless voice had instructed me to take. It wasn't as if I was hiding anything from Hugo. It was just that from time to time I needed to get away, lose myself in the dream, go window e-shopping.

My daughter Gina did the same thing, except with clothes. It was so simple, so harmless. You just put whatever you wanted into your electronic shopping cart—adding items until you ran out of time or your interest waned, and then with two strokes of a key, you could run the total and then make it all disappear. As quick as a hiccup, you could start over, any time you pleased, the whole exercise as cathartic, as healing, as a sand mandala.

Since Hugo was on the back forty, neglecting me, I simply took Marie's advice: I went online to brightideas.com and loaded the complete kitchen-planning tool. Every designer knows what marvels a new layout can do for an awkward space. And as it turned out, there was a tremendous sale on for Easter; things just got better and better. So while Hugo gave the property its spring tune-up, as he rode the lawnmower around the orchard, circled through the Summercrisp pear trees and the Jubilee cherries, the hardy Norland and the Parkland apples, the tall saskatoon bushes and the thick stands of raspberries and haskaps and highbush cranberries, I was landscaping, too: land-e-scaping.

Yet I wasn't ready to go down just any rabbit-hole; the first spread was too much, even for me, an oiled expanse of thick custom teak cabinets with notched-in handles and luminous soapstone counters, more like fine furniture than spaces to hide pots and pans or cans of green beans and tomatoes. Those over-the-top pieces would never fit our aesthetic, let alone our budget, if we had a budget for renovation, which we did not.

The fourth kitchen was bohemian chic, hip. That was more like it—I wanted to bring our house out of the 90s. I chose the same white cabinets the photos had, the ones with a slim Shaker profile. For contrast, I panelled the new island with rich walnut, topped it with a slab of Carrera marble, and slipped all that and five bentwood stools with chic crossed backs into my online cart. To balance the room, I added more veneer on the new pantry wall, kitted it out with double ovens, a built-in Espresso machine, and, of course, a convection microwave. Into my cart I plopped stainless steel appliances, as there are no fingerprints in fantasy, a six-burner gas stove and a glowing refrigerator with French doors and a bottom freezer. The island would feature a bank of drawers, including one for unwieldy items like my professional mixer, with a special hoist to lift it up to counter height.

I could feel the room evolve around me. The cabinets ran to the ceiling, and a small row at the top had glass doors and interior lighting for tasteful displays of our finest things. The backsplash of pale marble tiles rippled in a herringbone pattern. Unvarnished brass hardware would age with a delicate patina. Three hand-blown glass pendants hung centred in a row above the island. Acres of countertop would boast a large mango-wood bowl full of artichokes and a glass cube vase with pear-coloured hydrangeas or bluish-purple delphiniums or thin branches popping with pink ornamental plum blossoms.

The sun was low in the living room windows, and a band of apricot-coloured haze stretched long across the wooden floors. Lucky, still sleeping, lay zebra-striped, a product of light and shadow slanting through the dog gate. At last I was done. I checked my order, prepared to run the total. That was my favourite part of the online binge: the exorcism. The process reminded me of looking at cookbooks, where, after an hour of salivating over which treat I wanted, my head would swim, I'd feel tired of thinking, and I could relax into the roast chicken breast, whole-wheat pasta, and frozen peas that were really on my cardio diet.

As I looked over the order, I wondered how much money the store must be making to be able to offer such a sale and still turn a profit. Maybe it was the strange spring, maybe I was having a mid-life crisis. Blame it on the apocalypse—but as I clicked Total I felt a rush of pressure in my ears, that high ringing on the left side. Something shivered me from throat to liver.

The thing that was never supposed to happen happened.

The price was reasonable.

I couldn't think. Thoughts rushed by, a silver school of darting fishes. I had to slow things down, create order, no, really, that was the problem—*I must not* create the order.

The kitchen sale ended on Thursday; the bedroom event was starting on Friday for Easter weekend. Surely if we paid in instalments, we could afford it. Surely we could. Kitchens sold houses, that was common knowledge. Hugo would agree with me, he always did. Happy wife, happy life…didn't they always say that on those home reno shows? Honestly, could we afford NOT to?

I heard bootsteps on the back deck, followed by a loud clang-thud-clang as the door swung open and slammed shut behind Hugo. Suddenly he was there, stomping the grass clippings from his feet, tossing his gloves into the basket.

He called up cheerfully, "Delphine? Supper ready yet?"

5

IT WAS FRIDAY, GOOD FRIDAY, and though it should have been a holiday, the whole team spent the morning at the gallery, except for Nadine, who'd flown home for Easter. We'd been happy enough to open that day, as all the artists and stakeholders had finally found a date that they could agree on, and our manager, Jim, had arranged that the gallery would close on Monday instead. But the meeting had run long, every blessed thing seemed to go wrong, and I wanted to swoon with relief when I drew the cast-iron gate and clicked all three locks after the last of the group had sallied out the front door. For a moment I allowed myself to lean against the long brick wall. Then I reminded myself I needed to get home right smartly, make sure that Hugo and I were really all right..

Besides, if all was well, and I touched wood and prayed that it was, then we really *would* take the measurements and everything would be tippity-top, better than ever I could have imagined. And my dream kitchen would become reality.

I gathered my things and slipped out the back door. In the parking lot, my dusty old car sat neatly snuggled in between Jim's Volvo and Marie's blue van. Just behind it, though, in the alleyway, a group of teenagers clustered beside a young man in a small green vehicle, something zippy and new. Drat. That was going to make it impossible to back out. But my online horoscope had said that kindness should guide my day, and, in any case, it never paid to be rude in a small town, so I decided to wait a few minutes.

I slid into my car, looped off my long teal scarf, slipped off my leather jacket, and settled everything beside my bag on the passenger's seat. I checked my hair and face in the mirror, smudged a flake of mascara from below my left eye. The kids in the alley were still there. At last I turned the ignition, hoping they'd take the hint.

The pain in my chest took me by surprise. Yes, these last few days had been stressful, yes, I'd been worried, but now I had the situation in hand—and every single thing was coming up roses. Death was not an option.

I popped the lid and shook a pill from the bottle in my purse, slipped it under my tongue, and wondered how practical people did it, just flicked fear away as easily as a horse shivers a bot fly from its withers. Maybe if I breathed the way Nasrin had showed me the day she'd told me that the tests revealed I now had angina: count to five, hold for five, exhale to five. I was to call for help if the panic didn't subside quickly.

"Remember," she'd said, "DO NOT attempt to drive yourself anywhere when you are having chest pains, not home, not to the hospital. Try not to overreact. Most likely it will just be a panic attack; we've pretty much got to accept that you're an anxious person, even after all these years on anti-depressants. But now we have the added complication that you could be having a real heart attack, which means you could easily pass out and cause someone else's death, as well as your own."

As predicted, the discomfort eased off within a minute or two, though the distress I felt did not. Certainly Mom would never have admitted to worry: she was a doer. My "paranormal experiences," as Gina calls them, had to be a gift from Dad.

I was wondering bleakly whether you could buy hope online when my cell phone rang. It was Hugo.

"Del, you've got to come home. Paul is here," he said, and then his voice lowered. "He's on some kind of a tear. I can barely keep up with him. We're going to need help. NOW."

"On my way, love. On my way." I powered my window down and leaned out to ask the young people to move.

But there was nobody there.

6

TWENTY MINUTES LATER, I bounced the Toyota up our winding driveway. So many potholes, such deep ruts. When I opened the back door, I could hear Paul and Hugo in the living room on the far side of the house, their conversation echoing through the halls, Paul's twang mixed with Hugo's interjections. I eavesdropped for a moment before deciding that Hugo had been right—we were going to need help.

I slipped into the bedroom to make the call.

"So, Emma? Please?"

"Hmmm, I don't know. Are you sure he's really manic? He's an excitable guy at the best of times. Can't you just take him to Humboldt?"

"And what would they do there? They don't have a psych ward. And you're the one with all the experience, my dear, AND you're the oldest; he'll listen to you. I've never heard him like this, so wound-up, his conversation sailing free as the wind. He's brought a bunch of guns and ammo. I just heard him tell Hugo that since the long gun registry has been destroyed, it will be easy to stock up. You know Hugo's history—he's never gotten over Anders—and, well, I'm a little freaked out."

"Okay, well, the guns *are* a bit scary, though I'm sure it's nothing serious; he's been hunting forever, you know that. It's just his way. All right. I guess Geoff can take care of Dad and the kids, play the Easter Bunny, keep the home fires burning. If you're sure you need me—"

"Posolutely—"

"All right. Hang in there. It will take me an hour to get things lined up here and ready, but I should be there by ten."

"You've got your key, right? In case we're not back from Saskatoon, if we *can* talk him into going?"

"Lovey, of course I wouldn't lose your key. Such a worrywart! If you're not there, I'll let myself in, make myself at home, raid the larder, missus. Oh, and where do you hide the good chocolate? But they won't admit him—I'd bet your farm on that. Now take a deep breath. Breathe in, breathe out."

"Emma, thank you! Drive safely!—and—"

"Yes?"

"The chocolate is in the top cupboard beside the fridge, with all the goodies. Knock yourself out."

7

AFTER WE HUNG UP, I looked for something practical to do, a way to calm things down.

Maybe he was just *hangry*, as the kids say, hungry-angry. An old bachelor like him, living off the grid, who knew what his problem might be? I headed back to the kitchen.

Hugo must have been to town to do the shopping. I opened the new package of pepper salami and layered the thin slices on dark Russian rye, topped them with slabs of soft Camembert. I filled a tall glass pitcher with hand-squeezed lemonade, pulled out a fresh tray of veggies. Stimulants were not a good idea, not with all this stress, but we could whip up a decaf with the one-cup wonder machine—the latest toy Hugo had to have. Of course it was dreadful for the environment, trapping all those dandy compostable coffee grounds in little plastic pods, but we could hardly worry about that now, not with the way Paul was—

Right then I distinctly heard Fr. Lewis say, "Be here now."

You might think hearing the voices of the dead would be frightening, but I was used to it, at least to his, and had he said anything else, I would have welcomed his advice. But this time, his words just made the "here" and "now" cave in around me. Even with my eyes squeezed shut I could see it so clearly. I was surrounded by hideous white foil-covered pressed-board cupboard doors, cheap fake antique knobs, faux-granite counters, ancient mismatched appliances, the rickety old faucet. And in my mind I saw the glamorous renovation. I felt the horror of what I'd done last night and the night before. What I'd said to Hugo this morning. His reaction—

I tried to think of what to do. I could still hear the men arguing. Poor Hugo! How could I justify my recklessness when Hugo realized that I'd sent the order?

Let's face it, some part of me argued, *this place is the product of a mind focused on thrift.*

As if to support my point, the cupboard squeaked as I opened it to lift down the good plates and the tall glasses. I set Mom's silver on the tray, too, and carried everything out to the dining room table. I reminded myself that Fr. Lewis had been a model of thrift, always happy with the very smallest of treats, a cat's whiskers to tease, a sprinkle of cotton-candy-coloured Lavatera brightening his rows of string beans, a tiny pot of ginger jam to spread on scones for visitors. He'd even refused to let me replace a pair of boots that were two sizes too big, assured me they'd been a gift. *In more ways than you might think*, he'd added, the tanned skin crinkling around his eyes.

But it wasn't thrift that ran my world, not since I'd discovered the pictures. I'd tried to win him over when I first became involved with the research project, but he'd seen the danger right away, had pierced me with a shrewd, loving look as we sat at his desk in the tiny hermitage. I'd thought the provisional title, "*The Home Front: Glamour in Domestic Spaces*," would impress him, but when I said it he'd just flipped open his father's dictionary, read in his clear, dear voice, "glamour: magic or enchantment; a spell." And then he closed the cover and turned to me.

"What makes you think you won't be caught up? Remember Rumi: what we seek seeks us," he said, bending his head and shaking it in that mournful way, half mirth at the pitiful stubbornness of the human mind, half longing to prevent the pain he must have known it would cause me. I'd tried to explain, but within minutes the Abbey bells were ringing and it was time for him to go to vespers.

And that was the last time I would see him alive.

Remembering all this, for some reason I couldn't name, I suddenly felt galvanized. I had no more conflict than a robot as I set the table and strode off to tell the men that lunch was ready. When I reached the living room, things had taken a turn for the worse.

Hugo was trying. "Paul, surely we'd know if it were that bad."

"You think you'll be safe out here, on your little Shangri-La? When the people from the city run out of water? The glaciers are melting faster than anyone even expected."

"But—"

"No ifs, ands, or buts about it. The end is closer than you think. Haven't you read David Suzuki?"

We both had but I couldn't get a single word in edgewise.

"All types of things you need to stock up on—NOW—we have to be ready," Paul said. "No telling when we might have a solar flare or a pandemic or some terrorist attack. Take a good look, Hugo, you and Delphine, you can prepare. Still have time, of course, but it'd be foolish to wait—will be so much harder to get goods when things go bad. Buy goods that are hard to make, boots and running shoes and canned food and ammunition, weapons—"

"But you're basing this on?"

"The signs, signs everywhere. Just need to read 'em. Look at the move by General Motors after the government bailed them out in '08. Now they're packing-up and heading for

Mexico and the States. And Nestle, buying water in BC, you know how that works, international trade agreements and precedents..."

Hugo suddenly realized I was there and shot me a look that I interpreted as desperation, but only said, "Looks like our chef is ready. Come on, Paul, let's treat ourselves to lunch." He turned to me. "Rollmops?" he asked, his eyes hopeful.

"Not this time, Sweetheart," I replied, playing along. "We're all out. Couldn't get any, not for ready money. I went down to the market twice."

Hugo smiled at my wan little joke. Paul looked confused, stared first at me and then back at Hugo, so I explained. "It's just a line from a play, Paul. *The Importance of Being Earnest*. An old joke we make whenever we run out of something."

"Exactly my point," Paul yelled, slapping his knee. "We're all going to run out. The falling oil prices are going to hit Canada harder than—"

"Whatever you've prepared will be delicious, Delphine. You can't fault a man for trying," Hugo said. By then he was standing, and he gestured for Paul to rise and walk ahead of him.

We all went through to the dining room, gathering around the family table, the heavy antique Paul and I had shared when I was very little and he was living at home, before he'd been sent away and Mom had translated our world into Danish modern. Dad had given me the old table when he moved into Emma's house, and I kept a lace table-cloth on it, the one Mom used to use. I hoped this sense of familiarity, of formality, would help calm Paul down.

Hugo sat beside me at the head of the table while Paul settled on the far side. He showed no sign of stopping his rant. As I passed the plate of sandwiches around, I watched Hugo out of the corner of my eye. It wasn't easy for such a gentle man to know what to say at a time like this.

At last Paul paused and Hugo managed to say, "Thank you, Delphine. We had many a lunch like this at my *mormor*'s, watching rain trickle in little rivers down the windows. She had us name them, and afterwards we kids would don boots and rain gear and splash in the puddles until it was dark."

"That's all there is in Sweden, isn't there? Puddles and darkness?" I said, playing along.

"That world is finished," Paul said forcefully.

Hugo looked at me and rolled his eyes.

I started to pour Paul some lemonade, but he waved his hand over his glass, set his sandwich back on his plate. I tried not to look at the crumbs suspended in his moustache. "Unless we get set up in time, there'll be no idleness for the next generation, no leisure to listen to rain drizzle. We owe it to them to—"

Suddenly I couldn't stand it, something in me slipped. I didn't care about the President or Syria or Paul or his predictions. The whole world was blowing apart, and I couldn't follow along the path of this insanity a second longer.

My thoughts drifted and swelled. I admired the serene grey-green of the walls above the creamy wainscoting, the calm black-and-white prints of Swedish sailing ships that leaned on the picture rail, markers of a simpler time. The full white cotton curtains at the window I'd opened held the light breeze, billowy as surf. This was the room I'd designed for Hugo. Even the spring rain seemed Scandinavian. But how could the snow be gone so early in April?

Just then Hugo reached over and the weight of his hand on mine called me back. Paul was still going strong. "You need to—"

Hugo kept his gaze on Paul. "What we *need*, right now, is to get to Saskatoon as soon as possible," he said firmly, "if we want to make it back in time for Emma. We'll take my truck, okay, Paul?"

8

FORTY MINUTES LATER, by the time we had reached the junction with Highway 2, Paul had calmed down, and I was almost asleep in the warm crew-cab, but far from at rest. My relentless, ridiculous mind was running the tally of disasters, replaying the moment when everything had started to go wrong.

I'd been so engrossed with my online adventure on Wednesday that, when Hugo entered, when he called up to me, I felt like some intergalactic traveller, lost in space. I saw him at a great distance as he bent to unlace his workboots. I couldn't think, couldn't squeak out so much as a *hello* to him, and, when I didn't reply, he just straightened his back a bit stiffly, tossed his work gloves into the basket by the door. He stood and looked up the stairs, called me again, but I couldn't, I couldn't find my way out of the maze of mango-wood bowls filled with fist-sized artichokes tinged with bronze, walls tiled with handmade Italian tiles, smooth cool

46

acres of veined marble and gleaming hardware, all so real around me. I was floating.

I knew that Hugo must see me sitting there. I was trapped, everything whirled over and over and over, those slow-motion rolls. A memory. *Gina's stricken face gazed into mine.*

But this time it wasn't Gina—*I* was driving this wreck. And then WHAM! I was back in real time.

Someone said, "Älskling?" Hugo was standing in the archway, staring at me, his eyes naïve and blue as an infant's. "You okay?" he asked. "How's the coding coming?"

I must have replied, because he turned and went into the kitchen, started hunting for a snack. I must have reached over and closed the computer. I remember trying to appear normal, turning to my magazine. I forced myself to study an article, "Rustic Glamour in Gatineau." It should have made me sick, the old stone house undeniably proof that some Mephistopheles was playing tricks and I was Faust, yes, but the devil *was* in the details, raw timber walls and oiled barn-board floors, industrial pendants dangling from exposed beams. Rows of open shelves staged just so, soap-stone counters on miles of distressed claret-coloured cabinets below. The photographer had even captured the steam lifting the air above a black Japanese kettle, a-simmer on the matching AGA cooker, and above, from an aged iron rack, copper pans and tin pudding moulds hung, boasting just enough tarnish to testify to frequent use.

It was stunning.

I half-watched as Hugo dug around in the fridge for a beer, replaced it with a warm one, grabbed a handful of potato chips from the bag in the cupboard. At last he turned, leaned against the counter, took a long thirsty drink, wiped the dust from his forehead. He rubbed his neck, looked across into the dining room where I was still sitting at the table.

Munching, he said, "Well, I'm glad that's done. Soon started, soon finished."

"What?" I croaked.

Hugo looked over at me more intently. My hand was shaking.

"The grass, of course. I left it long going into last winter. I wanted to free the thatch up today so things can turn green right away, if this really is spring," he told me as he crossed to the dining room, bringing me a beer.

Waving the bottle away, I tried to say softly, "Thanks. Maybe later."

As the panic rose, it tasted like bile, it was that bitter. It dawned on me that I might have completed the order. On that last screen—had that really been a delivery date?

But I couldn't have—I hadn't filled out the shipping address or the financial information. I tried to reason it through. It had to be that troublesome smidge of OCD I had, the thing that made me fear that the straightening iron would burn down the house, even when I knew it was safe and cold, back on its shelf. That all-consuming fear. Surely this was one of those times. Surely.

Hugo came around the table and stood right behind me, bent over to look at the magazine. His nearness made it so much worse. I made myself leaf through the articles, flip after flip, tried to bore him away. I was sure I was going to be sick. It wasn't the first time I'd talked myself into wanting something so much it seemed real, but it was the closest I'd ever come to acting on it.

I heard his stomach rumble. I knew what to do.

I was surprised at how quickly the words floated to my lips. "You must be starving," I said brightly, forcing myself to look at the clock. "I had no idea it was so late. I'd better get cooking." As I pushed my chair away from the table, I felt lighter, buoyant. I squeezed Hugo's arm lovingly as I brushed past him on my way into the kitchen. In a voice as sweet as pie, I called back, "Why don't you go relax in a nice, hot shower? Surely you've earned it."

"Hmmm… that does sound great. What do you want to do about supper?"

"I'll just pop the frozen curry in the microwave, and put on a pot of basmati rice. Give me fifteen minutes or so," I said, though I didn't say, *to phone the store*—

But before I could locate the phone number, Hugo called to me from across the house. "See this, Del—it's landed on top of the power pole."

Landed? I had no time for some nature lesson. I wanted to say I was busy but knew he could hear the microwave whirring away.

The evening light was fading quickly. It was special in an eerie kind of way, I had to admit that. Quickly I grabbed my cell phone and snapped a photo. As I pointed to shoot, I could see that there was an owl-shaped dot.

When I looked at the phone I sensed a weird energy. The photograph was a dance of light, weird images bouncing back from the windowpane, the contortions looking like something Goya would paint. Against the fierce blue sky of nightfall, the reflection of the heavy balloon window shade appeared to oscillate—the folds cascading in golden ripples of light instead of the navy blue fabric I knew it was made of. In the corner our broom leaned like some witch's toy. The beige lampshade pulsed with pale blue vibrations beside a faint reflection of Hugo that looked like a ghost wearing jeans and t-shirt against the black treeline. Above that, the yellow light of the setting sun blared through his reflection. His head seemed to be blasted entirely off.

As it would, I thought, if he knew what I'd been doing.

Maybe Stan was right, maybe the world—at least *my* world—was on the verge of ending. The photo seemed to say so.

When the microwave rang, I was startled. I ran back to the kitchen. The precious minutes were gone and I was out of time—Customer Service would be closed—

Hugo called again. "You've got to see this—"

I wanted to scream, "WHAT NOW???" but something told me to pay attention. I dashed back.

"—there it is, see—it'll pass right by our window—"

It was unbelievable, the owl's body so massive, enormous. How was flight even a possibility? And yet there it was. We stood so still we could hear the feathers ripple as the great wings whooshed by.

My mind slowed at last. Paul once told me, "An owl changes your energy, puts you in the hand of God." And then anything can happen.

In the end, after all the excitement, I had to reheat the curry, but at last we settled down on the old brown sofa to watch the news, eat dinner with our bowls in our laps. I noticed that the raisins in the curry seemed especially plump and sweet, the chicken spicy, the pineapple tangy, the meal over before I knew it.

The whole evening was like something out of the *Twilight Zone*. Even *The National* seemed stranger than fiction. Apparently, in Israel, home improvement stores and malls were passing out gas masks. A woman told the reporter she'd only just discovered the government program while out shopping for patio stones, and she'd gone home so frightened she forgot to pick up anything but the twenty-five gas masks she needed for her extended family. And still, the announcer said, only forty-five percent of all Israelis were equipped. Worse, their bomb shelters had been locked up or turned into artists' studios, community centres, and such like, and they couldn't just be refitted overnight. Officials were reluctant to open up the ones that were locked, in case they, too, might be filled with the wrong people.

Wrong people?

The news droned on and on, but I couldn't listen. As soon as I could, I excused myself and went to the bedroom. The store's robo-message firmly assured me that Bright Ideas was closed and would reopen at eight-thirty the next morning. And then Hugo found me, ready to call it a night.

As I fell asleep, my last thought was of the Israeli woman, trying to gather her family.

9

A ND THE NEXT NIGHT, when I could have come clean, I had calmly talked him into it, made him think we'd dreamed it up together. Hadn't I always, always wanted a new kitchen, a new space, a fresh and lovely place of beauty and solace and comfort? Wouldn't it be right for us?

And the entire time I knew there was no choice—the decision was out of our hands, or it certainly felt that way once I finally managed to make the phone call from the gallery that afternoon. After I'd wrestled through all the rules and logistics and possible outcomes with the immoveable Jürgen at Bright Ideas, so polite as he explained the restocking fee of ten percent, thousands of dollars, if we didn't go through with the order, time had snaked, hours and seconds and minutes weaving together, rubbery with bands of possibility.

I fried up a thick sirloin steak for supper, medium rare and running with juice, just the way Hugo liked it. I baked some potatoes, set out the fixings, and tossed together a Caesar salad from a package. As always, we settled down to eat on the couch, and by the time we'd finished eating, the news was done. But when Hugo flipped to *Mountain Men*, more people escaping civilization, I fled, too, the show yet another reminder of the impending apocalypse.

Before I left, though, I couldn't stop myself from prodding poor Hugo. "How in the world can a sweet soul like you—an animal lover, a man who longs for life in a high rise—be amused to see those crazies run around on skidoos and float planes, trap and hunt relentlessly, chop down old-growth timber?"

Hugo looked surprised for a long moment, then he just said, gently, "Well, it makes my troubles—ours—seem pretty tame. These guys sell everything, choose steep pastures far away from coastal flood plains or fault lines. And the old ways they use are pretty interesting." He seemed to want to convince me. "It's harmless, Del—a diversion. You should be able to understand that."

I was already sorry I'd snapped at him, but I could hardly confess what my problem was. I shook my head and headed into the kitchen. I tried not to think as I cleared the counters and brushed the cobwebs off the dated frilly tri-light fixture. I wiped the stove-top and cleaned the microwave, packed the dishwasher, and swept the floor. As I worked, I thought and thought of what I should do. Could do.

By the time Hugo wandered in a half-hour later to see what I was up to, I was as calm as Christmas.

"So," I said brightly, leaning against the sink. "What do you think about the kitchen?"

He looked around.

"You've cleaned up! It looks great." He came over and took me in his arms. When he bent to kiss me, I just turned my face and smiled gently. I didn't have time to be distracted by romance, so I pulled away and asked again, "Seriously, Hugo. What do you THINK about the kitchen?"

He glanced around, eyebrows lifting.

"So what's to think? We had a nice meal, you've done all the work, I'm grateful." He faced me again, blue eyes laughing. "What's this about? What colour of paint do you want now?"

I hoped he would remember the many men we'd seen on home-reno shows—they always gave in sooner rather than later. And after thirty-odd years, though none had been so odd as this was shaping up to be, it should have been clear to him that if I wasn't happy, no one else would be, either.

Another part of me wanted so desperately to tell him the truth, but those words wouldn't come. I just couldn't abandon my dream kitchen. Not now, not when it would be so perfect, not when we really could have everything, not when it would cost so much NOT to have it.

As if on cue, I heard the iPhone commercial playing sweetly on the TV in the living room: "I'm livin'…I'm livin'…I'm livin' the life of dreams…"

I started out slowly. "I've been thinking about that gooseneck faucet we bought last year, the Kohler. Maybe you could install it? This one rocks in all directions."

Hugo frowned, tried the tap, and sized up the trouble, then he squatted, opened the cupboard door, and twisted the coupling. He stood. As he lifted the tap, a stream of water poured out, smooth as anyone could ask for.

"Better?" he asked proudly.

I pinched him lightly. "Yes, better—if you hope to evoke the age when Neanderthals roamed."

"Hey!" he said. "I just heard that Neanderthals and Homo erectus co-existed, interbreeding at will. Plenty of people today have Neanderthal DNA. So we're right on trend."

I gave him the look, friendly but stern. "You know—"

"All right," he smiled. "Sure. Why not? I'll install the new tap next weekend. I guess it should have adapted to its new environment by now."

I kept at him. "Like hardwood that has to acclimatize? But wouldn't it be a shame to put that gorgeous new faucet on such a marked-up old fibreglass sink?"

Hugo peered at me, puzzled, then looked at the stain-dappled surface. I knew he'd never even noticed it before. "Well, look at that. Huh. I guess I could pick up a new one—what do you have in mind, stainless steel?"

I shook my head. "We can't put a new faucet and sink into that awful counter. It's so dated. Faux green granite? And that ugly strip of white on every edge? So early '90s."

Everything I was saying was true, but at this last point Hugo took a step back, crossed his arms. "Hey there, missus. New counters would run three or four thousand dollars, wouldn't they? Have we won the lottery? Where are you getting that kind of cash?"

Exactly, I thought. *Exactly*. How would I account for the money to restock the order if I couldn't talk him into it?

That was my opportunity. I burst out, "Can we afford NOT to fix up this room? The layout is beyond awkward— Honey, every time you want to fetch a beer from the fridge, I have to step away from whatever I'm cooking to let you by. We could put the new fridge where the stove is now, fit double ovens into a wall of floor-to-ceiling cabinets. An induction cooktop over there. This refrigerator hasn't worked right for ages, and we've changed the oven thermostat three times. Who has twenty-year-old appliances?"

I was in the zone.

"They're not even Energy Star rated. Think of the environment!"

Hugo walked around the room, looking at the stove and peering into the fridge. "Delphine," he said, his face worried, "you're joking, right? There's nothing wrong with this kitchen."

I was almost there. He was trying to reason against it. I had him now, if I played my last card right. "Even your mother thinks we should renovate! It's the first thing she said when she saw the place. And we need more storage, Hugo, you know we do."

He blinked as he turned to look at the ugly countertop, so crowded with the carbonator, the Mixmaster, the toaster, the electric can opener, the grinder, and the coffee maker. His eyes widened as I pointed out the plastic foil bubbling up on the bottom of the cupboard door above the heating vent, the place inside the cabinet where onions bled yellow stains, the shelf with the trim cracked and starting to peel, the corner cupboard door with the broken hinge. I showed him the cracked crisper bracket in the fridge, the frozen milk, the bag of baby carrots gone slimy long before the due date. I reminded him of the three times we'd had to switch out the oven's lower element, and I walked him through the work triangle, pointing out how easy it would be to replace the lower cupboards with drawers for easy access, add an island for extra storage and counter space, and abracadabra! We'd have that little bistro we'd always dreamed of, our own European-style café. We would admire it—and one another—whenever we lingered over lattes in the peaceful light of dawn or during lazy sunsets.

Hugo looked like a man who had gone to sleep in his own bed only to awaken on Mars. "But Delphine—" he said, "we're tired of living in chaos, aren't we? I thought that was why we left the city, the consumerism, that style of living. What happened to the simple life you were talking about? The books on monasticism?"

I watched him, let him play on the line like a fish tiring himself out.

"And what in the world would all this cost?"

I had no intention of giving ground. Better a terrible end than a terror with no end, Hugo always told me. I was no longer sure that applied, or what it meant, but I couldn't give in.

I simply said, "What will it cost to keep patching things up, year after year? You know that the place will never sell, not looking like this. Why shouldn't we renovate now, when we can enjoy it, enjoy ourselves? You're always saying you want to move to a condo some day. When we finally find jobs near the kids, will we have time to fix things up? Kitchens sell houses. You know they do. Unless we renovate, you'll be tied here forever!"

Hugo stepped back and leaned against the counter by the sink. He looked around the room, rubbed his neck, looked as though he were about to speak. Closed his mouth. Finally he asked again, "How much will it cost? And how would we pay for it?"

I knew then that I had him. This part I had an answer for.

"There's that money from the commissions I painted last fall. And the term on my retirement GIC is up this month. That'll be a start. And Bright Ideas has a great sale right now; no interest if you use their credit card and pay it off within twenty-four months. We'd need to charge twelve, maybe fifteen thousand."

Hugo exhaled with a whistle, shook his head, walked to the far side of the room. "You'll have to pay tax on that RRSP, and what about our retirement? Are we going to live on cat food through our long golden years in our glorious bistro?"

I knew better than to follow him around the room, but I couldn't give way, not when I'd almost won. "And we could pay it off, five hundred a month. And there's that money I expect to get back on my income tax. That should be four or five thousand."

"Sounds as though you've put a lot of thought into this idea. Sounds like a done deal," Hugo said. His eyes, usually so gentle and mellow, accused me. He seemed almost like a stranger, his features distorted somehow, his tanned face almost crimson. His dark hair more grey at the temples than ever I'd noticed before.

I forced myself to say, "Honey, we *need* it. I need it. You've always said we'd do a kitchen. Just one. Just this one. It will be good for us. A little spot of European magic on the bald prairie."

Hugo stayed put, still leaning against the stove, and shook his head. He rubbed the back of his neck. And then at last he raised his eyes, looked straight into mine.

"Okay, Delphine," he said. "You win. You can have your new kitchen." He looked around as if he were seeing the room as it would be, renewed.

"Maybe we should celebrate," he said, walking over to stand in front of me, resting his hands on my hips. "Where'd you put the liquor when you cleaned up? I could use a drink."

10

B Y THE TIME I WOKE ON FRIDAY, everything about my mood had changed. I needed to tell Hugo what had happened, dig into our small savings to pay for restocking, let the pain turn this into one lesson I wouldn't soon be able to gloss over or forget. It would be the end of the dream, that was certain, because Hugo would never, ever, agree to a new kitchen, not once he knew I'd thrown all that money away.

The worst part was that I'd made this mess all by myself. I'd been too clueless to tell him the truth when he found me on Wednesday. Was Fr. Lewis right? Had I been under the spell of glamour? Or had the fear of losing what I wanted so much once and for all pushed me too far?

Strangely, I didn't even want the renovation anymore. I felt changed, as if I'd recovered from an illness. Something heavy had been lifted, and I'd sailed back to the world of the sane.

I gently pushed back my side of the bright duvet, and abandoned the warmth of the bed, felt the floor cold on my feet. I shivered a bit in the morning air, and pulled my robe around me, Mom's robe—I'd kept it all these years—as I softly padded out of our room.

When I turned on the hall light, the mirror flashed at me.

My mother had found me. But, instead of vanishing, she was looking back at me with a yearning so steady. In my morning face, my short blonde hair, there she was. Unmistakably. It was the first time I'd seen her in Saskatchewan, or on my face. Staring as hard as I could, there was no message, no sign other than her presence. Before I could figure out what to do, my eyes squeezed shut just for a second, and although I scrabbled out an old tissue from my pocket to blot the stinging tears, when I looked again she was gone. I was staring into my own face, more lonely than ever, the circles dark around my eyes, the unfamiliar weight on the figure I had never learned to like, even when it was slim.

Mom always knew what to do, always. She just plunged in, distracted us with some scheme, a trip to the mountains or a bonfire in the backyard or a painting bee in a room that needed a lift, and all would be well. Why wasn't I more like her?

I slipped into the dark bathroom, ducked my head under the tap, ran my fingers through my short wet hair. As I rubbed my head with my towel, it came to me that this wasn't just the latest version of the same old grief. I knew something new.

Mom was no nomad, she hadn't been lost, travelling with strangers. All those years I ached for her presence, she'd been there, as close as could be, waving hello. Right inside me. And if she was a woman of enormous courage—

11

I MADE MY WAY DOWN THE DARK HALL and into
the kitchen, prayed for the words I'd have to find to tell
Hugo. I set a cup of coffee brewing, but as I lifted the spoon
to add sugar, suddenly he was right behind me. I jumped,
startled, but I made myself turn to face him. He looked so
dear, so carefree in his loose grey t-shirt and navy pyjama
bottoms, his dark hair tousled and face creased with sleep.
He really had no idea, none at all. I couldn't bear to see the
trust in his eyes, so I put my arms around him, rested my
head on his chest, and then, after a few moments, I lifted my
face to his. Praying that he'd understand, I gave him a long,
loving kiss.

He held me tightly and said, "Well, that's a fine good
morning! I should agree to renovate more often."

My stomach lurched, but I went on. I had to.

"Houston, we have a problem," I tried to joke, but he
looked puzzled, so I said, "No, I'm not lost in space. Well, er,
maybe. Honey, listen." I took a breath. "I've made a real mess
of things."

He peered at me. "What mess? You tidied up."

"Oh, you know me. It's the kitchen, of course. I—"

"But it will be great, better than ever! What has you worried now?" He released me to reach into the cupboard, fetched out his favourite mug—a strange thing, the head of an old sea-farer. "Any trouble looks better after coffee." He slipped the pod into the machine, reached into the fridge for the creamer.

I was trying to find the words when he spoke again. "I wondered how you had taken the measurements all by yourself. We can check this afternoon, after your meeting. Then we'll have the whole long weekend to figure out just what we want."

The long weekend. My three days of rest and relaxation. I squeezed my eyes closed, hard. I took a breath. The words came out in a whoosh. "I've already ordered it."

There was a pause, and then Hugo turned to me. "What did you say?"

"I've already ordered it. On Wednesday, while you were cutting the grass. Only I didn't mean to. I was window-shopping online, and then you came in and something crazy happened and I panicked. I don't remember doing it, but I wanted it, and somehow the order processed. I thought I'd hit Save, when I must have hit Ship. You can't—"

Hugo looked at me sideways, just for a half-second, then he hugged me and laughed. "You're a real card, Delphine, such a joker. For a minute I thought you were serious. Remember when Tom invested five grand in the stock market without telling Lara, and lost all of it? Like she said, how could you ever trust someone who had done that? It was the end of their marriage."

I tried to swallow, but my throat was closed. I cleared it with a cough. I knew I had to confess before things went any farther. "I'm sorry, Honey," I said, looking down, "but I did order it. It was such a good deal."

Hugo paused for a moment, then laughed, scrumbled my damp hair with his hands.

He chucked my chin gently. "Listen. I guess you'd better stop spending so much time with Marie. No one has a poker face like hers; she can say the most outrageous things. Joe says her jokes take him to the brink of despair." He shook his head, and then his face grew serious. "But if you want to put the order in yourself, you go for it. It's your vision. But let's stick to the budget."

"Honey. You've got to believe me. I don't want it any more," I said, frantic.

His eyes narrowed as he stared at me again, blood rising to his face. "Oh, no. No, no, no. We are NOT going down *this* road, just because you have some other plan for that money, some new daydream you want now that you're tired of this one. After what you put me through last night?" He braced himself against the counter.

The telephone rang. I saw Hugo's jaw tighten as he answered.

Marie greeted him loudly. Hugo said a few words and passed the receiver to me.

She was going full speed. "Delphine, can you bring hard-copies of the agenda? The server and the wi-fi are down, Jim tells me. And don't be late! Why are you still at home? Better get a move on, my dear."

"Sure, sure. I'll be there shortly. Can I call you back? I'm in the middle of something right now."

"Aaaah, romance? Don't be late, Juliet, my ducky—or you'll be a dead duck," she laughed as I hung up.

Star-crossed lovers we might yet prove to be. Hugo was wary. "Your co-conspirator calling to check up on you, see how the joke is progressing?"

I tried to explain. "Well, Marie was the one who helped me measure in the first place, but—she has no idea. Nobody's joking here. Honey, really. We can't afford it. Gina will need help with university, and we need our retirement, and—"

All of a sudden, Hugo's face, his voice, was unrecognizable. I'd expected him to be confused, upset, but he was far angrier than ever I'd seen him; he was done, finished with me, maybe for good. "*Skit, också*, Delphine. You want the kitchen, you'll get the kitchen. You'll get your way, you always do. End of story. And then can we forget the whole thing? *För fan I helvete!*

För fan I helvete. For the devil in hell.

There was silence. I turned away, quiet at last. There was nothing more I could say. My tears fell but I couldn't feel them. Almost instantly his arms found me again, embracing me. He rested his chin on the top of my head.

We stood absolutely still for a few minutes. When at last he spoke, his words were almost too quiet to hear. "Älskling, I shouldn't have said that. I'm sorry. You've got to believe me. It's just that you've talked me into it. I can't go through that all over again when you find some new thing you want, and then another, and another. Let's just build the little bistro. And enjoy it."

I pressed my damp face against his T-shirt, my forehead resting just below his throat. I couldn't tell him. I couldn't lose him. And what difference would it make? I had made a mistake, after all—it was an accident. The only real harm I'd done was in not clueing him in right away. Hugo was right. We'd get the work finished, stop focussing on material things, enjoy our lives. Our home would be a sanctuary.

Someday I'd be able to tell him the whole truth.

He'll laugh, I know he will.

12

I KNEW WHEN WE PASSED THE GUARD POSTS over the second slough that we were only twenty-five minutes from Saskatoon. I stopped torturing myself and started to listen to the conversation in the front seat. The men were talking about the water table, the conditions for seeding, and the difference between frost dates here and in P.A. Paul seemed calmer. Me, I was worn out with worry—about Hugo, about Paul, about the kitchen, about the world poised on the brink of impending catastrophe. I had to calm down, so I turned to stare at the panorama of fields patchwork-quilted before us. The land was already greening up in the south-facing pastures. Herds of cattle, red and black and dirty blonde, were lying down, slowly chewing, savouring their afternoon cud. As the car crested hill after hill, the rhythm swept me along, and I could feel the worry start to drain away. The worst was surely over.

But when Hugo cranked the radio way up, my gut wrenched again. I could see his eyes in the rearview mirror—what had conjured that look of anger? Had he finally figured out what I was trying to tell him that morning? But the announcer only said, "Following years of outcry against the federal deregulation of railways, the government today promised that there will be a barrage of criminal charges laid concerning the train derailment and explosion that caused the deaths of eleven people almost two years ago."

"One very convenient thing, that explosion," Paul said loudly, turning to stare first at Hugo, then swivelling around to seek me out as I sat behind him.

"What on earth do you mean by that?"

"Well, the President won't sign the pipeline agreement because folks think it's too dangerous, and all of a sudden there's this explosion that makes the risk of transporting oil by train seem downright deadly, all of a sudden your pipelines look good. Had to be a human hand in that."

Oh good God. Was he more ill than we thought? Paranoia went with schizophrenia…

"You're not saying someone planned the explosion? Killed all those people on purpose?"

"You don't think they wouldn't, with the amount of money at stake? Have you not heard a word I've said? Think about car recalls—the big five auto makers only send out a recall if the cost of paying the families of the deceased or maimed is higher than the cost of the repairs."

"And you're saying all those lives weren't worth more—"

"Than a multi-billion dollar project? Worth more, absolutely. Cost more, no, I don't believe so. Not where big oil is concerned. There are other pipelines, all our new trade partners want them. Just makes so much sense: some puffed up nut—or moron— thinks he's top of the food chain planned this. Think about it. What're the odds we'd have a catastrophic *train* wreck just when so much money stands to be made with pipelines?"

Hugo and I exchanged glances in the rear view mirror.

Afraid that anything I might say would wind Paul up further, I averted my head, turned away to look out the passenger window. At first I saw just the red willow branches that lined the ditch shaking in the breeze. As I looked more steadily, I could see a few does moving through the trees at the edge of the field beside us. The sun emerged from behind the clouds, a sudden dance of shadows.

If he was right, if people could be that heartless, maybe the human world did need to pass. But of course Paul couldn't be right; he was ill. I felt ashamed of myself at that thought. I wished it were more difficult to dismiss him that way, but whatever doubts I'd had earlier, this afternoon's performance had convinced me. He couldn't be held responsible.

I sat there staring as we surged over hill after hill.

I TRIED NOT TO THINK AS I WATCHED THE CLOUDS. They were still woolly, but breaking from time to time—bursts of light and deep watercolour shadows blotting the fields as we passed. I half-listened to Paul and Hugo talk about the persistence of bubonic plague in the southern U.S. My thoughts wandered to all the times we'd been to one hospital or another.

It had been at a hospital when I had found out—at last—what Paul had meant to confide to me after Mom's funeral.

I had intended to stay in touch with him. Standing there, in the parking lot of Denny's in Clareview, the little restaurant where we'd had supper as a family that last evening after the burial, it all seemed so reasonable, so possible, so necessary.

Feeling shy, I handed my big brother my phone number, saying, "We need to stay closer. Call whenever you can." And he hugged me and promised to do so. But of course we didn't.

In the end, another crisis pried him off the land many years later.

Hugo and I were still living in Edmonton. It was noon on a Saturday, and I was putting the news to work, for once, or at least the newsprint. I'd mixed plenty of vinegar and warm water and just a dash of dish detergent; the kids were helping me wash windows when Paul called from the hospital. Theo's diagnosis was silicosis, a disease I'd never even heard of. I was sorry to hear it, and more than a little curious. Who was this stranger Dad had kept away from us all these years?

I wove my car through the crowded parkade. I finally found a spot on the top level, and made my way down the stairwell and back inside, onto the busy pedway of the hospital. I waited through the line-up at the information desk, and followed the elderly volunteer's directions to the third floor. When at last I located the room, Paul was already there, awkward in the green vinyl chair beside the large window, watching the man who must be Uncle Theo as he slept.

He was in his mid-sixties, with a silver buzz cut, a thin rough face that would make him look at home on the cover of a paperback western. So that's where Paul had picked up the cowboy act.

Theo was clearly having a hard time, each breath shallow and wheezy. Paul himself looked older, old even, weathered. He must have been 41, nearly 42, I calculated quickly. More grey than brown in his hair—but before I had time to find out how he'd been, Dad came in, and I was shocked to see tears in his eyes. I rushed over to hug him, but I'd barely released him when Dad walked right over and clasped Paul on the shoulder. For once he was glad to see his son.

When we took the nurse aside, she told us that Theo's disease was caused by fine silicate, rock dust, and Dad said, "Where in God's name would he have been exposed to that? Theo's always led life out of doors—the original back-to-the-land type, if ever there was—"

Paul just shook his head and said, quiet as could be, "He worked a few summers on a rock crusher, down in Morinville. Needed the cash. Told me ranching horses was not what you'd call the most profitable of enterprises. And he wouldn't ever ask for help."

Dad shook his head, wincing. "He never said a word, and I was too busy to see it. Guess I'll sit here, hope he wakes up. I can wait all night if they'll let me."

And wait we did, but after two hours, I couldn't bear to watch Dad watch Theo. Paul's fidgety hat twirling was getting on my nerves, too. I suggested that Paul and I get some coffee from the machine in the lounge. We stopped at the desk to ask the nurse to call us if Theo came to, then we found the sunroom with its pair of dusty-rose chenille recliners and a multi-coloured sofa that defied description. The TV was on and we couldn't find the remote. Some sitcom was blaring. I think it was a rerun of *Three's Company*, with its canned laugh track burbling over our words.

I was curious about Paul; I wanted to know my brother. He certainly didn't look dangerous. I'd heard the gossip about jail time, the scandal, and still I remember how scared I was as a child when the police came to the door to arrest him for selling dope. And all the stories we'd heard after his release, the break-ins, the trouble in Calgary and Vancouver.

Paul looked as though he could hear my thoughts. He sat on the sofa that had the best view of the doorway, and fiddled with the brim of his hat.

I asked him how he'd ended up at Theo's place.

"Yeah, you were pretty little—maybe ten or so—when Dad kicked me out. I was at the lake a lot, ran into Theo at the Co-op store in town there, and he invited me to come and camp at his place. Sometimes there for weeks at a time. He didn't mind, left me free to come and go." He paused. "Helped me fix up an old Ford 150, made me earn it, taught me the ways of a small farm. But sometimes I just needed to bust loose."

He shook his head. "One night about nine years later the RCMP in Boyle caught me joyriding. One of the cops thought I was too old for such hijinks. Set me up with a doc. Turned out it wasn't acid or speed or pot that was making me high."

He read the question on my face. "I was manic, they told

me. Three stays in the psych ward. Electroshock therapy. A dance-card of anti-psychotics 'til they found the right cocktail, and tinkering to find the right dose."

"AHAHAHAHAAA...." The TV burst forth in a crazy laugh track but Paul kept talking. I seized on his words *Haldol* and *Risperidone*, I'd heard those on medical dramas on TV. I couldn't process what he was saying, my mind was standing still—and then whoosh, it was a slide projector, scenes clicking by, one after the other.

"I was 25 when I found out. You must have been 19."

The year Mom died.

Paul was still talking. "Theo kept me on the path, helped me forge some sort of a life."

And Mom? Had she guessed? But all I had the courage to ask was, "Why didn't you tell us? We would have understood, maybe Dad would have let you come back—"

Paul shook his head sadly. "Theo didn't believe that Dad could handle the news, no sireee sister. With all his strict rules and regulations, a son in the nuthouse? A never-ending source of shame."

I had to concede that maybe Paul was right. How in the world would Dad have ever dealt with that? As if he'd guessed my thoughts again, he said, "But I did tell Mom—I couldn't lie to her, not again. Remember your first year of university? The folks were so proud of you and Emma, didn't want me near you, always afraid I'd corrupt you or bring some unsavoury element into your orbit, but Mom agreed to meet me for coffee on Whyte Avenue. Before I went back to Theo's, she knew, and promised to keep my secret."

Ba-dum-bum-bumm. There was the TV again. Hilarious laughter followed. Really, I thought, *sound effects*? I couldn't stand it, pieces snapping together faster and faster.

Mom hated to keep secrets. But she wouldn't have told Dad, even if Paul had given his permission. The stigma would have been unbearable. So when Paul confessed his secret to Mom, when she had no one and no way to express her fears, she had done as she always did, started a project.

That very last bout of decorating, the crazy colours, violet and coral and fuchsia and brass. We'd all thought she was trying to keep up with Francie.

I had to slow down, think things through. "Don't jump to conclusions," I heard the TV say.

Just then our truck hit a rough patch in the road, fish-tailed a bit, jolted me back to the present. I grabbed the door handle. The sun was shining bright on the seat beside me. Out my window, broad fields of grey-gold stubble were drying. Almost-bare windbreaks glittered by, some of last fall's lacy dried leaves still dancing in the hedgerows, and up ahead, the bands of cloud had given way to my favourite prairie sky, a pure cerulean arch.

And before I knew it, we were rushing down the back of the last hill as the highway divided and the city opened up before us.

Saskatoon.

Home of Bright Ideas.

13

I WAS SHOCKED TO SEE HOW RUNDOWN the hospital had become. We abandoned poor Hugo in the emergency waiting room, left him surrounded by crying toddlers and their impossibly young and bedraggled parents who appeared to be on the verge of joining in. One woman, who looked no older than a teenager herself, was trying to reason some kind of syrup into her croupy screaming two-year-old, his cries bubbling and choking; most of the medication was on his face and overalls. Paul and I took our place at the end of the queue while the two young receptionists wandered back to their cubicles after a smoke break, their ponytails swinging while they chatted breezily about their plans for the weekend. As we stood in line, Paul seemed different. He was calm, cool, and collected, a regular Marlboro Man, more sedate than I had ever seen him. You'd think he'd never had a worry in his life, or a moment of excitation.

It took at least twenty minutes to reach the workstation, and when at last the paperwork was all filled out, the receptionist just nodded us over to a smaller waiting room, where the chaos seemed somehow more contained. As we crossed the hall, I could see Hugo but couldn't catch his eye; he'd given up his seat to a very pregnant woman and was leaning against the wall, deep in conversation with a young man on crutches who looked something like Erik.

Within moments, Paul and I were seated. I wasn't about to touch the magazines—they were covered with contagion, I was sure of it—and I didn't feel like talking, so I had plenty of time to think. The change in Paul was so alarming, all his irrational belligerence, the great stash of weapons he'd brought, the strident call that we arm ourselves, his grandiose conspiracy theories, all gone.

Just like Dad. The thought was sudden, surprised me. But no one had ever called *him* ill. No one would have dared.

Now that we were here, now that Paul was so calm, I wondered if we had only convinced ourselves that he was ill this time. Hadn't we done our own bit of prepping for disaster? But once we were in the little waiting room, Paul's mood changed again. Oblivious to my concern, he started using his hat to play peek-a-boo with a baby in a stroller while he chatted with her mother. A haggard blonde nurse appeared from time to time, ushered patients into one of two tiny examination rooms.

When it was finally our turn, I noticed that the examination room walls, once white, were smeared with a paste that I hoped was only mud. The linoleum floors were crunchy with sand and debris. The soft vinyl seat of my chair was disturbingly warm, presumably from the fevered patient who had been there seconds before.

Fifteen minutes later, a doctor no older than Marc and Erik knocked and came in. His untidy black hair, the bags beneath his eyes, his stubbly beard and wrinkled scrubs all testified that he had been on call for days. He looked at the chart, sat down on the rolling stool, and introduced himself.

"I'm Dr. Wilson. What seems to be the problem, Mrs. Boudreau?"

Worried that that would set Paul thinking of *his* Mrs. Boudreau—Abby—I jumped in more quickly than I intended.

"I'm sorry. This is Paul Boudreau. I'm his sister, Delphine Almquist. Paul has been off his meds for at least three months. I gave the nurse a list." I paused as the doctor put the electronic chart on the table, tucked his feet under the stool, and turned towards Paul.

"What seems to be the problem?" he repeated, trying to catch Paul's eye. "Can *you* tell me why you're here, Mr. Boudreau?"

Paul was hunched forward, his elbows propped on his thighs, hands clasped. He glanced down at his cowboy boots, and then looked up abruptly, lifting his grey eyes straight to meet the doctor's. "Well, God's own truth is that none of this is my idea. My sister here has always been a worrier." He drew the last word out so it sounded like "warrior."

"What brings you here today, then? Are you having suicidal thoughts?"

"Hell, no, not at all. I feel fine," Paul said, his gaze steady.

"How about racing thoughts? Hallucinations? Illusions?"

Paul squinted, acted puzzled. "What's an illusion?"

My jaw clenched. Emma had warned me about this. With such obvious questions, Paul would avoid anything he didn't want to answer, smile that broad mesmerizing smile, his eyes would seem clear. He knew how to turn on the charm, there was no doubt about that.

"Deceptiveness," I said angrily, "is one of the symptoms. And bipolar patients are charismatic, especially if they're in the hypomanic phase." I cringed inside, knowing I sounded like the entry I'd read on Wikipedia. "Paul always has had a way with strangers. I really think he needs to be back on his anti-psychotics," I protested. "This morning he was raving about the end of the world, stocking up on guns and ammunition—"

The doctor, his back to me, cut in, "Paul, what about your sleep? Waking up early?"

"Sure, I'm up at dawn, stoking the woodstove. Morning is the best part of the day."

I felt myself grimace. I was certainly not going to say that I was the one who couldn't sleep.

"What's this about guns, Paul?"

"Trying to live off the land, be self-sustaining, you know, green. No crime in owning a rifle or two. A man has to eat, and the deer are fat as butter this year."

"But stockpiling weapons and gasoline. Going without electricity, satellite, or telephone. He was diagnosed—" I couldn't stop myself from interrupting.

"But Delphine," Paul said gently, peering around the doctor at me. "You know I have my solar and wind set up! I have electricity, keep my radio on all the time in the evenings."

I opened my mouth to protest, but just then Dr. Wilson turned around. He looked at me steadily, saying, "Well…I'm not sure I share your concerns. Nothing crazy about living off the grid. Sounds like a little bit of nirvana to me. And there's a whole subculture prepping for the end of the world as we know it. They don't all have mental illness, Mrs. Boudreau."

"It's Almquist. Dr. Almquist," I corrected him, desperate to add whatever weight I could to my opinion. Immediately I wished I'd kept quiet. Now he was certain to ask what work I did. Wouldn't he be impressed when he heard I worked in one of the two art galleries in Humboldt?

"I keep up with the news," I hurried to say, "who can avoid it? But Paul has been on medication since he was a young man, well, 25, in any case. His wife, uh…moved away, a few years ago now, and, since then, he's been less likely to take the pills." Moved away—now why had I used that euphemism? Pretty little Abby had grabbed her things and fled the province while Paul was having a manic episode. A year later she had him served with the divorce papers. But the doctor didn't have time to hear all that.

"If he's this calm after being off medication for three

months—that's what you said first, wasn't it?—then maybe he doesn't need treatment. Let me try one more thing."

What in God's name? Did he think Paul couldn't hear him?

"Paul," the doctor said, turning back to face him, "I know people are preparing for the zombie apocalypse—how would I go about that?"

I barely stopped myself from launching my purse at his head.

Paul laughed. "Zombies? No need to fear the dead: it's the living you gotta watch out for." He frowned. "Government, big business, big banks, what's happening to the global economy, the air, the water, the planet. Eighteen-trillion-dollars in debt in the States. Austerity measures. Massive migration. The chaos in the EU. Climate change."

"So you're spending lots of money getting ready," the doctor prompted.

"Not at all," said Paul, shaking his head. "I'm trying to save money. Become self-reliant. Bring the family together."

The doctor stared at him, then gave a nod. "Sounds like a plan. I wish you all the best."

He turned to face me. "I don't think there's any cause for worry, not at this time, Mrs. Boudreau. Paul seems lucid to me. When was he diagnosed? And by whom?"

I refused to correct him; I'd just answer his questions, keep my replies short, so he would listen. "About thirty-five years ago. He's sixty-one now. He was in Ponoka for awhile."

"And how many episodes has he had since then?"

"He's been hospitalized three times, but he's hypomanic at times, even on medication."

"He's not displaying any symptoms now. Let's leave it and see how he goes. If he *is* elevated, he should see a psychiatrist, though that might take a year or more, at least in the city." He paused. "I am concerned about you, however. It's not easy being a caregiver for an extended time. Perhaps you could use something to relax, Mrs.—"

I bit my tongue.

"I mean Dr. Almquist," he finished, on his own. "A little something for anxiety won't hurt and might help you relax." He paused. Wait for it, I thought, and I wasn't disappointed.

"What do you do for a living?"

I fought down a groan, saying, "This is not about me. You've got to help my brother."

He typed into his tablet and scrolled through files. "Hmmm...Let's see. We'll give you a trial of the Xanax. You can see if that helps things for the weekend, and go to your doctor on Monday." He scribbled on a pad.

"Don't you mean Paul's doctor?"

He looked up quickly. "No, I do not. I mean yours. You're agitated, your speech is pressured, and, frankly, you're a little aggressive. If Paul did have problems once, you may be a candidate, too. Mood disorders often run in families." He pressed the paper into my hand. "It'll help you to sleep."

I took a deep breath, tried to steady my voice. "Thanks," I said, rising. "Paul, let's go."

The doctor stood up. "Things will seem better when you've—"

I opened the door and led Paul away. The doctor's voice faded and we made it back to the overfull waiting room to fetch Hugo. Noting the paper in my hand, he smiled at me. "So? Success?"

"I'll tell you all about it. Later."

14

NOW THAT THERE WAS NO ONE TO FOOL, Paul was exuberant; he couldn't stop greeting strangers by doffing his hat. By the time we reached the truck, Hugo must have sensed how worn out I was. He suggested that Paul sit in the front again, leaving me to nap in the crew cab. As Hugo manoeuvred the vehicle through the parkade and out to the street, as Paul waved his hat out the window, I saw how perfectly he fit the pattern Emma had described. Bipolar patients were masters of deception. For short bursts of time they could calm themselves, play the victim, and then just as swiftly shift back into elation, or fury, or colourful flights of fancy.

And yet, to be fair, I had to admit that I really knew almost nothing about Paul's disorder, only what I'd read on my phone after hearing Emma's predictions. Why had I not informed myself sooner? Maybe the young doctor was right, maybe the meds had been keeping him down all these years while he'd gradually learned to cope with his illness. Not that I was convinced. Maybe the doctor was bipolar—so much sympathy for poor misunderstood Paul. In any case, there was nothing I could do, not until I could get him in to see my own doctor on Monday. Nasrin would believe me. She had to. And Emma would be there. She knew Paul so much better than Hugo and I did. We'd only really spent time with him since he'd bought Pépère's homestead up in northern Saskatchewan, two years ago.

The warmth of the vehicle quickly made me drowsy. For a little while I looked when Hugo pointed here or there to things worth admiring, like a hawk mousing from atop a huge round bale, or a flock of geese wheeling in a large V heading north, or two blackbirds chasing a raven. A skinny long animal, a weasel, maybe, dashed across the highway and Hugo managed to spare it. Paul rattled on about his plans, and I deliberately tuned said plans out.

Exhausted, I fell asleep, and when I woke I realized we had passed through Humboldt already. We were headed south, just passing the landfill. From there on, the fields were as flat as a map: Marc liked to joke that you could see your dog running away for a full twenty miles. It took me a minute to register that Paul was still talking. Did he never intend to quit? But I started to listen, really taking in the gist of what he was saying.

He was speaking calmly enough. "Course we won't have to stand watch, just keep the rifles loaded. Had my team dig the wire around the perimeter, put in an 8-foot bison fence, roll of barbed wire on top. Can't be too careful. We'll electrify the whole shebang. Electricity will likely be the first thing to go when the crunch comes, so we'll have to stay off the grid. Dedicated a dugout, two pairs of small windmills and a solar array to power the fence and make power for the heating system and a water pump and a small refrigerator—"

I leaned forward, tried to say that we'd better pray that electricity was NOT the first thing to go, but there was no way to edge in a word. He just wouldn't quit, that was apparent, so after a few moments I closed my mouth again.

"Going to be an adjustment," he said, "not being able to run to the store for a can of coffee. Theo says we should use chicory root, but that's an acquired taste. Have to make sure that we've laid in all the seeds we need for healing herbs and substitutes from Rainers' garden store."

"Theo?"

Even ever-calm Hugo turned to stare over at Paul, who just pulled his hat down to shield his eyes as he peered out the passenger window into the sloping sun. Hugo cast a quick look back my way in the mirror, and our eyes met.

"Look at that!" Paul shouted, pointing. "Jesus! There's a whole field of them!"

Hugo's eyes swivelled back to the road as he braked, swerving to miss two young does crossing right in front of our truck. I looked out my window and saw another twenty or thirty whitetails in the field to the west, nosing the windrows, dining on the remains of last fall's swathed grain, left in the fields when the snow flew so early.

For a moment we just watched in wonder. But I couldn't let this opportunity pass, I had to find out. In what I hoped was a sympathetic voice, I asked, "Paul? What were you saying about Theo?"

Paul might be crazy, but he was no fool. He saw right through me. "Geez, Delphine, can't you just for once take in all that gentle energy?" he said. "And be grateful?"

His eyes on the road, Hugo said, "I'm just grateful we didn't smash into all that gentle energy at 110 km per hour."

"Me, too, Sweetheart!" I patted his shoulder. "Me, too." I turned to look at the road we'd passed, watched the deer cross, two and three at a time bursting or just wavering across the width of the empty highway behind us. Then the whole herd took flight, bouncing and zigzagging over the hardtop and into the darkening field to the east.

My neck was sore by the time they were done, so I turned around, looked at Paul through his sunshade's mirror. "I still want to know about the chicory, Paul. Is it something Theo used?"

"No, we planned to, but never got around to it. Then last week I was unpacking my things when a column he'd clipped years ago about nature lore jumped out at me, mentioned chicory, lots of other plants. It's as if he sent it to speak to me."

That was a kind of crazy even I could understand.

"And beside the column was a piece about the new weapons. I took that as a sign, too."

Hugo turned to stare at Paul. I watched the road as he had other things on his mind. "Delphine and I will NOT be stocking weapons, Paul, get that through your head, now and forever. You know what happened to Anders."

Paul wouldn't back down, not even to humour Hugo, but he didn't press, either. "See you might feel that way, given the circumstances. Must have been hard to lose a brother like that."

I was angry to hear Paul speak so casually of something that had torn Hugo apart. Paul knew that Hugo had never gotten over Anders' murder. To this day, Hugo and I blamed the gun culture in the States. His younger brother was the only other member of his family who had come to live in North America. If Anders hadn't pulled a gun to defend himself, the mugger in Chicago might not have wrestled it away from him and then shot him to end the struggle. Hugo hardly ever spoke of it these days, but I knew that Paul's ideas about guns as protection were more than he could bear.

Wearily, Hugo said, "Guns do nothing but make you a target. Are you willing to murder all comers? How many? And what in God's name happens when you run out of ammunition?"

"It's not murder if you're protecting your family, is it? And we'll need guns for game and even to slaughter our animals, you know?"

Hugo said nothing. I could see his knuckles blanch white as he tightened his grip on the steering wheel. I leaned forward and rested my hand on his shoulder. Surprisingly, Paul had the good sense to shut up. We were all silent as Hugo turned the truck off the highway and sped down the grid road. At last he cleared his throat and spoke. "I'm not changing my mind, and that's that. But it won't make any difference to us what you choose to do."

We were only a few minutes from home, though the strained silence made the trip seem longer. Soon the little house was in view to the north, its row of porch windows glowing gold in the evening light. We wound our way up the driveway. With the sun at that angle, the grass in the pasture already seemed green, and the horses were dreamily cropping each spare millimetre.

When we stopped, I tried to lighten the mood. "Here we are for where we're going. All in here for there get out," as Dad always said when we were kids. Hugo smiled wanly at me, and then he and Paul walked over to Misty and Commander, who had both trotted over, nickering and rattling their noses in their black rubber oat buckets and then lifting their heads, moving their tongues and lips to mime oat-munching as they showed the men what they wanted.

15

AT LONG LAST, JUST AFTER 10:30 P.M., I heard Emma's car drive in, and I jumped up so quickly from the card game that my knee knocked the table, hard. The crib board shimmied, and the men looked at me with surprise.

"It's just that I haven't seen her for so long," I said. "I'm okay. You two stay here for now, and Paul," I added, my eyes firmly meeting his, "You make sure Hugo doesn't cheat. I'll get Emma settled and then we'll all have time to visit."

As I hurried away, Lucky looked at me curiously, then tangled past me to reach the door first. He never barked; we had so few visitors it wasn't in his repertoire. Hugo called out, "Enter safely all intruders. The dog will show you where the valuables are."

At the back door, Emma's face shone under the porch light, a dear, clear vision amidst the familiar darkness. Just inside the door, she set her suitcase down and gave me a long hug. It was more than relief. We seldom talked and lived so far apart; it was wonderful to be together again. I hung her jacket on a hook by the entrance, and led her to the narrow staircase to what was now, after Gina's departure last fall, the guest room. When I teased Emma about the weight of her luggage, she grinned. "I always pack for the unexpected— especially when I'll be a province away from civilization."

Hugo and I kept Gina's loft room just as she'd left it. It was too hard to think the nest was really empty, and I held out hope she or the boys would come and visit. When I lifted the door to the loft and we entered, Emma exclaimed, "Ah!" and I felt a wash of pleasure. The walls and gently slop-ing ceilings were covered with shiplap painted *Devonshire Cream*. The dark wooden floor had been softened with a worn fuchsia carpet, the faint pattern still rising through. The cast-iron bed looked cosy with its soft blue and white linens, but what—

Oh my God.

There it was, the toile duvet cover I'd purchased online from brightideas.com last February.

That was surely the reason the kitchen order had processed.

It had seemed like such a good idea at the time: apply for an account and receive a twenty-dollar discount on the first purchase charged. With the free shipping, the thing was vir-tually free. Who knew that once the address and the billing method were entered, the express checkout was enabled, and the second purchase would be only a click away? Disaster a click away...

I stood there, frozen, but Emma didn't seem to notice. She just sat down on the navy velvet bench at the foot of the bed, and patted the seat beside her. "You've done wonders, Del."

I had no idea what she was talking about. She couldn't know what I'd done.

"The place seemed cramped and run-down when you first moved in, but now it's a cute little place, a nifty little resort. You've got the touch. Mom never shared her secrets with me."

"Or me," I said bleakly.

"Her projects just always seemed to fall into place without any effort or deliberation on her part at all, like when I asked her how to make lemon sponge pudding." I tried to listen as she rambled on, but my mind was on the toile duvet.

I forced myself to respond, change the subject. "She was always a miracle-worker. And speaking of miracles, let me tell you, it's been quite the day."

I presented what you might call a carefully edited version of the doctor's comments and then sketched my own theory of the truth. I wanted to hear Emma's professional opinion. She was the one with all the experience. She nodded, "He can put on a fine show when he wants to. On the other hand," she added, "the fact that he's playing cards seems promising enough."

"Well, he hasn't so much been playing crib as lecturing—or hectoring—us. He has plans to invite all of us up to his place for Christmas, and he's already got poor Hugo roped in, hog-tied, I'd say. Paul told him he wants to dress the cabin up with a Swedish theme this year."

While Emma laughed and joked about what the others would say, I was dying to tell her my problems: she was the one person I could share my kitchen woes with. But as I was about to tell her everything, she patted my leg and rose to her feet. As we creaked our way down the old staircase, she said, "Let's see how it goes. Did you say you had leftovers in the kitchen? I have to say, I'm starving."

16

I HAVE ALWAYS THOUGHT HUGO A MIRACLE worker, but he must be a mind reader too. By the time we'd arrived in the dining room, he was in the kitchen, nuking a bowl of chili for Emma. I went down to fetch a bottle of Merlot from the basement. I knew Paul shouldn't self-medicate, but if ever there was a time for a bit of a nip... The doctor's recommendations had put him on top of the world—he'd never take his pills tonight. A little wine might calm him down, lull him to sleep. When I returned to the kitchen, Hugo had already set out the glasses, piled the acacia wood board with crackers, the cheddar biscuits I'd made for supper, some Emmentaler, a piece of Gouda, and a wedge of Blue. I dug around in the crisper for snack carrots and snap peas, while Hugo and Emma waited behind me to get out the plates and cutlery.

I heard her say quietly to Hugo, "Paul's in fine form. Sounds like you've had quite the introduction to the exotic side of life with Les Boudreaux."

She lifted her voice in my direction. "It would do all of

us some good to relax, especially you, Delphine. What can I do to help?"

"It's been a crazy, hectic week," Hugo answered for me. "And you know how she worries."

Paul joined in from the dining room, right at top volume. "Of course she worries—with her job? Time to get out of this rat race. Go back to a simpler time. Days spent in the garden or in her studio, evenings in front of the fire, none of this corporate liberal arts bullshit. What kind of job is that for an artist, analyzing trends in home décor? Life would be a lot simpler if there were no online shopping."

I tensed instantly.

But Hugo just said, "Give Emma a chance to settle in, Paul, and then I want to retain my honour at crib. I think I have you on the run at last."

I forced myself to finish up in the kitchen. Hugo seemed completely at ease. He sat down, took up his cards, and played a six of spades. "Fifteen two." He moved his pegs. "And by the way, Paul, Del's situation is a little more complicated than you make it sound. We can't just abolish the internet."

"How complicated can it be to set yourself free?" Paul asked. "Emma, Hugo and I were just talking about how *Pépère* came over. Now he was a pioneer."

"Paul, it's your turn," Hugo prodded.

Paul played a six. "And another thing—"

Hugo interrupted, "Twenty-one. Now take your points. That's a pair."

Paul looked over at the pile of cards, folded his hand and tossed it onto the table, saying, "When's the last time we all got to visit? That's enough crib for tonight. I surrender."

"And that's an offer I will graciously accept. My record stands untarnished—three to none," Hugo said, "at least for tonight." He gathered the cards into a deck and took the crib board over to the old credenza. By the time he returned, Paul and Emma were talking. He was telling her about the house he'd found, the one we would all love, he was certain of that.

She smiled and nodded, but when Paul rose to pass the plates around, she looked behind his back at me, spread her hands palms up and mouthed, "Now what?"

I took some comfort in thinking that she could see some of the symptoms I'd read on the internet: "Patients exhibit an inflated ego during manic or hypomanic phases. Racing thoughts cause pressured speech, rhyming, possibly confusion, and some patients may have auditory or visual hallucinations. Grand schemes, impulsiveness and spending sprees are common. Patients may be secretive and sleep less than usual. Stress seems to be a trigger. The first event may be a depressive episode and therefore missed."

As I reviewed the list on my phone, I hated to admit that the resident at the hospital might have been right. Paul's behaviour did not match the model precisely. For one thing, he was hardly secretive. If anything, he was exhausting us with details, wanting to share every element of his plans in full glorious technicolor. But he was certainly racing; our conversation hopped and pranced from idea to idea as we tried to catch up on all the news.

Paul was dreaming aloud. "Of course Emma and Geoff will bring their crew—and Dad—at Christmas, too, and I'm hoping Delphine and Hugo will bring the whole fam-dam-ily, as Theo used to say. By then we'll have the place settled, and we can all relax around the woodstove with rum and eggnog—what's that drink, Hugo, *glögg*?—Del's shortbread cookies and Hugo's special *pepparkakor* and those buns shaped like Lucia cats—"

"*Lussekatter*," Hugo replied with a smile. "Made with saffron. Should be able to find crocus stamens even after the apocalypse." I kicked him gently under the table, and he looked at me, surprised. I shook my head. No sense in making Paul think we agreed with his predictions.

"Dad will love it," Emma said. "We all will. Hugo can take us all on an international cooking adventure."

"Baking with the woodstove *is* going to be a bit of adventure, that's one way to put it," Paul added, laughing. "No microwaves or convection ovens at the ranch. Probably have to take the yeast dough to bed to make it rise."

"Wait. Are you trying to get us to come visit, or talk us out of it?" Hugo smiled.

17

WE'D ALL LOADED OUR PLATES, and Hugo had just opened the wine when Paul asked us if we wanted to hear the story he'd been telling. "We were talking about *Pépère*. Yes, sneaking back to France before he'd proved up was quite the risk—he could have lost his homestead—but on the return trip to Canada, he met and fell in love with a little Irish gal. Hard to believe that Granny was ever young, or indentured. Who'd ever have thought they could keep a hold on a dynamo like her?" We all laughed, remembering the stories Dad had told us in our youth: she'd made the whole family tow the line.

"They had to court through the mail, wrote every week until she paid off her bond in Québec City. Took her two years, but then she came out West for the wedding. The one beautiful day in June that year, or so they said."

Emma smiled at Paul's version of the old story, and

glanced up. "And look where that got him! The way Dad tells it, Granny really kept *Pépère* in line. She marched over from the place they were billeted before the wedding to inspect his progress on the house. He was out on the homestead, supposedly building, but she found him sawing wood, all right, no, not with a saw, but snoring, his head propped up on a log."

Paul reached over to refill his glass. "Theo said the way Granny told it was, 'Can you imagine? There he was, himself, fast asleep in the dappled wash of noon, the sun filtering slowly through the first sap-green leaves of May.'"

Emma smiled. "I thought I had the Irish, but listen to you! Even Dad says she gave Émile a piece of her mind. She never caught him at *that* again."

"Oh, she kept him under her thumb."

"I can just imagine."

"But she was a spiritual warrior, if ever there was one," I said, as I rose to reposition the cheeseboard so that Paul wouldn't have to reach across.

"Spiritual? A witch or a seer maybe. She was a fearsome little thing," he added. "Five foot nothing, 95 pounds, all piss and vinegar, Theo said. By the time I made it to Athabasca and could have gotten to know her, it was too late. All those strokes. All she could do was sit in a chair." He cut two pieces of Brie for himself, and passed the cheese board to Emma.

Hugo said, "I've always heard that *Pépère* was a quiet, gentle man. In the pictures, he's as thin as a rail and bald as a billiard ball, just a wisp of hair on top. He looks like a man who never, ever, stepped out of line."

Emma laughed. "Well, he had his ways. And Granny had her reasons. When we were kids, the two of them were in the nursing home, though only Granny needed care. He was with her because that was the practice, then, to keep couples together."

Hugo paused for a second, and then added, wryly, "Well, separating them might have been a relief for him."

"Hugo!" Emma objected, laughing.

Paul jumped in, "He knew how to handle her—*Pépère* used to bury himself in a book and turn his hearing aids off when he got tired of listening."

"What did you say?" Hugo asked quickly, smiling.

"Very funny," Paul said, turning to me. "Better watch out. You don't want our Hugo to learn new tricks." He tapped Hugo on the back in a little stutter.

I smiled. "Don't even think about it, Hugo, or you, Paul. You never miss a thing. Yes, *Pépère* was quite the character. Dad said he never contradicted Granny, but always had a strategy. Actually, Hugo's quite like him."

"Well, not in all ways," Emma replied, and shook her head. "Nor would you want him to be."

"Oh?"

"*Pépère* woke up one day just as mad as a hatter, when he was in his early fifties. Had to be committed for a full year."

"What? I never heard that before," I said, looking over at her suspiciously.

"Neither did I. You just making this up?" asked Paul.

"Nobody knew why," Emma admitted. "Just went off his rocker. It must have been all the trouble. Sure, he had it good, some would say. They wouldn't let him enlist in WWI because of his deafness, but that meant constant explanations. Life on the homestead couldn't have been easy, and then the Great Depression came. It would have been late in the Dirty Thirties when he got sick," Emma paused.

"Really, it's hardly surprising. Sure, at first it must have seemed like a lark. But after the adventure, the newness wore off, and the reality of chopping wood and hauling water, ploughing with horses from dawn until dusk, raising and butchering pigs and chickens, and so on, well, how could a city-boy like him deal with all that? The never-endingness must have sunk in," she continued.

She pushed her bowl to the centre of the table. "Dad told me that when Émile arrived in Canada, he took the train to Saskatoon, got off, had to walk a hundred miles to Prince Albert and find the camp of the acquaintance whose letters had lured him there. Found his fire by climbing a tree and locating the smoke. They tented all winter, and you know what winter up by P.A. can be like. Rarely a day warmer than -40. Snow always four or five feet deep."

"That's the story I've always heard. But nothing about being crazy," Paul said.

Emma nodded. "They hushed it up, all right, but last year Dad hauled all the family skeletons out of the closet for me. One of the perks of having him live with us, I guess."

"That, and his love of cooking bacon and pancakes. He tells me you have breakfast for supper at least once a week now. He's pretty proud of his new skills," I couldn't resist teasing her.

"And Edmonton is still a great place. You three should try it again," Emma replied, smiling.

"Not on your life!" Paul exclaimed. "I'm planning to lure you and yours out here."

Emma's eyebrows arched gracefully as she helped herself to the wine. "Anyway, they settled on the land a bit to the south of P.A., where the farming was better. Once the cabin was built and the homestead proved up, *Pépère* made a living by logging, you know, chopping trees, running a sawmill, and hauling lumber to market on foot with a team of horses, and hanging out with gangs of men all doing the same. Dad told me *Pépère* was a bare-knuckle boxer—and a good one, made extra money in the camps."

"Always knew he was an adventurer," Paul said, refilling his own glass. "What's that jingle I heard Hugo singing tonight? About rebellious pioneers?"

"So what went wrong?" I asked. "Dad always told me. 'People simply don't snap.'"

Emma shook her head. "They never knew. In those days they just called it a nervous breakdown. Now we'd call it a psychotic break. All I know is that he spent a year in the mental hospital in Weyburn. Granny moved to P.A. while he was there, lived with Dad, who was teaching then. Of course they didn't visit him—the stigma! By the time *Pépère* was released, she'd sold the farm and set up a tiny house in Prince Albert for the two of them. Not much bigger than your living room, Delphine."

"Aha! If it's not my living room," Hugo winked at me, "guess I won't have to paint it."

"Well, let's lift a glass to them," Paul smiled. "Can't imagine finer role models. Here's to adventure!"

"To NOT living in sod shacks!" I said.

"To NOT having four children in five years!" Emma added.

As we laughed, we all clinked glasses. Hugo asked, "How did they ever manage to stop at four?"

Emma was matter of fact. "Granny shared a bed with their daughter, Auntie Élise, and *Pépère* bunked with the boys, and that was that."

"Ouch!" Hugo said. "Sounds brutal. No wonder he went crazy."

18

AS WE JOKED, EMMA COMMENTED that Dad seemed to have buried his own demons. Paul shook his head, "After a lifetime of paranoia?"

My own mind was ticking like a bomb. Were they telling the truth? I wasn't so sure that *Dad* had ever been crazy, though yes, now that she mentioned it, I had noticed a change, that his taste had altered in such a radical way.

"He always buried himself in politics, but of late he's become omnivorous," Emma told us, "devouring the latest Hollywood memoirs and books on extraterrestrials and ancient history and avant-garde poetry. All his nationalism, his political fire, his conspiracy theories—now as cold as well-stirred ash."

Hugo admitted she might be right. "The last few times I tried to talk to him about the news, he just grunted and said, 'It's all just so much hype. They said the oil would be gone by 1980.'"

About the time we'd left Edmonton, Emma, who always copes by filling her life with projects, had helped Dad clean out and sell his house and convinced him to move in with her, Geoff, Janey and Ewan, where he'd set himself up in his neat suite in her basement.

She said, "How betrayed he and I felt when the buyers declared that the first thing they would do would be to repaint the kitchen. It's true, Mom's *Flamingo* was not for the faint of heart, but it hurt all the same."

I was surprised that Paul knew the rest. "Fortunately, Geoff is pretty laid back, because Emma and Dad are two of a kind, each thinking her- or himself the best driver, the best mathematician, and the most savvy reader. And each thinks the other the next best, so they make what you might call a fine mutual admiration society."

Emma protested a little. "Hey! There have been benefits all around. Ewan and Janey were still in elementary school when Dad moved in, and he devoted himself to keeping them away from video games. He taught them to build an electric motor using a wine cork and helped them perform chemistry experiments, like that erupting papier-mâché volcano that spewed smoke and lava all over Geoff's pristine garage." She smiled, but gave a theatrical sigh.

"How's that workin' for ya these days?" Paul drawled.

"Well, what the hell," Emma replied. "He's gonna do what he's gotta do. At least I caught him before they started making the chloroform."

We talked and laughed until at last Paul tossed his sleeping bag out on the couch and settled himself snugly into it, his hat covering his face. "C'mon, you kidlets," he said. "Early bird gets the worm."

19

THE VERY NEXT MORNING, I wondered if all our trouble had ever even happened.

As I went softly down the hall into our kitchen, the grey sky was already light. Our lunatic brother had made himself at home, whipped up a batch of his famous flapjacks, filled the air with an invitation of crispy bacon and strong black coffee. I pulled my robe tight against the chill, but couldn't help smiling as I said, "For God's sake, Paul, 6:35? It's Easter Saturday!" He grinned at me as he adjusted the stove, but instead of replying, he just walked over to holler up the stairs at Emma and told me to go fetch Hugo.

He wanted us all up and at it so that we could go and see that house he couldn't stop talking about. "It's *ir-re-siss-tible*," he drawled. "Be perfect for you and Hugo and the kids when you come up to the homestead."

The hair on the back of my neck flirted with the idea of rising, just a smidge, but the plan seemed harmless enough. Now that he was no longer threatening us with the imminent demise of humanity, what could it hurt to let him dream?

The jolt of his arm around my shoulders washed a bit of my coffee over the rim and onto the floor, and he quickly grabbed a rag from beneath the sink and crouched down to wipe it up. Even if he was a bit of a whirlwind, this was a side of Paul that I could admire. I shook my head and laughed as he buzzed between the coffeemaker, the stove, and the refrigerator. He waved the tongs at me cheerfully, pointed at the cupboard and nodded. I caught his meaning and took out some mugs.

I heard Emma call, "Good morning! That smells fabulous," as she descended the creaking back stairs. She was wearing her robe, too, a purple satin kimono that set off her still-ginger hair. My sister and I make no secret that, like our mother, neither of us will go grey while there is a bottle of hair dye to be had. Paul, Emma and I bantered and teased as the last batch of pancakes cooked. Emma turned to me inquiringly, eyebrows lifted, as she noticed the empty brown bottle beside the mixing bowl.

"Don't worry, Em. Beer-batter flapjacks, better even than sourdough. You'll love 'em," Paul said as he turned the last batch of half-crisped bacon, poured some of the fat into the pancake dough. "Keeps them from sticking."

"Oh, I bet they're delicious. It's not the pan I'm worried about them sticking to; a second on the lips, a lifetime on the hips," Emma said, and clutched her breast in mock distress. "And a shorter lifetime—accckkkk—I feel my arteries congealing." Of all of us, she really was the one least likely to worry, as well we knew: in seconds, all smiles, she lifted a piece of bacon from the paper towel and crunched it down noisily.

I laughed and took the white plastic spatula from Paul's hand, turned the pancakes as they lost their shine and the bubbles broke. He put the second batch of cooked bacon on the plate and laid new strips in the pan.

"Coffee...Must have coffee..." Emma murmured, as she advanced towards the counter.

Before long Hugo heard the racket and joined us, and we talked and joked our way through the whole little feast. The kitchen was completely dishevellized, as Gina would say. Paul looked at the clock and slid the last flapjack onto Hugo's plate. While Emma ran upstairs to fetch her Salish sweater, I hurried off to put on a little makeup. From the bedroom I could hear the clatter in the kitchen. Paul and Hugo must be man-stacking the dishes, knives and forks spliced between my favourite plates, the whole thing a towering invitation to disaster. *Never mind*, I told myself; *there will be plenty of time to clean up later.*

And to verify that the measurements Marie and I'd taken for the kitchen were correct? I thought, suddenly anxious. I only had until Tuesday to adjust the order or pay the cancellation fee.

By the time Emma and I made it back to the kitchen, Paul was ready, decked out in cowboy boots and flannel-lined jean jacket. He soon shepherded us all through the back door and out. We took Hugo's truck again. Paul rode shotgun (he was the one who knew the directions), and Emma and I visited in the crew-cab. By ten after eight we were zipping along, admiring the breaks in the bright clouds that cruised the spring sky. "There's enough blue to make a Dutchman's pair of breeks, eh Emma?" I said. "The weather should change at last."

"I, for one, have had enough of these ongoing precipitation events. Lots of flooded basements again this spring," Emma replied. "They're really worried about Calgary, too. Or so Marc told me." She consulted her phone. "But praise be to God: the Weather Channel is forecasting 20 degrees here today."

I thought it was strange that Paul hadn't said anything about climate change yet and I certainly knew better than to get him started. We were entering Humboldt, and Hugo slowed right down, let the aging coffee-row jaywalkers dawdle and greet one another in safety. At the Petro-Canada station we turned right, cruised slowly through the little city. On our way out of town, Hugo cried, "Look!" pointing up to the north. Huge ragged Ws and Vs of birds wheeled above; Spring really was here, a full four weeks early. But though the rain had melted the last few drifts, the pasture to the northeast was still white, this time with snow geese, lifting and settling and rising again as the cars whizzed by.

"Remember the first time we drove this road, Hugo?"

But he wasn't listening to me. We were caught in a line-up, ten cars trapped behind the largest seeder I'd ever seen.

"Shit," Paul said. "Forgive my French. We're sure to be late now."

"He'll pull over, give it a minute." Hugo looked in his mirror and winked at me. "That house of yours is not going anywhere, Paul."

Paul said nothing but removed his cowboy hat from his head, tweaked the brim. We were trapped. It was impossible to pass with so many vehicles coming towards us, truck after truck zooming past. We crawled along behind the monster machine for another kilometer or so, but soon the farmer turned south off the highway and we were back up to speed. Hugo slowed down as we passed through Engelfeld, the next town, then pushed it back up to 100, and before long he had turned right at the dogleg just before Watson.

On Railroad Street we all gazed with surprise at the enormous red and white figure, his backdrop of poplars and evergreens rooted in the tall thatch of last year's dead grass. There was a sign declaring Watson "The Original Home of Santa Claus Day" and a sheet of plywood featuring freshly-painted elf bodies with holes for faces so that you could take family photos. Bizarre as that might seem on Holy Saturday, there were no half-measures in that town: even the liquor store sported giant candy-canes and every fire hydrant was hand-painted, a different elf on each block. The trees boasted green buds and the Nanking cherry bushes were almost ready to blossom. A lanky man out picking up bottles in the ditch turned his head as we drove by, his stare following us as if we were the strangest things in town.

Hugo always drove the speed limit, even when there was more chance of winning the lottery than finding a cop. In Saskatchewan towns, it was 40 km/hr. Paul was not so fastidious; he urged Hugo to step on it. "If we're late, we'll miss out. Crying shame. Deals like this just don't come along every day." So Hugo looked all around, scanned the side streets for cruisers, and finally, reluctantly, pushed it to 50. But all was well. At Main Street we turned, followed Paul's directions south and out of town. Soon we were on the gravel doing 75. The road was freshly graded, and as we skidded a bit, I quietly seized the handle with my right hand and hung on, pressing my left palm against my belly, hard. No one appeared to notice. Five km straight, then east, and then Paul said, waving his hat with a flourish, "And Bob's your uncle, and there she be."

A Suburban blew past, kicking up broad veils of gauzy dust. We couldn't see a thing.

"Should be right here," Paul repeated. He craned his head out his window, peered back and forth down the road.

Giant black spruce and struggling poplars lined the road where the turn ought to be. I played with the thought that maybe we weren't meant to find this house, after all. But within minutes, the dust had settled, Hugo found the break in the trees, and the driveway opened before us. Up ahead, the two-storey house with its dark cedar siding looked deserted, but no, there was a figure in the window, and the curtains fell back into place.

"At least there's somebody home," I said, relieved for Paul's sake. "The property seems nicely kept."

The gardens along the drive were tilled and raked smooth, and tidy half-barrel tubs flanked either side of the doorway, ready for bedding plants. A dark rail fence marked off a lawn cropped short and starting to tinge up with green. A beagle and a shepherd-lab mix danced and barked around our truck and a man opened the screen door and walked out to the porch.

"Whoa there, Baxter. Spinner, you settle down. That's enough."

Paul opened his door, abandoning his hat there on the seat. With the truck windows rolled down, we heard him call as he walked over, "Mornin'! This the Weston place?"

When the older man nodded, Hugo, Emma and I piled out of the truck.

"It is. I'm Jack Weston. Who's asking?"

Paul walked to the porch, and we came up behind. "I'm Paul Boudreau," he said, stretching out his hand. "Called a few days ago. Planned to come yesterday, but something came up. We were detained. These are my sisters, Delphine and Emma, and my brother-in-law, Hugo."

Jack frowned. "We waited all last afternoon. You're catching me on my way out, now, but I guess you can have a look, if you don't take all day. Come in, come in." He held the screen door for Paul, and walked in behind him.

Hugo caught the door and held it, slipping in behind Emma and me. The one window in the porch faced north, and light filtered in through the green plaid curtains. The air felt sharp, at least ten degrees colder than outside. In the dimness I saw a separator, a couple of cream cans. Two old wool jackets hung below a shelf of ball caps and toques and sheepskin mittens.

Paul boomed, "How old did you say this house is?" I was sure I heard the window rattle a little. If Jack wasn't hard of hearing before, he might be now, I thought, but Jack just replied, "Depends when you start counting. She's been redone three times."

He opened the second door, the one into the house proper, and the others walked through. My shoe had come untied, and, my fingers suddenly numb, I fumbled with the laces like a pre-schooler. At last I opened the door and stepped inside. Everything tilted. I had done this before, I had stood knee deep in the calm pools of light that flooded this kitchen.

20

I FELT A TERRIFYING, EXHILARATING DÉJÀ VU. The only other time I had experienced anything like it was in a conversation all those years ago, when the thought of moving to Saskatchewan was first presented to me.

My friend Fiona and I had finally found time to meet for coffee in the large bookstore on Calgary Trail in Edmonton. She was such a dear soul, a poet who loved art as much as I did. We had met years ago, in our first-year Art History class, and she was the only close friend I'd made in university with whom I still stayed in touch. We saw one another three or four times a year, and emailed in between. I wanted to hear how her family was, what her latest manuscript was about. She had been away on a tour, and was eager to tell me about some college she had visited.

"It's this perfect little campus, hidden in plain sight on the prairies. A hundred and fifty students, a liberal arts focus. And the retreat facilities—just ask any writer about Muenster. There's a tall cedar maze around the monks' graveyard, so eerie and Gothic. It had snowed just the night before. We walked it in the fog, so serene, otherworldly in the best possible way. When we emerged, we met the Abbey's hermit, dear Fr. Lewis, the most darling old man. He told us that fog and storms and even Northern Lights mean that some hurdle has been overcome by those seeking spirit. He said that the things that hate light react against spiritual progress, try to punish us by hiding the physical world, or frightening us. Of course once we know the secret, they fail, because the very sign of their revenge shows us that we're winning."

"Uh-huh," I said. "That's quite the theory. How was the reading? Did you have a good turnout?" I wondered where she was going with all this.

"It's a have-not province."

"Hmmm...." I was fretting that we had such a short time together.

She smiled and tried again. "Property is dirt-cheap. Lots of charming old houses. Turn of the twentieth century. If you and Hugo are looking for a challenge, why don't you apply to teach out there?"

I was struck by déjà vu at this moment. I had done this before, lived this moment. Everything around me slowed down, the people drinking coffee at the tables around us, the shoppers browsing through the shelves of books, and yet my thoughts flew by, ricocheted faster than I could think. It was all so familiar.

"A Benedictine order built the college."

So there was synchronicity, too; that was so bizarre. I'd been reading about monasteries, had just picked up *The Rule of Saint Benedict* in the university library. I had always been fascinated by saints, particularly after that program on PBS last week featuring Monte Cassino.

"Maybe you and Hugo could find a charming old house on an acreage near the college, grow your own food, get back to nature. Didn't you say he's just taken a position as an online instructor? If he's working from home, does it matter what province?"

"I don't think so. And budget cuts and rising class sizes have certainly made teaching in Edmonton a misery for me. Three hundred students this term in one section."

"And life in the country might be like a return to those blissful summers at the lake."

"What is it you always say—that thing that Joseph Campbell says about the chance to break away, return to what matters?"

"Follow the pollen path," Fiona beamed at me.

WHEN I ARRIVED HOME, Hugo was curious, and I was eager to sell him on Fiona's idea. We arranged a trip to Saskatchewan to meet with the president and the fine arts director in February. It was almost a day's drive, but, as we followed the sweep of the road down the hill and across the ravine and over the creek at last, the great brick building seemed a grand thing, a mirage or a castle. Double rows of grand and graceful elms, enormous black spruce rose high above the gravel drive, hundreds of trees, all perfectly spaced; each one planted and watered by hand until, like the monks who tended the abbey, it had grown firm in the belief that the prairie was its home.

We entered through the tall west door, and I left Hugo seated in the foyer, thumbing his way through the stack of yellowing *Prairie Messenger* newspapers. It was Reading Week so the college was deserted. As I poked around, looking for someone to report to, I admired the old maple floors, the classrooms lit by fourteen-foot windows. What was that scent in the air? Could there really be bread baking somewhere? Eventually I found a young woman in a storage closet, sorting through a box of files. She took me to the president, Dr. Yvette Belanger, who asked her to fetch Jim Fredericks. Soon the three of us were settled into cosy chairs beside the table. Yvette cleared a spot in the stacks of books, art, archaeology, a biography of Leonard Cohen and a copy of Walter Benjamin's *Illuminations,* and, within minutes, the young woman from the storage closet was back with a tray of china cups abloom with gorgeous red and yellow roses, a large teapot of fragrant chai, and the most delicious apricot gingersnaps, made, Jim assured me, in the Abbey kitchens below the college.

It was all so mysterious, so perfectly welcoming. There was a guest wing where those who couldn't afford a room could work half-days to pay their way by weeding the enormous vegetable gardens, picking raspberries or saskatoons, or helping out with routine painting or maintenance. The monks had been hand-feeding the chickadees for sixty years, and the birds flocked to guests who brought seeds and nuts to feed them, especially down by the graveyard. We talked about the importance of nature and art to civilized society, the interdisciplinarity possible in a small institution, the benefits of a life organized around the principles of mentorship and hospitality. They were not a bit surprised to hear I'd been reading *The Rule of Saint Benedict* when I'd first heard of the college's existence.

At last there were only two cookies left on the plate. Yvette told me of the pleasure they'd felt when they'd reviewed the dossier I'd sent them, and Jim finally inquired about my education and teaching interests. This was my chance. My teaching reviews were excellent, my research fit their offerings, and I'd always been told that my communication skills were strong. And after we'd spent another charming fifteen minutes discussing my focus, the relevance of art in healing, Yvette smiled as kindly as anyone ever had at me in my entire life, and said that she had no positions available.

About to ask when classes started, I stopped, closed my mouth, and tried to breathe. What had happened? They'd been perfectly friendly, yet what could Yvette's words mean except no work for *me.* Trying not to shake, I rose, thanked them politely for the lovely visit, and gently asked them to keep me in mind should an opening arise. I could still smell the bread baking as I made my way back to the foyer.

I collected Hugo quietly, and when I pushed open the heavy wooden front door, we almost bowled over an ancient monk, pulling from outside.

He introduced himself as Fr. Lewis, and asked whether we'd like some feed for the birds. It wasn't until later, when I'd emailed Fiona to tell her about our fiasco of a trip, that I realized he was the same hermit she had spoken about, the one who had told her about the meaning of fog when she was there for her reading.

After my disastrous interview, I felt like I was dying, but Hugo had no idea about that yet, so he said "Yes, please," and the old fellow passed him a handful of split peanuts, telling us to stand with one palm held out just so, until one tiny bird after another flitted over to delicately clutch a finger with its claws, snatch a seed, and swoop away. We stood in silence, our breath bright clouds in the cold air. When the monk left us, he chirped, "See you soon!"

Ha! I thought bleakly. *Not bloody likely.*

Thirty minutes later, we were back in the nearest city, Humboldt, drinking strong black coffee at the Bella Vista Inn. I still couldn't understand what had gone wrong, but I managed to tell Hugo the story, and he became quiet, protective. In the end we didn't even open our menus, just ordered the special, some kind of cheddar soup with pastrami sandwiches on rye. I had the strangest feeling, I just couldn't pin it down. It wasn't the déjà vu I was familiar with, if you could be familiar with that kind of thing, but there was something about this trip, it reminded me of something I couldn't quite remember.

And as we looked out the window at the blue showing through the low clouds sliding across the rec centre's football field, Hugo suggested that we shouldn't go home yet, not without looking at houses.

21

A S I STOOD IN THE DOORWAY to the Weston house proper, I knew that Emma and Hugo were to the right of me, talking quietly. I heard their voices but couldn't make out the words. Had I dreamt this? It all seemed so familiar, not just this place, but everything, these people, this kitchen, this moment. I tried to shake it off, force myself to look around.

Every wall was a soothing pale colour I couldn't quite place. *Shantung*? *Spring Celadon*? High ceilings rippled with waves of reflected light. Wide plank floors shone white in the sun. Ropes of garlic and onions and clusters of herbs draped a large frame in the corner. There were tall oak cabinets on three walls. A window over the farmhouse sink looked out over a little orchard where well-pruned trees swayed in the wind, almost ready to bud out.

For a moment I was horrified. Paul was opening the drawers, apparently trying to slam them shut. They glided slowly back into their frames. Emma said to me. "Very nifty. Must have been upgraded relatively recently."

"Put in a new kitchen in 2002," Jack said, coming up behind us. "Sure has served us well. Never thought we'd leave, but there you have it. The kids don't care to take over, and even when I promised we could redo the house again, the wife won't stay. Happy wife—"

"Happy life," Hugo chimed in. "Ain't that the truth?" he grinned at me wickedly. He turned to face Jack again. "The outer walls are pretty thick. What's the story there?"

Jack proudly explained that the construction was double; they built a whole new structure over the old one. "Lots of old farmhouses are redone that way. Cool as a bunker in the summer, cozy all winter long. We've a woodstove in the living room, and another linked to an oil furnace in the basement. Go on down and have a look. Keeps the house from freezing when the power goes off. Seemed like we'd be here forever. This is where the kids grew up," he said, looking around the room. Paul and Hugo clambered down the stairs. We could hear them chatting, but the words were out of reach.

For a moment Jack looked around, seeming lost, then he straightened and gathered himself. "But plans change. We're moving to town." He turned to look at me. "My wife has had a bout of cancer."

"I'm so sorry," Emma and I said, almost as one.

"She's in remission now, but we need to make the most of our years together. Had enough work. Our friends have invited us to winter with them in Palm Springs. If we like it, might buy a place down there ourselves, rent it out when we're not there. Still a few good deals, in spite of the way the American economy is recovering."

Hugo and Paul came upstairs, back to the kitchen, and we all walked through into the living room. "Look, Delphine," Paul said, quietly for once. "That's a real library." Raising his voice, he called to Jack, "Would sure be a chore to shift all those books…maybe you could leave them with the house?"

Jack seemed surprised. "Well, I'd need my Zane Greys, of course, and a few others. But fifty winters on the farm, the reading material does pile up. Might be able to work a deal."

Emma quietly pointed at the bookcases themselves, tall with glass doors, so like the ones I'd admired at the stores in Edmonton. These were custom. Before long, we had inspected the entire house, trying not to say too much: the fine airy kitchen and open main floor, the four spacious bedrooms with dormers upstairs, the decent-sized four-piece bathrooms on each level. The closets in every bedroom were generous, too.

"It might seem silly, getting excited about closets, but you know—" I said to Emma.

She understood. "As nice as you've made it, those little hundred-year-old houses have no storage," she shook her head. "I don't know how you manage, my girl."

"I manage by rotating the clothes our tiny wardrobe will hold—it's the vacuum-bag relay race, the dance of the seasons, upstairs, downstairs," I joked.

As the others climbed the stairs to the bedrooms, I could hear Paul talking to Jack; he was using his charisma, all right. When they arrived at the top, Hugo and Emma and I gave them the space, descending to the living room. We returned to the bookcases.

Emma looked lovingly at the shelves. "Jack has been too modest about his reading taste. There's a good collection of nineteenth century novels, plenty of twentieth century American and Canadian, and all kinds of history and practical how-to stuff."

Hugo nodded and said, "And look at this, the all-encompassing *Encyclopaedia of Country Life*, full of arcane entries, everything from how to choose a good alpaca—you've always wanted one, haven't you, Del?—to how to make candles or mix paint or get bread to rise in a draughty kitchen."

I glanced into the dining room, and I had the sensation that the sun had come out from behind a cloud, only it hadn't, the sky was thick again, damp with mist. The west windows were cracked open, their thin lace curtains waving gently.

The room held an antique oak table with eight mismatched high-backed wooden chairs. A trio of pink and purple and magenta African violets sat atop a fine lace doily on the table. I was surprised to see a white orchid, two full stems of flowers and a spray of buds on a ledge beneath the window to the east. I couldn't remember when I'd felt so at home.

Paul and Jack were back downstairs now, standing in the kitchen over by the back door. Paul was loud as usual, and even Jack's voice carried. "That might be okay. We hope to sell this spring. I have a buyer for the land, all six quarters, on condition that he can seed in May. But we'd have to have time to get our things out before you can take the house."

"It's already the first week of April. Seems like quite the rush. What're you thinking?"

"Well, we're half-moved into town. We've a nice bungalow there, been in the family since my parents retired thirty years ago; no sense putting things off."

When Jack named his price, Hugo nudged me with his elbow, whispered, "Couldn't build it for a sixth of that. Paul says it can be moved and set up with geothermals. With the solar/wind combo up on the homestead…"

I saw what he was up to, recognized that look. I poked him back and hissed, "Cut that out!"

Hugo whispered, "You're always complaining that we don't have enough room."

Emma was about to step in between to quiet us down when we were startled to see a woman come out of the door from the basement. We presumed it was Mrs. Baxter, her grey hair short and stylish. She was wearing jeans and a pin-tucked lavender tunic, carrying a laundry basket topped with a homemade quilt. She stopped in the kitchen to make a pot of tea. By the time she arrived in the living room with a tray of cups and saucers, we three were back on our best behaviour, relaxed and friendly.

"I'm just going to have a bit of a rest over by the south window," she smiled at us, "But you're welcome to join me." As we followed her over to the long sofa, we chatted about the house, her flowers, their upcoming travel plans. At last she said, "You have children?"

"Twin boys and a girl, but they've grown up and flown away," I told her.

"I have two of my own," Emma added. "A boy and a girl. Definitely still underfoot."

"This place would have room for all of them to visit, something we can't manage now." My own words startled me, reminded me that we were supposed to be finding flaws, not getting excited about *living* here. Why on earth would we move up to Paul's place?

It might be good for him to have some company, I caught myself thinking. As I looked over at the kitchen again, for a second I indulged myself, imagined all of us gathered around, Paul, Dad, Emma, Geoff, all the kids, too, helping to cook, laughing and joking, not just at Christmas or Thanksgiving, but every day. And we could fix it up, make it our own. I envisioned the whole place repainted, white walls and upper shelves, lower cabinets grey or claret or rich green or indigo, long butcher-block counters, new flat black hardware and a backsplash of cool fresh tile. A large island with room for high bistro stools. A bouquet of pink tulips, a cool marble board for rolling pastry. An espresso machine. Lattes by the woodstove in the evenings after long days outdoors.

I shook off my nonsense and said, as firmly as I could, "But this is for Paul. It just wouldn't make sense, not for us."

Mrs. Baxter just smiled, excusing herself to go to the kitchen for more hot water.

We noticed then that Paul and Jack were talking earnestly, their voices rising, and Paul was shaking his head. "Well, with moving, setting up, and all...not going to be cheap. And if you can't get the house off in time for seeding, your good friend Jonesie will walk away, you'll lose the money for all those sections. I heard of people letting houses go for a dollar, just to get the property free and clear. The land's where the money is, as I'm sure you know."

Jack looked over at his wife for a second, then turned back to Paul. "Well, that wouldn't feel right, giving our home away like that. Make me a reasonable offer."

"We could have your house moved in less than three weeks, say the 24th of April." As he outlined his offer, Paul's confidence startled me. He finished, "We'll take the whole shebang."

"We?" Hugo said sharply. "Paul! *We* haven't said we'd do any of this." He rose and started to cross the room.

Paul waved him away. "I mean *I* will, I'll take it. I'm buying her for the homestead."

Emma and I looked on, concerned, while Paul continued. Hugo backed off, came to stand beside us, his eyes wide.

"Reckless overspending is a symptom," Emma said softly.

"The thing is, he's *not* overspending," Hugo said, turning to her, his voice low. "He's getting one hell of a deal."

22

IN LESS THAN TEN MINUTES JACK AND PAUL reached an agreement. The proposal was too sweet for Jack to pass up: Paul would pay cash and guarantee to have the house off the land in time for seeding.

We heard Jack say, "With the house off our minds, Lorna and I can sign up for that European River Cruise, then, when that's over, just follow our feet. See where life leads us."

Paul could have most of the library and whatever was in the shed; there was a good wood cook-stove and a collection of hand tools. The various outbuildings could go, too, so long as they were off the land by the date agreed. At last Paul came over to us, smiling broadly. As if to prove that he was no madman, he asked Hugo to help him, and the two men moved from room to room with the book of graph paper and a pencil, measuring, making note of windows and doors and orientation. When that was done, we headed back to the truck.

Once we were on the road, though, Paul's true glee surfaced quickly. "So, what d'ya think? I've kept most of the money I got for my land, Theo's land, in Alberta. This is hardly a drop from the proverbial bucket."

Emma was cautious. "It *is* a gorgeous house, Paul, but how in the world are you going to get it moved and set up in such a short time?"

"What seems sudden to you is really the end of a long hunt for me. I knew I wanted to get another house on the home place this spring. I did my research, have a team of geothermal experts booked and the machinery to do the digging once we've picked the site."

"And this *we* is—?" Hugo looked as concerned as I had started to feel.

"Don't you worry about a thing. Already booked an appointment on Monday for a consult with the house movers."

Sitting beside me in the back, Emma could see I was worried but, of course, she couldn't guess why or feel my terror. What could I do with my Bright Ideas order if Hugo really wanted to head for the bush? She reached over to take my hand. "Don't fret, Del. It's a project for Paul to busy himself with. He'll set up a commune out there in his never-never land, and we'll just have to make sure he doesn't install a roller-coaster or a safari park stocked with lions and tigers. Oh my!"

I shook my head. "What I'm worried about, Em, is a little different." Different, that's the word for it. I faked a smile, but I couldn't relax. This was hardly the place to spill my worries, so I focused the conversation on Paul's move. "I have a feeling that unless we can decide whether we're signing on right smartly, he'll design the place all to suit his end-of-the-world sensibilities, and somehow, no matter what the rest of us think we want, we'll all soon be toting rifles and roughing it in the bush. And what will Hugo do without his television?"

"Well, men like projects. And honestly, I'm amazed that you're not smitten. Don't you want this house? It's fantastic, truly. Roomy without being extravagant. Must be 1300 square feet on each floor, and upstairs, the lovely dormers and sloped ceilings like we had when we were growing up in Woodcroft. And truly, Delphine, I say this with no disrespect: compared to the Weston house, your present place is a chicken coop."

I had to stay calm, or at least act that way, so I nodded. "Jack's house, I mean, Paul's new house, does have a special feel to it. The light is stunning. And if half of what Paul's told us about the way he's setting things up turns out to be true, the view will be pretty spectacular."

Emma laughed, "And there'll be squirrels, Del. Lots and lots of squirrels."

"Then there'll be nuts, too," I said, poking her ribs. "We'll fit right in."

23

PAUL WASTED NO TIME ONCE WE MADE IT BACK to our little grey house. He urged us to get hustling, put together enough warm clothes for an overnight trip out to his place: he had some ideas about where to set the new house, but he wanted our six cents' worth, and four heads were better than one, after all.

While we packed, Hugo told me he was surprised, even impressed, by the way Paul had handled the negotiations.

I replied, "Well, people like Paul tend to be enthusiastic, creative. I saw it on Facebook, so it must be true."

"People like Paul? Just how are you categorizing him? You mean Sagittarians?" Hugo laughed, trying to flick me with the pair of longjohns he was holding.

"No, I mean people born on the 28th of the month. Geez, what do you think I mean? Do you really want me to spell it out? After yesterday? The bi-polar bear?" I threw two pairs of socks at him as I dug through the dresser for another heavy sweater.

As I stashed our underclothes and pyjamas in the duffel bag, crammed in bunny-hugs and jeans, nothing seemed real. Some part of me knew it was important to decide what to do. The new house drew me, I had to admit it. It felt like a gift from the universe, right from the first moment I'd entered that kitchen. I had been a bit lonely in the little house, especially since Gina had left. Hugo and I had only Paul, really, for family, and if he went into seclusion up north—

Maybe Erik had called it that New Year's Day five years ago. He has my knack for saying the most outrageous things that somehow turn out to be true. Even before we knew about ISIS or Ebola or the way the government was monitoring all communications, I'd remarked one day that it was going to be an interesting century. In that matter-of-fact way that Erik has, he replied: "Mom. If you find it *interesting* to watch jackals eat our entrails, then, yes—for sure this century will be interesting." And he smiled wryly at me, and went back to playing his video game.

Hugo and I didn't have our heads in the sand; we had done our own bit of prepping, not for civil unrest, of course, but we'd taken the last Ebola epidemic seriously. The swiftness of it scared us, its immediacy had changed our focus. Oh, yes, we were casual as spies among the aimless Friday after-supper shoppers. Without really having a plan, we found ourselves quietly adding jugs of chlorine bleach and laundry soap to first one cart, and then three, gigantic packs of toilet paper, cases of baked beans and end-of-the-world staples like canned chickens and tinned picnic hams and stew made with mystery meat, the type you'd only eat if you really were facing the apocalypse. I had added as many packages of thick yellow rubber gloves as I could find. Peroxide and Polysporin and Bandaids and rubbing alcohol and Strepsils too. The virus wasn't the only thing you could die of, and hospital visits would be impossible, likely the epicentre of the pandemic. Hugo tossed in boxes of blood-thinning baby aspirin to prevent strokes. We already had gauze and painkillers and fever medication and odourless garlic capsules and slow-release vitamin C to fight infection, and soon our stores of canned, bottled, and frozen food overflowed the cold room in the basement. For weeks Hugo casually fetched case after case of cans of Green Giant green beans and Campbell's Hungry Man soup and large jars of marmalade, leaving them clustered in bags on the floor in the kitchen, where I had either to trip over them or find them a home.

When the television reports worsened, we began to worry in earnest. Statisticians said there was only a small chance that Ebola would be in Canada by the end of October, half of what Spain's chances were thought to be. But the grim epidemiologist on *The National* warned that unless people were quarantined before they left West Africa, all the questionnaires and fever checks in the world's airports would only make us *feel* safer.

We were in Canada, for God's sake, not in Europe or Africa, and at first we didn't know what to do. Emma wasn't concerned. I knew my friends would dismiss me as paranoid—they always did. It's true that my earlier fears had failed to materialize: instead of soaring oil prices and interest rates, the reverse had happened, and there'd been no solar flare or electromagnetic pulse to disrupt satellites or the fry the electric grid. But with Ebola, even the ever-calm Hugo was concerned. And then Peter Mansbridge announced that the Marburg virus, another haemorrhagic fever, had broken out in Kenya.

Yet none of that had destroyed civilization.

Hugo broke into my silence by asking whether I'd packed for a change of weather. It could be -20 with blowing snow tomorrow, or +20 with a light breeze. Soon we had stowed even more clothes in the duffel bag. Emma, who is always more organized than the rest of us, was already in the kitchen, helping Paul heat up last night's leftovers. We joked all through lunch. Paul, who is always full of tall tales when things are going his way, kept us laughing, but as soon as we finished eating, we set out again.

24

THIS TIME WE TOOK TWO VEHICLES and headed for the homestead that Paul had purchased for his off-the-grid compound, the site he had decided to reclaim from the folks who had bought it from *Pépère* when he sold up and retired. The remoteness and the family history made it the perfect choice. There was a good creek, plenty of trees, and yet the folks who had lived there had kept plenty of fields cleared, so that he could pasture animals, raise hay and grain, he told us. I travelled with Hugo, and Emma rode with Paul in his old blue beast. The drive took us through the rollercoaster of hills again, except that unlike the day before, this time we turned north at the junction and headed towards Prince Albert. Despite his law-abiding nature, Hugo kept up with Paul's pace, and in thirty-five minutes we reached Domremy.

The village, barely a hamlet really, had a Co-op grocery, a gas station, a post office, a general store, and the Domremy

Inn, which, I told Hugo, might be a blessing if we needed to escape Paul's world. We stopped at the Co-op and I lined up to pay while Hugo gassed up the truck. I looked around, thinking how different this place must be from the little settlement that *Pépère* and Granny knew in their day, but it still seemed French. Named for the birthplace of Jeanne d'Arc, Hugo told me. He'd just seen a special about her on the learning channel. I wondered if that was a sign. I've always had a weakness for saints, especially mystics and visionaries.

As I ruminated about all this, I watched the woman in front of me purchase a string of four lottery tickets and wondered how she could afford twenty dollars for that, yet refuse her son the chocolate bar he was asking for.

The girl at the checkout seemed to be having the same thought. She gave the woman a grim smile, then turned to me. Her face warmed as she asked, "Just the gas?"

"I'll have one of those lottery packs, the one she had, too." I had no idea why I said that; I never gambled anymore, but for no reason I could name, I wanted to vindicate the previous customer. Surely there was little enough thrill in her life, and I enjoyed scandalizing the smug small-town cashier who'd had the nerve to assume I was on her side.

After I paid, Hugo and I climbed back into his truck and the little convoy set off again.

Paul turned east on the grid and took the back roads for half an hour or so until we reached the homestead, just north of Pelican Lake and overlooking the Muskeg Creek. Hugo and I hadn't seen the home place for quite some time, and we noticed that a broad new gravel road replaced the old cutline that we had always used to guide us. When we reached Paul's cabin, Hugo parked beside his truck. Emma and Paul were already out by the time we'd opened our doors.

Hugo whistled at Paul and asked him, "Won't clearing the brush for that road take away some of your privacy?"

"Thought about that. Can't be helped. In a few years those willows and poplars will sucker and fill in, and no one will see us. Be better if folks didn't know we're here, but the sad fact is that my shenanigans are already making quite the stir in Domremy. I need the road to move the houses and outbuildings in. The fortifications will just have to keep people out, if it comes to that."

"Hous*es*?" I wanted to ask, but Emma was already talking. "Fortifications?" she said, one eyebrow lifted. She looked around.

"Yeah, fence and such like," Paul said, pointing. What was invisible from the road was obvious enough when we looked from inside the property. We could see the tall thing clearly, the roll of barbed wire on top.

"In the meantime, it's handy to have the hamlet nearby. It's a nice little community, and, until things do get tough, it's still useful to have a place to buy grub and hardware and get the mail," Paul added.

After the exchange at the Co-op, I wasn't sure Domremy would be much help, even if we needed it. Would the hamlet folk help a bunch of strangers, especially looney-tune survivalists?

"You really think the end of the world is on its way? Years after the so-called Mayan Apocalypse?" Emma laughed. "What a joke that was, just like all the others—the fizzle with Y2K, the Jehovah's Witnesses' predictions—"

Paul's face grew serious. "You think I'm crazy? Ask Delphine, she knows I'm not—go ahead, ask her, just had that confirmed yesterday. Even the doc said there are tons of people preparing. Societies always come to an end. And of course the collapse won't happen tomorrow, the Mayan thing was a metaphor, a warning shot from the elders. On the other hand, might be just as well to go green asap, get used to doing things the new way, take what worked from the old. Think about all the fuss when a satellite turns the wrong way, shuts down the internet, can't use debit or credit cards."

Paul went on. "And all those cyber attacks on the banks. Space junk. China's growth slowing. Russia refusing to admit it's taking over Ukraine. North Korea and her rockets. Iran. Syria. Israel. ISIS. Something other than our tiny li'l first-world problems will touch us, sooner or later. Civilizations crumble. Ask Hugo. It's history."

Hugo couldn't resist. I knew he'd heard all of this on television; he watched shows about prepping for doomsday just to tease me. I was surprised when he nodded and said, "Well, some do say it's not a matter of if, but when. Look at the States and their deficit—and don't get me started about the Eurozone—"

"Right," said Emma. "So don't get started." She winked at me.

But Hugo was on a roll. "I'm more concerned about the drop in oil prices, though it may be a good thing, might mean the world will finally turn to green energy. If they can't make money on oil, all of a sudden it will seem uber-important to save the planet. And when most of what you export comes from holes in the ground, what are you left with when what you've dug up won't sell? It's not Swiss cheese, folks. Canada is facing a real recession."

Hugo nodded, and Emma jumped in again.

"How in the world do you three manage to get up in the morning, thinking that way? The Prime Minister has negotiated trade deals with China and India—"

"Exactly!" Paul slapped Emma's back, a little too hard. She shot him a confused look as he continued, "What about China and India? Poor li'l Canada'll be no more than a chunk of meat, kiddo, raw meat dangling between starving tigers. Might not be the end of the world yet, but..."

I couldn't even start to say what I thought, the laundry list of problems sounded so impossible to deal with. And yet here the sun was shining, the clouds now just a slim bank far to the south, and we were surrounded by the racket of spring birds and wavering frogsong. And again, I couldn't escape that feeling of déjà vu that had dogged me all day.

A porous sun, the sky white, the outline of snow in the air. The first snowfall.

I tried to shake off the ghost, forced myself to speak. "The planet will keep turning. All we can work with is today."

Even to myself I sounded like some tiresome self-help guru. My chest was feeling tight. More than anything, I needed to change the topic.

"And if the world is about to end, why the fancy new mansion?" I asked, poking Paul gently with my index finger. "Wouldn't it make more sense to build another log cabin out here, or bunk us all down in a longhouse?"

Paul looked down, studied a tiny black frog as it hopped across his left boot. He started to speak, stopped, then raised his clear grey eyes into mine.

"Would you have come out here for a log cabin or a longhouse, Delphine? Would you?"

"I haven't said we'll come for the dream home."

Paul looked at his boots again, but the frog was gone. A noisy cloud of red-winged blackbirds landed in the bush behind us.

At last he said, "Okay. You wonder why I worry things will collapse. Maybe it won't happen, not in our lifetime. But like I said, empires always break down, one time or another—" He gestured to the south slope down to the creek, lifted his left hand and our eyes followed to the canopy of thin birch and aspen branches just on the verge of leafing out. He turned and looked at us with some emotion I recognized but could not name.

He panned our faces as he said, "We'll hope I'm wrong, then, I can testify to that, but tell me the truth: have any of you ever seen a finer place?"

25

WE WALKED TO THE FAR SIDE of the small clearing where Paul's cabin stood. The water was singing off to the south, the afternoon sun was hot. The almost-leaves were flickering slips of green light, and the breeze from the west felt fresh, invigorating. In the distance, white-throated sparrows were calling, with chickadees and a grey jay joining in, while a woodpecker rat-a-tat-tatted in front of us on a spruce. We could hear a sage grouse, far away, drumming.

A sudden burst slanted by me, lovely but strange, leaves outlined in snow. I heard someone say, "The road is closed. Have to bring her. Can't hurt to have her with us when Delphine comes around."

The voice sounded like Paul's, but when I looked, Hugo was the one speaking. He was talking to Emma about solar panels. Paul was already way up ahead, leading the way through the bush. "Let's have a look at the sites I'm thinking of, just for fun, then," Paul called. "Say we'd want to be close, but still have a bit of privacy."

Paul gave us the tour as we entered a glen down along the creek. "We'll have backup solar arrays, just in case one fails, and we'll share the windmill set-up I installed last fall. Smaller units to prevent headaches and suchlike that some people complain of. Use woodstoves for cooking, nothing like wood heat for comfort, though it takes a bit of experimentation to learn to use a wood-fired oven. We'll have rechargeable lights as long as we can; have some fine solar lanterns ready. 'Course, we can supplement with kerosene until the collapse comes and we run out."

Emma and I both started to speak, but he reached between us, gently redirected a spring-drowsy bumblebee away from my face. "Why not take up the old ways, as much as we can? I've been learning. Can keep our own bees for pollination and honey. Stealing too much wax from the hives is no good, but by mixing beeswax with tallow, adding alum, we'll dip hard candles." He paused. Emma, Hugo, and I were all looking at him as if he was from Mars.

Hugo cleared his throat. "That's great Paul, you're a veritable fountain of information. But even if we did buy into your scheme, how would Delphine and I earn a living?"

Paul looked at him for a moment, then shook his head slowly from side to side, laughing hard, his hands braced on his belly. "For such smart folks, all of you seem so awful slow, it's painful! I'm talking about spending your *lives* living. And how would you use money, 'specially money in banks, after the crash?"

He paused, then straightened up, launched right back into his lecture, as if he'd been dying to share his plans. He had the whole thing figured out. "Even if this monstrosity you call *civilization* succeeds, we won't need cash out here, not once we're set up. We'll have a great big sunny garden not far from the water, and keep draft horses for ploughing and transportation, a few cows and a bull. Might as well keep some pigs to turn our food scraps into bacon and ham. We'll want some sheep for mutton and wool, and, of course, we'll need chickens. If all else fails, we can live on deer and moose. Plenty of grassland for grazing."

He gestured around. "This here quarter is *Pépère's* original, the homestead he settled, and—as you can see—she's got a good stand of timber for lumber, case we want to build. The three other quarters he cleared were kept up by the folks who sold them back to me. See what we need and what we can handle. What we can't use'll go back to bush, help us stay out of sight."

My head ached like nothing I had ever felt. I could hardly think. It did seem that we'd spent our entire lives chasing some event, a shifting target always on the horizon: new jobs, new houses, new furniture, even the new kitchen. Wasn't that the way Hugo and I had lived, hopscotching after things? Were we ready for a completely new—a completely old—way of life? What would the kids make of it?

Hugo and I fell behind. He draped his arm over my shoulders, walking quietly at first. I couldn't read him at all. The sun was hot, and I asked him to stop so I could take off my jacket.

At last, I said, "Well, we are used to isolation; that's pretty much the way we live now. As Emma demonstrated last night, Lucky doesn't have a clue what a knock at the door means. We still don't know our neighbours and—"

"Hey," he said, squeezing my shoulders, "speak for yourself. I know the ladies in the R.M. office." He leaned down to nibble my ear.

"Oh you do, do you?" I freed my hands, swatted at his chest. "And you think I should know that they'd miss you?" He jumped away and I chased him a bit, launched myself at him as I tripped, and brought us both down to the spongy ground. We bantered as we tussled, and then, after we realized the others were already far ahead, we rose, brushed the leaves off, and jogged to catch up.

Paul and Emma were spreading their jackets in the sun and setting out the little picnic we'd packed. The salmon sandwiches had stayed fresh in the cooler, and there was plenty of iced tea. Hugo said, "This saving the world is thirsty work," as he filled our plastic cups. Paul helped himself to some sliced beet pickles and passed the container.

But mostly we were quiet; there was so much to think about. I looked away to the creek, caught the light dancing, and tried to remember how long it took to boil water on the woodstove up at the lake. We ate slowly, soaking in the sounds of the wind in the treetops, the creek splashing, the birds rejoicing, and I couldn't help but drink in all that peace. The home place.

AND AFTER WE'D FINISHED, Paul led us up to a small plateau at the top of a gentle rise. "If we put the house up here, you'd never have to fret about flooding." As he spoke, I saw him pause and look at the slope of the land, the trees. "Where would you set the house, Del?"

I knew this was our chance to recreate that sensation of light I'd loved at the Weston farm. I felt shy, a five-year-old again, like the time Paul took me out on the back porch and had me try out names for our new kitten, calling to see which one suited best. After much dithering, we settled on "Fluffy," a trite enough name for a cat, but the two syllables sung well, and the cat didn't seem to mind.

I thought for a moment and then gestured to the side.

"There?" Paul said, pointing slightly over from where I'd indicated. "Del, you surprise me. Good for you. That sets the living room over here, and the windows 'll take in the same light as they do at Jack's now."

"Well, with the leaves filtering the light, the effect will be even better out here," I told him, feeling a little less awkward. "Could we look at the floor plan you two drew?"

"Hugo, where's the tape measure?" Paul asked, pulling out his papers.

The men had drawn to scale and noted all the important details, including how the house was positioned. Paul said he had to have his ideas firmed up by the time he met with the experts, so he'd know what was left to be done, what to ask them about. Soon he had us all helping, adjusting here and there, marking with stakes and pegs and rocks, trying to envision what the view would be like from each room, which trees would need to be cut away to get the truck in, and which ones to leave. If we could bring the house in on the grid and up Paul's road, our own driveway (would you call it a driveway if there were no cars?) wouldn't need to be too long. Any trees sacrificed could be saved for lumber or firewood.

He insisted that we check out the other site, the one closer to the creek and to the east, but it didn't have the same charm. The first place was the best one, with its large wooded hill. Paul planned to cut a swath around the houses for fire protection but lots of trees could be left for walking within a reasonable distance, except where the creek lay to the south. That was shielded from the road by the forest on the far side. "Not crazy about having men see the place, even though they're like-minded people, but me and Leland are gonna have to work ourselves into shape, no time to waste in moving that house. Got to be done—terms of the agreement. Besides, we'll be busy. We'll need a barn and a farmyard built near the compound for the homes this summer."

"Compound? Homes? That's pretty ambitious, Paul," Hugo said, shaking his head. "Even if we decide to come, you know I'll only have weekends, and you can't build all that out here by yourself."

"Well, don't fuss about that. You'll have your own work— selling your acreage, packing up. You'll probably want to part with your horses, too…not heavy enough or trained for farm work. Like I said, I found a pair of Clydesdales, some three-year old Percheron fillies, a stallion. Can use those for logging and farming, breeding as we need. And we'll rotate the pastures. That three field system goes back to medieval times, Leland tells me."

"Aside from the fact that we haven't said yes, Paul, that's the second time you've mentioned this Leland. What are you talking about?" Hugo asked.

"Not what. Who. John Leland. My consultant." Paul's gaze was as clear as rainwater. "Specializes in intentional communities. I know him through friends who set up an eco-commune in northern Manitoba. Put me onto this whole scheme in the first place. He helped me figure out how to go off grid, what order to do things in, where to get the best deals." He paused, eyes narrowed. "You didn't really think I got all this from TV—that's your brand of crazy!" As if he could hear my thoughts, he said brusquely, "This ain't rocket science. All been done for thousands of years. Jesus, our own grandparents did this less than a century ago. We've just forgotten." He turned and walked ahead.

Forgotten? No, I was spinning with déjà vu again; I was sure we'd done this before. Such gentle swirling. I felt so odd as I stared at the scarred poplars. A dead leaf here and there filtered its way down, landing lightly on the snow, piling in drifts around me, more real than the greening crowns of moss beneath my feet.

26

A S SOON AS I HAD CLOSED MY EYES that night, I saw Mom open the back door, separate inside cats from outside cats, gently work her way through the tall weeds out to the barn, and lift the lids off the metal bins that housed the alfalfa pellets and the oats. The horses nickered at her. The palomino pawed at the ground below his bucket, snorting and jerking his head. I helped pitch thick flakes of timothy hay from the loft, the dust floating bright in slow-mo, and then we climbed down, made our way back to the house. As we sauntered by, I bent to the rustling magenta lilacs, the French grafted ones of my childhood, still fragrant after fifty years.

We entered through the back porch, littered with canvas runners and red-trimmed black rubber boots, and went into the kitchen. The table was covered with a plastic cloth, blue and orange and yellow floral. Bottles of ketchup, mustard, relish, Worcestershire sauce, barbecue sauce, horseradish, HP, jars and bottles of every blessed condiment you could imagine, all standing guard in the middle of the table, despite the day's heat. Two or three flies buzzed in slow circles against a hazy window filled with sun. Mom pulled a bottle out of the icebox and reached into the drawer for the opener. She handed me a tall glass of ginger ale, fizzing, and one of Granny's old china plates with the tiny pink roses, the gold fluted rim, a maze of fine cracks. She passed me a pack of Peek Freans, the sugary ones with the jam centres, then smiled and told me to sit. When I turned to the table, Fr. Lewis was there, looking as natural in a plaid shirt and beige workpants as he would in his black habit. He was sipping a cup of tea. "Stop looking at the pictures," he told me, his eyes a-twinkling. But then there was a harsh sound, and a raven lit on my shoulder.

I woke lightly to see the log walls of Paul's cabin, the early light filtered by rag-thin curtains, shadows of the willow's limbs swaying like slim dancers in the blush of dawn. I didn't care how lovely it was; I wanted to go back to that other place. Drowsy beneath the grey wool blankets, I let go, drifted off.

Fr. Lewis was there, this time in a plain pine coffin, the condiments like votary candles in front of him, the plastic tablecloth spilling from beneath the box. He smiled from ear to ear. The choir sang, "Thank God I'm Free at Last." There was a magazine on the table, open to an ad for the newest thing, black stainless appliances. I was in a panic. I couldn't find my mother.

When I woke my heart had lost its rhythm. I couldn't catch my breath. As I lay there the beats soon resumed a regular pattern, and I slipped on my glasses, glancing at the relic of a clock radio on the wooden chair by Hugo's side of the bed. It was 6:35 a.m., just like yesterday. Must be my new magic number. Hugo was still snoring steadily.

I slipped out of the bed as quietly as I could and headed to the kitchen. Even through the socks I'd worn to bed, the wood floor felt cold on my feet. Outside the window, in the shadow of the trees, twenty meters away, there was a slight figure in black, his hand lifted, palm to the sky. A chickadee dipped from the air, lit, took what must be a piece of peanut, and another little black-cap landed as the first one left. Was I still asleep? There was grit in my eyes, I didn't want to blink but— When I looked again, the trees were empty and still.

An hour later, Hugo and Emma were still sleeping. Paul and I stood on his south porch, forearms resting on the top railing. "Visiting the past is hard," he said softly. "After Abby left, I tried living there. It gets easier when you learn to let things be." He turned his head, looked off towards the bank of the creek. The water was noisy, the stream gushing with the spring runoff. I drained my coffee cup, turned the heavy ceramic thing in my hands, admired the bright splash of glaze, the solid heft.

But I couldn't make sense of the past, the present—surely not the future. We stood there for a long while, until Hugo came out to join us.

27

AT FIVE MINUTES PAST FOUR on Monday afternoon, I left Paul people-watching in the waiting room, and went in to seek my doctor's advice. Although her practice was closed, I had managed to convince her that this was a real emergency. After all the weekend's events though, I couldn't decide whether Paul *was* ill or not. He had completed the miraculous purchase this morning, after all, and Hugo and I had talked of almost nothing but the proposed move. We both had the sense that we were being led, and yet here I was, dithering again, all in a panic.

I asked the doctor, "Would we be crazy to abandon everything?" We'd worked so hard on the little house, it was ours. "But is there really any alternative, given the way things are going? But how can we sell it—such a final step?"

"Why not *rent* your home, Delphine?" Nasrin asked me gently.

"Well, shouldn't we invest in the life, not keep one foot out the door?"

"Should you say 'should'? What does your heart say?"

"That's just it—I don't know anymore. Paul seemed so paranoid, so crazy, all those preparations felt so extreme until we saw the place. I was sure he was manic. Now it turns out he has a business consultant, one who's set up other sustainable farms and even large-scale green communities. But that's no guarantee he isn't manic. Isn't it insane to be so full of fear for the future that you leave everything behind?"

"You're asking me? Canada is quite a change from Iran. I could never have imagined Humboldt in winter," Nasrin smiled.

"But you came *to* something, not to run away from an impending apocalypse."

"We left for a variety of reasons, but yes, we ran towards a dream," Nasrin said. She checked her watch. "About the illness—"

"Of course. You want to hear about my lunacy first?"

Nasrin nodded. "Now why would you say that?"

By the time I'd explained about the kitchen, about my disorientation, the déjà vu, Nasrin's face was grave. She nodded. "It can run in families, certainly. But how do you feel? Do your thoughts race?"

"That's the kind of direct question the Emerg doctor asked Paul! But if you're manic, do you know your thoughts are racing?"

"Ideas can appear like bright bubbles that burst before you can catch or follow them. You would feel exhilarated or euphoric, and that might switch abruptly to red-hot anger."

"Well, it's just—I feel so—overwhelmed. On the other hand, when I saw Paul's new house, it felt like home. Did I tell you about—" I stopped mid-rush, suddenly embarrassed.

"Delphine, it's true that your plan to move to the woods doesn't sound quite rational, but I wouldn't say you were experiencing mania. You have great insight into your own mental state, and that is not a sign of illness. What you long for is at odds with what you think you should do. Why not consult a spiritual advisor?"

I shook my head. "There's no one left who'd understand since Fr. Lewis passed two years ago. Stan, my co-worker who I talk to now, is actively awaiting the end of the world, but for some reason I can't make him take my ideas seriously." I stared at my hands, remembering. What would Nasrin make of my theories about spiritual attacks?

Nasrin said, "Delphine?" and I saw she was looking at me intently. I said, "Wild as it seems, I do want to move, I really do. It would solve so many problems. Maybe out there, away from it all, I'd finally be able to stop looking at the pictures."

"Looking at—??"

"I told Fr. Lewis about the so-called 'shelter rags' that Marie and I study in our research. He said I was addicted, ridiculous as that sounds. He took it seriously, told me it was a form of pornography."

"You see and then you want to do? Let's think about this. The lovely and exotic seems natural, attainable, inevitable. Why do you think you want the new house so much? Aren't your ideals, your desire for retreat and peace, at odds with the splendour of the house? What appeals to you about moving to Paul's community?"

"It's more than the glamour this time: the idea of family is irresistible to me. If the kids would come—"

Nasrin nodded. "Have you asked them?"

"No, not yet. But it's not the perfection of the house, it's that it's perfect in being offered to us, just now when we're on the brink of so many dreadful crises. Am I reading too much—"

"You might be suffering from what Buddhists would call *attachment*. Or perhaps you are in the throes of a metamorphosis. But remember Kafka!" Nasrin smiled.

"Well, there will be plenty of dung out there if I do become a beetle!" I laughed.

Nasrin laughed, too, then returned to her usual calm. "I should see Paul now. Please send him in on your way out."

After Paul had gone in, I seated myself in an almost-empty part of the waiting room and pulled out my phone.

There were half-a-dozen work emails, a message from an online astrologist who'd been pestering me about the luck that only he could bring me, and several ads for sofas I'd admired at The Bay. When the receptionist sent me back to Nasrin's office, I arrived to find Paul chatting. He gave me the two thumbs up. "Quite the wise woman you have here, Del. Think we should we recruit her?" he asked, glancing from my face to the doctor's.

"Thank you, Paul. Humboldt is quite rustic enough for me," she smiled.

"So? Are we on track?" I asked, looking at her.

Paul jumped in. "Slightly elevated, the doc says. Put me back on a low dose of Zyprexa."

"Yes, it takes about six months to lose effect, and you might find yourself quite ill before long unless you start it up again. Perhaps you and Delphine should take up yoga."

Nasrin stood, gave Paul his prescription, and shook our hands. "Remember. If you are not sleeping, if your thoughts tumble quickly, if you become angry or depressed or see things that aren't there, you must tell Delphine, so she can contact me. You wouldn't want to end up in a hospital just when you are starting your new life."

"If there *is* a hospital," drawled Paul.

"Precisely. Work through this stressful time without breaking down. Take your pills and make an appointment to see me in two months."

"All-righty. Will do!" he said, standing to open the door.

"Good luck. Call if you have any concerns," Nasrin smiled as we left the room.

28

IT WAS ALMOST 5:00 O'CLOCK when we reached the parking lot, and, as I looked up at the sign above the hotel next door to the clinic, I had an idea.

I phoned home and Emma answered, full of questions. "Well, what did she say? I was starting to think she'd rushed one or both of you to the psych ward in Saskatoon," she joked.

"Oh! Everything is fine. Paul is a little elevated, she says, but he's agreed to take his pills, at least until there aren't any pills to take," I said, raising my eyebrows for Paul's benefit. He grinned, and I continued. "Has Hugo started supper yet? Do you two want to saddle up and join us in Humboldt for a bite?" I asked. "It's prime rib night at the hotel."

"Hugo is out doing chores, I think, but no, I don't see any signs of supper. I've been reading all afternoon, relaxing and loving my time away—this really is the life! So many good books, so little time," Emma said. "Why don't I find him and we'll meet you there in half an hour?"

"Sounds good," I said, nodding at Paul and pretending to fork food into my mouth. "Tell Hugo we're at the Pioneer. We'll go get a spot."

The dining room in the hotel boasted a bar, seven booths, and an assortment of tables. It had a cosy air, with brick and wood-panelled walls and lights in sconces. While we waited, Paul and I looked around at the other patrons. Our booth was dim. As I squinted at my menu, Paul pulled out his BIC to light the hurricane lantern, and when that didn't cast more than a dim glow, he held his lighter above the menu.

"Paul! Are you crazy?" I whispered.

"You heard what the doc said," he grunted. "Perfectly sane! But hungry."

"Put that away. You'll start a fire. Besides, I thought we wanted the special."

Before long the western décor set Paul talking about Theo, and then one thing led to another, and suddenly he wanted to talk about our uncle's terrible gasping death. I could hardly stand to remember.

"The pain and fear must have been unbearable, yet Theo's eyes still had enough twinkle to tell me I would have liked him had I made the time to get to know him. It was too late by the time we met," I told Paul, thinking of Mom's death, her relentless afterlife, and Fr. Lewis's. Surely even the dead crave connection...

Emma and Hugo arrived, and the waiter came by to recite the details of the special and take our orders. I tried to distract Paul, change the topic, but nothing worked. When our prime rib arrived, glossy with jus, Paul had just reached the part about his last winter at Theo's Alberta farm near Athabasca, the coldest in fifty years, week after week of forty below, the wind chill worse than minus -50.

"Week after week of piercing blue skies, trees spectacular with hoarfrost, blew off every day, grew back twice as thick next night. Even with the sun, the air was brutal. Those shaggy mares stood like some circle of musk ox, the young herded to the centre."

Paul told us there had to be some reason Theo had left him his place, some reason he was there, unyielding though the winter was. There had to be more to it than just owning things, taking care of a dream that somebody else, even someone as special as Theo, had wanted.

"That's what Hugo and I thought when we came to Saskatchewan, Paul. We must be here for some purpose," I told him, as I ladled gravy over my whipped potatoes.

"Purpose is all around us, Del, all around us. And still so much to run from. But Theo, he understood, knew me like no one else ever seemed to."

He continued. "Theo was the original wild child, chasing his brothers and sister round the home place with the tail of an old coyote they found in a trap. Thought he'd outgrow it, but his tricks never wore off. Told me once he asked two girls to the same dance, and, at the last moment, had to get Dad to escort one while he took the other."

"It wasn't all fun and games," Emma said. "At another party, Theo pretended he'd been drinking moonshine. Staggered around, pretending to be blind. As his older brother AND a chaperone, Dad was doubly obliged to keep an eye on him."

"Went just livid," Paul laughed.

"Delphine," Hugo said. "Let's back up a minute. What do you mean, we're here for some purpose? You know, right? We succumbed to what you and Marie call the *Downton Abbey* effect. We were retreating to the life genteel in our country resort, all the boomers do it…"

"*Downton Abbey*? What's that?" Paul asked.

"It's a TV show, set in a manor house in England, a hundred years ago. With its elegant costumes and furnishings, the intrigue and sub-plots, the lives of the aristocrats and their servants, it's very, very addictive," Emma explained. "Geoff and Dad always watch with me."

"You do know that the weather up north will be a discouragement to servants," Paul teased. "But we'll battle the elements together."

He put down his knife and fork, looked serious. "That winter before Theo took sick, one night the horses broke into the granary, gorged themselves properly on barley chop meant for cattle. Barley's too hot for horses; thought sure they'd founder, and a foundered horse might as well be a dead horse. Heat destroys their feet, hooves grow long as skis, curl up in front, so much pain you can never ride them again."

"So what did you do?" Emma asked. "You didn't shoot them?"

"Well," Paul said, shaking his head, "sure thought we'd have to, and losing the herd would have broken Theo. But the wind chill was -50 that night and worse the next day, an' the clever beggars just stood, legs to the knees in the snow banks, tails to the wind. Every blessed one pulled through. A miracle, a real miracle." He looked up as the waiter reached past him to take his plate. Paul made a pouring gesture to him, and pretended to drink a cup of coffee.

The young waiter nodded. "Right away, sir."

"Miracle—" I said, "that's what we thought when we found our Shangri-La."

Hugo smiled at me. "Even before Delphine heard from her friend that property was cheap in Saskatchewan, we were looking for a challenge. We looked at the gorgeous old places near the university. Ha! The most dilapidated house there was more than half a million. Even with land, character houses cost only one-tenth of that here."

"But you can't hide there from the kind of trouble the world is facing now." Paul was loud again, and I looked around to make sure no one was watching us but the dining room was almost empty. "Take the fella who killed the militia-man, stormed Parliament, had all the MPs afraid for their lives. More lunatics with weapons every day, all around the world. And ISIS—"

I glanced at Hugo; I could see where this was heading. I waved the dessert menu, and Emma must have guessed my plan. While I distracted Hugo with the promise of the tangy raspberry cheesecake, she talked Paul into sharing the triple chocolate explosion. Nothing succeeds like one's just desserts, that's what I've always said. Before long we were all laughing again.

PAUL RODE WITH ME ON THE WAY HOME. As we drove past St. Scholastica, five minutes from home, the old white church seemed to jump out from behind the massive spruce and tall poplars that protected her, the steeple tilted ever so slightly against the sky, the little graveyard outlined on two sides by new plantings of evergreens. I felt startled, on edge. Why would a cemetery, especially this familiar one, trouble me? Or was it Paul? He was still talking.

"Course I was mortified to be in trouble again, at nineteen. Just didn't know how to stop—"

"Nineteen? The year Mom died?"

"No, I was twenty-six when she died. I'm talking bout the year you and Mom had just settled yourselves for the summer at the lake. Remember? You were thirteen."

"Thirteen? Okay...right. Mom never really explained why we were returning to the city. 'Dad's done with studying at last,' was all she said. 'Hallelujah! He's pitched the books,' she cheered, danced a little jig."

I signalled the turn onto the grid road, then continued. "When we got home I could see that he'd *pitched* the book, all right—slammed it so hard it smashed a hole in the dining room plaster." I could still see the textbook lying there, twisted, when we arrived home. *Adolescent Storm and Stress*.

"Never thought about it, I guess."

"Well, there's a little more to it than what Mom let on. She came to see me, in jail, told me the police had stopped by the house to report that I'd been breaking into cabins again. When Dad heard that, the uselessness of his courses hit him. None of it ever helped me; he decided the whole lot was absolute bunk. Quit his master's program that afternoon, stormed up to get you, and home you all came, pronto."

The end of my blissful summers at the lake. The he-man display with the fireworks.

Paul continued. "Mom told me at last she'd realized the apple didn't fall far from the tree. More was needed than Polyfilla and lath to fix Dad's wounds. Of course I hadn't been diagnosed yet. And HE would never go to the doctor..."

I could fill in the rest. "But, as always, she had an idea. He had been painting landscapes for years. We thought she chose *Bone White* paint as the height of modern décor. She must have wanted to give him a blank canvas, room for more art, on a larger scale, a houseful of portraits, something else to focus on."

"You ever wonder why he painted those lakes at spring breakup, when the ice was going out? Mom told me. He picked that time to visit the place, knowin' it would be deserted then—too ashamed to face the neighbours whose cabins I'd broken into." Paul said.

Dad had done painting after painting of lakes after that, moving from realism into the abstract, sophisticated studies of light. We never questioned why he sometimes sat up all night after finishing a piece, just looking at it.

Of course sleeplessness was a symptom.

I always thought he was marvelling at the wonder of what had come through him.

29

I LONGED TO SHARE MY SECRET WITH EMMA, oh, how I did, but the last thing I needed was to scare her—or risk her letting the cat out of the bag to Hugo. After we tumbled into the house, the four of us stood in the kitchen and talked. I could see Hugo eyeing the fridge. Soon the men were digging out the beer and snacks, and I seized my moment, leading Emma into the living room. I turned on the silver lamps and we curled up beside one another on the old couch. As she rested her head on her arm, I wondered if it might just be better to have this chat tomorrow, not right before bed.

"Why don't you stay and visit, take a few days off? It's such a long drive back, and you could use a break."

"Well, Lovey, now that Paul is under control, I'd better get back, though it seems to me the real excitement is just starting," she smiled. "But I'll be back in December to bring Geoff and the kids up to Paul's little village. It will be great to see everybody all at once. And don't worry, Del—I'll make sure Dad leaves the chemistry set in Edmonton!" She winked at me.

"Please, Emma? I need your advice, I don't know what to do." I looked around to make sure the men weren't in earshot.

"Really? You knew what to do in here. Look at the colours, the warmth, the style. You and your artist's eye—all those books and antiques, the room feels like a well-loved library, some European hideaway. Such a good little house. Choose your renters wisely, young one."

Of course she had no idea what I was worried about. How could she ever guess that I had accidentally ordered a kitchen? "Emma," I said, "The other day when I was—"

Hugo and Paul walked in, beer bottles in hand, munching nacho chips. Hugo walked over and proffered the bag to us. I shook my head. I tried to brush the moment off with a joke, saying, "I see you found something you like in the kitchen."

"Well, yes, I was telling Paul how last week you were planning a new little bistro here. Now I'm not sure. Kitchens do sell houses, but if we're moving—"

If only I'd had time to get Emma onside. I had to stop him from trying to back out.

"We have to do the kitchen, Hugo, we've been through this. The house won't sell in this state, unless we want to take a loss. Besides, no tenant would think twice about leaving a dilapidated rental in shambles. The broken hinges alone make the place look like a dump."

Hugo set his beer and the chips down on the end table, and came over to stand behind the couch. He put his hands firmly on my shoulders. "I know, I know. I haven't forgotten your 'our kitchen is a disaster' seminar, believe you me! But what if renters trash the NEW kitchen? Have you thought of that?"

Paul smiled, shaking his head. "No matter how many times I tell you I've got plenty, you two always think money is the route to every kinda freedom." He shook his head. "Independence is great, you need that, but there's a time and a place. And what use'll money be in the future? If you won't think *Star Trek*, think Caveman." He smiled. "Life after solar flares or cyber-crime."

That seemed pretty random. Nasrin had said he might get worse before the meds started to work. Was he cycling higher? "The whole plan is a gamble, Paul. I'm starting to think—"

I wanted to say, "We should stay here," when, miraculously, Hugo made that unnecessary. "Paul's right. We'll hardly need money once we're set up, and, well, so what if the new reno acquires a few dings? The distressed look is still in style, no?"

"That's true." I felt a little bubble of hope. "And people will pay more rent and take better care of a beautiful place. That's what they always say on *Income Property*."

"You do realize that home-reno shows are the engines of the capitalist world you're planning to escape, don't you, Del?" Emma laughed, and Paul nodded, frowning.

"But we can't just abandon this place." I felt my face start to flush.

"Now, Älskling," Hugo said, patting my shoulder. "You know we're teasing. Once again we'll fix our place up for someone else's enjoyment, but can we do it on the cheap this time?"

Speechless for a moment, I scanned their faces. The kitchen was either coming, or it wasn't, and the price was not open for debate. I was amazed at how easily the lies floated to my lips. "The price I quoted is as cheap as it gets. This is the last week of the sale." Well, last week was the last week. "Delivery will take eight weeks. We can start prepping anytime."

I decided to distract him. "And whether we're going to sell or rent, the whole house should be refreshed," I added, as Hugo rolled his eyes. "We'll need to start by painting." I paused. "One step at a time, right? That's what Marie always says."

"Who's Marie?" Emma asked.

"One of my office mates. She's working on the research project with me. She teaches all over the province and still finds time to work at the gallery, never seems to feel any stress. It's amazing what she can do. She's teaching me to ramp up, take on more high-pressure tasks."

At least that was the truth. And it was her fault that I'd started the renovation file.

"It works beautifully," Hugo said. "For her, at least."

Emma was yawning. She reached over, gave my arm a squeeze. "I'm sorry, Lovey, but I've got to hit the hay. I have a long drive back to Edmonton tomorrow, and I can't go home without my beauty sleep. We don't want to scare the children!"

part two
30

WHEN I WOKE THE NEXT MORNING, for a few seconds, I felt perfect peace. I had dreamt about our first year in Saskatchewan, when I'd started work at New Horizons and Stan, who had been at the Abbey for three years before finally deciding he wasn't quite their kind, had told the monks about me. Curious, in the nicest possible way, they had invited me to dinner and seated me by Fr. Lewis. He was such a dear, wry man, a natural confidant. We hit it off. He explained that he was a hermit—a *solitary*—devoted to the life lived apart, though he nourished the community of spirit. As I would discover later, he sustained a huge number of friends and acquaintances from across Canada with his faithful handwritten letters, offering each person the solace and counsel they needed. He listened attentively and responded with generosity to anyone lucky enough to speak with him. He loved the stories of the lake that I told him that night, and I loved him.

The dream took me back to the first visit I'd made to his hermitage, past the enormous horse barns, past the acres of gardens, and through the deep swath of forest. I relived how honoured I felt, blessed, really, as I emerged from scrubby brush of willows, birch, and poplars that cloaked the trail, and saw him standing, his face lit, one chickadee after another plucking broken peanuts from his ancient paw. He waited until his hand was empty, and then we advanced on our way down the leaf-littered path and into the tiny house. The chickadees settled in a flock amongst the lilac branches that snugged up to his front window.

"But obedience is the key to our unfolding," he told me, after we'd spoken about how lovely it was to see one another and I had admired his home. "Just this spring I was ordered to move back into the Abbey."

"Oh? What for?"

"Well, the Abbot thought it best," he said carefully, mirth in his eyes. "After the attack."

"Attack?" Who would attack a man his age, especially one hidden out here?

"It might be construed," he said, "as a physical attack of a spiritual nature."

He had all my attention. He seemed so frail, yet he had that look, a twist of defiance. He made the tea in his Brown Betty teapot and poured it, offering me a cup and a dainty old china plate piled with the treats he'd liberated from the Abbey kitchen in honour of my visit. I asked again, "Attack? What in the world do you mean?"

"It means I have developed an aortic aneurysm. That's the medical term for it. But it was definitely an attack from the other realm." He took a bite of his oatmeal cookie.

"Why do you say that?"

He chewed for a moment, swallowed. "IT loves to interfere with my work, my spiritual work. Now I must live in the Abbey, do chores, wash dishes, make myself useful," he wrinkled his nose, "attend three meals every day, and community functions. IT takes so much time, and busy-work agitates, destroys peace. It's exactly what IT wants."

"It?" I said, sipping my tea.

"No, IT."

"Oh," I said again, but inside I was wondering. I seized the chance, though every bit of caution in my mind was shouting *no!* and I confessed that I used to think I was a mystic, perhaps a minor prophet. He surprised me by not laughing. I told him that everything seemed hell-bent on driving Hugo and Gina and I away from Saskatchewan. Our first summer had been "crowded with incident," to quote Lady Bracknell: the car accident, the horse hijinks, the lightning strike while I'd been in the shower. "And in all of this, I wasn't hurt; it was a miracle."

"An excellent description of an early spiritual attack. Read Teresa of Avila," he said, his eyes twinkling. "*The Interior Castle*. There are several copies in the library, I believe it's also available online."

I scribbled the name in my notebook. "But what about you—how dangerous is this aneurysm?"

"Oh, the next attack, or the one after that, will kill me." He smiled mischievously. "They have me on the third floor at the moment. All those stairs, it could happen at any time. Not used to climbing, you know. Which only makes it more urgent that we should meet again soon, let's say next Tuesday at 4:00 p.m., in the little parlour of the Abbey, after you've read *The Interior Castle*?"

"Home décor?" I asked hopefully.

"For the spirit," he said, as I set my mug down. I can still see the pale green lusterware, the dregs of tea leaves on the bottom. He rose and led me to my jacket, which was hanging on a peg. When I stepped outside, he followed me, standing just outside on the little porch, breaking peanuts for the flurry of chickadees that waited to reclaim him.

He waved cheerily when I turned back for one last look.

And then I woke up.

31

I COULDN'T GO BACK TO SLEEP; my thoughts were racing. What would Fr. Lewis say now? Was this attack leading us on or were we in danger? Images drifted and tossed, other visits with Fr. Lewis, Paul's revelations about Dad, the night Hugo and I announced our plan to move out here to Saskatchewan.

Emma and Geoff had been surprised, but Dad seemed taken aback, offended.

"First Paul, now you and Hugo and Gina? Do you have any idea how long it took your mother and I to build the good life in the city for you? You're such a bunch of yo-yos, you kids! Well, I guess you come by it honestly enough." And he recited the story his own father had told him the winter Dad was eleven, how odd it all seemed, Granny beside them rocking and knitting the coarse wool she spun herself, my grandfather crouched down, their four children squeezed onto two chairs beside the woodstove in the sod shack where they were all born.

Dad said, "We'd always thought *Pépère* was a farmer by birth. He was so at home on the land, so patient. But you can imagine how surprised we were to find out that his father had been a surgeon major in the French army, and that at seventeen years old, the boy who would become our father had been a student at a boarding school in Lausanne, Switzerland, almost ready to graduate and go home to take a position in Paris, when all of a sudden a letter came, saying his own father was dead. And that all of their social connections had died in the same epidemic."

"Social connections?" I asked.

"That's what we wondered. How could *Pépère*, who wore coveralls every day, who'd told us he had to borrow a suit for his wedding—what *social connections* could he have had?"

"And?"

"And the loss of his father meant the loss of his middle-class life. He knew he would find only low work, a room in a grimy boarding house back in Paris, far away from the social circles he'd known. And if things went wrong, it would be the workhouse, or life on the streets—"

"And just why did life in a sod shack in the frozen wilds of Canada appeal?" Emma asked.

"The freedom, of course," Gina offered.

"At least in part, at least in part," Dad nodded. "But I think it was also a lark, an adventure, a place to test your mettle as a man. A classmate—who had a cousin, who had an acquaintance—said that land was free on the Canadian prairies. Free. It turned out that it wasn't FREE, of course. The work was never-ending, the weather blistering hot OR freezing cold, depending which of the two seasons you were in, and, if things weren't so bad starting out in 1906, the Dirty Thirties hit soon enough. But of course he couldn't foresee that, so off he set, part of the land rush. And of course none of them thought about the treaties." Dad continued. "And that was that. Once set in motion, events must play themselves out. My father led his life as a farmer, and I did my best to get out as quickly as I could. I never understood why someone as high-spirited as Theo settled for a farm, but his life was almost as different from *Pépère*'s as mine has been. Paul—"

I jumped in. "Paul's the real homesteader. Hugo and Gina and I won't be farmers—we're acreage owners, living the Life of Riley on our fine little estate." I looked at Hugo, leaning back, nursing a glass of Schnapps. He smiled and nodded.

Dad peered at us across Emma's dining room table, the chic mid-century Danish walnut that Mom had been so proud of.

I could feel his bewilderment, I could see our schemes through his eyes, could imagine how we looked to him, the three of us, full of ideas and hopes, escaping the city where he'd worked so hard to build us a fine home, to make himself feel at home.

WHEN WE LEFT FOR SASKATCHEWAN, we set off in a convoy that was more like an ark: Hugo drove the 24-foot U-Haul, with most of our worldly possessions in the back and Gina's thirteen guinea pigs in two cages in the front; Gina drove our ancient Buick with the dogs panting and slurping at the windows in the back seat, and I brought up the rear in what was then the new Toyota, our two caged cats crying with breathless vigour for the full seven hundred kilometers.

We'd surrendered sessional teaching, abandoned Hugo's dream of an ultramodern condo, forsaken our large city house with ease. At least I had. The poplars and maples on our new land had not yet burst out in full leaf, but we could see the buds swelling, and as we drove closer to Humboldt, the vista looked the way I had always imagined that Paris would look—soft white clouds with indistinct edges, patches of brightest turquoise in between, trees blurry with the shiver of April winds.

Within weeks of our arrival, however, we were dismayed to discover just how far from free our own lives would be: it cost nearly a thousand dollars to fill the propane tank every two months, and groceries cost double what they did in Edmonton. We needed two telephone lines, one dedicated solely for Hugo's work, and the Internet and satellite cost another couple of hundred per month. The list ran on and on and on. Insurance was supposed to be cheap in Saskatchewan, but it turned out to be twice what we had paid in Edmonton. Between hauling our own garbage and fetching home building supplies, it soon became apparent that we needed a truck. There were the repairs to the house and barn, the taxes were going up that year, and the price of gasoline was rising. And somehow, with all of this, we needed to keep some of our capital for retirement.

I was determined not to worry. There was plenty of work in Humboldt, so long as the oil and potash booms continued. So what if I had to work for Big Field and their intensive pig operations, or man the check-out at the friendly 7-Eleven Petro-Canada gas station? I could set my hair in pin-curls and wear a fine mesh hairnet like they did in the 60s, fry chicken and chips for take-out between sales of Lotto 649 and cigarettes, even at eighty years old.

But that day had not yet arrived, so Gina and I poured over the stack of old magazines we found in the sun porch and wondered if there would be money in some kind of cottage industry, custom carry-alls or re-upholstering, paintings done on commission, sandy fields of lavender— there had to be some way to make money.

We set the worrying aside. We rushed to prepare the barn for our new horses—a strong dun gelding and a sorrel grade mare. Hugo built fine box stalls in two days while Gina and I worked in the house, unpacking boxes, arranging furniture and setting things in order. When at last everything was done, I checked my email and, surprise of surprises, there was one from Jim Fredericks, the fine arts director I had met at the college.

His one-line email simply read: "Where would you like your contract sent?"

It wasn't a teaching job, but words couldn't express the relief I felt at finding work, any work. I would be a program coordinator at the Humboldt New Horizons Art Gallery, an outreach started by the Benedictines. Yes, I would have to leave Shangri-La, re-enter the world again, but at last we'd be secure and I had ten days before they wanted me to start. There's nothing like a deadline to focus the energies. The acreage had been empty for over a year; if we wanted to taste our own farm-fresh produce that summer, we'd need to attend right smartly to the thigh-high weeds in the garden.

The three of us spent two long days in the garden, clearing dried scotch thistle, sow thistle, red clover, wild sage, and absolutely verdant quack grass, the garden a far greener plot than the yard. It was backbreaking work, but Gina and I reminisced and planned and teased just as Mom and I used to, and on Saturday at about five o'clock, we stood up and stretched our aching backs. Hugo had started planting the potatoes and it was clear he was determined to finish, so when Gina and I went inside, he just smiled and waved as we left him in the land of classic rock, his iPhone ear-buds blasting out Genesis.

While I rooted around for pork chops in the freezer, I remembered that we'd polished off the last of the ice cream at our campfire three nights before. What was supper without dessert? In an instant, Gina and I decided to take the new Toyota out for a quick spin and fetch a pail from the Co-op store in Humboldt. We scrubbed the garden from our hands and faces and brushed the tangles out of our hair. Gina put on a touch of mascara and lip gloss, and ta-da, we emerged transformed.

She loved to drive and I was happy to ride shotgun. As we settled in and admired the new-car smell, she turned the ignition, slid the car into gear, and we glided down our rough gravel driveway, floating above the stubborn strip of grass that ran up the middle. The 5:30 news was all about the crisis in the Middle East: Israel was re-occupying large parts of the West Bank, apparently as a protest to the rockets from Lebanon. Determined to worry about that later, I popped *More Best of Leonard Cohen* into the CD player, and soon Gina and I were singing along at top volume.

We didn't see another vehicle on the highway to Humboldt. Gina veered sharply here and there to avoid the numerous potholes and breaks in the pavement on Highway 20, and we kept an eye out for deer and moose. The trip was peaceful, the air hazy with ribbons of dust. In field after field, farmers circled the land with enormous tractors pulling harrows and air-drills, most likely listening to the news and awaiting the suppers their wives or daughters would soon bring out.

When Gina and I pulled up, the Co-op parking lot was deserted. A teenaged clerk was leaning against the single open checkout counter, fixated on the bright pages in an issue of *People*, her dark brown ponytail swishing like a horse's tail when she looked up and around. "Closing in five minutes. Need help with anything?" She gave us the once over as she squinted into the sun that slanted through the glass doors behind us.

"No, thanks," I said. "Or not really. We're here for ice cream. Anything on special?"

"Hmmm…Dutch Apple and Double Chocolate. In the back freezer."

Gina and I love to try new flavours, and the first did sound like apple crisp and whipped cream without the trouble. I asked Gina to go back and fetch a gallon while I scanned through the rack of magazines by the till. *Country Living, Hobby Farm, Elle.* There was one called *Modern Quilts by Design* on the lowest shelf. Gina might enjoy it. As I bent down to pick it up, I saw a magazine wedged in behind, one I've never seen anywhere before: *Homeward.* It featured a gorgeous section on country kitchens.

I glanced to see what time it was on the big clock behind the till. It was six. The clerk was staring out the windows and then she looked down the aisle, ran her fingers across the edge of the counter, and rubbed the dust on her uniform. Gina came up behind me and whispered, "We'd better get going. She wants to lock up."

"When you're right, you're right, kiddo. Let's buy this magazine—my mother used to quilt," I murmured, feeling a rush of something I couldn't identify. I looked down at my hands, saw the home décor magazine, the farmhouse issue, and an odd feeling drew me. Pale shantung walls—was that the colour?—faced me from the cover. My throat felt fuzzy, and I cleared it, saying, "We might as well take this one, too."

We decided to make up some time and take the grid road home, the shortcut that ran past the Vintage Museum. We knew that Hugo would be starving, hangry, or he'd have filled himself up with nachos and beer and wouldn't want supper at all. The sooner home, the better. Besides, the interior of the car was hot and the ice cream had already started to melt. I withdrew the two magazines from the plastic bag. The condensation on the ice cream pail would spoil them, and we wouldn't want that.

We went the posted 40 km/hr through town, but once past the last house, its black flowerpots sporting neat pink geraniums, silver Dusty Millers, and spindly white petunias, Gina picked up speed. She commented that the new car was nice, it had oomph. By the time we reached the grid, I'd changed the CD and the two of us were singing, just a bit off-key, to John Denver's "Thank God I'm a Country Boy." When Gina accelerated, I realized the car wouldn't straddle the ruts, the wheelbase was too narrow, and as we neared cruising speed, my stomach lurched as we bounced. The sun was sinking in the west beside us, the little particles of dust glowed bright and free as the car hurtled forward, and I kept my eyes on the road ahead, held my left palm firmly against my waist, my right hand on the door handle. My mouth opened, closed, then opened again. Closed again. I stopped myself from speaking, from warning her to ease off the gas.

Gina was as cool as could be. She knew what she was

doing. As if to prove this point, she slowed down, the car flowed along, and soon we were both crooning to "Some Days are Diamonds."

A truck blew by us from behind, a thick choke of sand and rocks. Gina pulled onto the shoulder. It was instinct, anybody would. The deep ridge of gravel left by the grader not fifteen minutes earlier sucked us right over, and before we could feel, or say, or do anything, the car was nosing off to the right and into the ditch, floating on waves of brome grass as lush as never we'd seen before, except maybe in the garden.

Gina hauled left on the steering wheel, hard, trying to regain the road.

And then silence. Weightless, the car was a space capsule. Ever so slowly Gina withdrew the key, turned gently to me and I peered back, our eyes fixed on each other's faces, yes, we were all right, the car was rolling with all the leisure of fate and over and over and over. The spin lasted forever. Just as we were settling gently to rest on the right side of the car, my hand glided slowly by in front of my face, barely touched the glass on my window, and that, in turn, little by little, bit by bit, quietly tinkled into a magnificent pattern of the most fascinating cracks. I stared with wonder as two or three tiny red drops of beautiful blood slowly trickled down the back of my right hand.

We pushed up and out of Gina's door, the two of us backing up at last to have a look at the damage. The only mark on the vehicle's body seemed to be a shallow dent on the roof of the passenger side. My side. A deity's thumbprint left as he or she had tossed us with the skilled hand of a practiced gambler. And though the engine would likely need work, there had been no harm to either of us, at least nothing we could see. As we hugged one another I thought of the tales I'd heard about rollovers, the cracked necks, paraplegia or quadriplegia, or simply death.

The Boudreau luck had always been too good to be true.

As I followed Gina away from the car at last, I heard a

male voice pronounce, as clearly as could be, "a great weight has been lifted from you."

You mean the car? I wondered, as I peered around to see who was speaking. Gina was six feet away, standing by the gravel ridge, her hands on her hips, staring at the dusty black truck that had driven us off the road. It was pulled over up ahead. Probably excited by what they'd just witnessed, the three young men, babies really, advanced towards us. I stood there, squinting, shaking my head, strands of hair waving about my face.

Then I remembered the ice cream was still in the vehicle. Sprinting back to the ditch, I heaved myself into the car headfirst. I could just reach the pail, sitting safely closed on top of the magazines. *Homeward* drew my eye as it lay there, that world of perfect rooms and perfect homes and perfect gardens.

I pulled it out.

After I called the CAA to send the tow truck, I alerted Hugo, and looked over to see Gina interrogating the boys. We needed names for insurance purposes. Reluctantly, I held out my hand to the oldest boy, the driver, surely no more than sixteen years old. But before I could force out a syllable, the youngest spoke.

"You're the new lady at the art gallery, aren't you? The artist?"

A throng grew at the scene of the accident. Pickups pulled over and people gathered in clusters, slapping backs, talking of baseball and weekends at the lake. The boys finally agreed to say what they'd done; with a crowd that size, anonymity was hardly an option. In the end they gave a statement to the police. But best of all, by admitting their sin, they were free to tell all about the spectacular crash, how fast that little car had spun and bounced. It was just like a stunt in a movie, over, and over, and over, three times in all.

When Hugo appeared, we thanked everyone and headed back home in his truck, and Gina and I told our version of the boys' story. Hugo was calm, and in ten short minutes he delivered us home. Out by the garden, he built a fire, and the three of us collapsed on our red Adirondack lawn chairs. The ice cream was soupy, so we slurped Dutch apple milkshakes and talked the whole thing through. The last of the sun shot apricot fingers between the poplar leaves, and robins serenaded their mates while white-throated sparrows and chickadee calls hung in the faint breeze.

"Oh, and Mother," Gina said, slipping a marshmallow onto a willow stick she'd just sharpened, "risked her life for her precious magazines!"

"Hmmmm, hogwash," I said, taking a swig of my shake and poking the fire with my own stick. "No risk involved. But yes, my precious. Out on a big adventure." I felt odd, defensive. "And the dark riders did chase us from the path. Someone had to retrieve my purse. I was careful."

Gina rotated the marshmallow. "Not nearly careful enough, Mrs. Underhill," she replied. "I know what hunts you," she said, wagging her stick at me.

Hugo poured another round of Dutch apple, and I picked my magazine up off the damp grass. I wanted to look through it, but the fire was almost down to coals. There was not enough light. Then the coyotes began to howl, first one, then a burst of calls, close by in the trees to the west and the north.

We leaned back and listened for a full half-hour, free of all fear, thrilled as the deepening night fell all around us.

32

THAT WAS THE START, and how close we three had grown since we moved out here. But the boys? How on earth would we lure them up to the life *rustique* out on the homestead?

If all those blessed home reno shows had taught me anything, it was that there was always something you weren't seeing, every single time. The vendors said the electric had been updated but new outlets covered the knob and tube wiring behind the walls. That great rain-showerhead and elegant tile job? Corroded plumbing and soggy gyproc. Open concept? Had they put in a beam to replace that loadbearing wall? But the real danger to our home, the thing that had driven us out here, the thing Hugo and I couldn't fix, was entirely of our own creation.

We were still living in Edmonton when Erik and Marc had finished high school. We had never doubted that the kids would all stay close, share Sunday dinners, we'd all play cat's cradle with the threads of one another's lives. But after surrounding ourselves with the finest things we could afford the whole time they'd been growing up, it should have been no surprise when the boys looked for careers that would allow them to live life large: Erik was off to study architecture at McGill in Montreal and Marc secured a spot as an apprentice electrician in Calgary.

How do you surrender your children? I stood by, numb as a post, while Erik efficiently edited his possessions, dropped off boxes of clothing and Lego and Construx at the Goodwill store, returned books and keepsakes to friends and family. When he'd filled his new used Audi with just the few items he couldn't do without, it finally hit me: he wouldn't be back, not even for a visit, not for a long, long time. His career would consume him—for years at least, if not forever.

I remember the aching bewilderment I felt looking at the two boys, no, these two young men, as finally I read their future and ours. Both were tall like Hugo, Erik dark-haired and serious, and Marc, a zany ginger like Emma and Granny. Marc's choice was just as final as Erik's. Along with his bed, he had loaded the old sofa we had banished to the basement two years before, a tidy array of kitchen utensils, boxes of miscellaneous goods, and, of course, his video games, all neatly arranged in the back of his spotless truck. Though he'd be only three hours away, he'd work twelve-hour days, party on weekends. What would it take to bring him home once he was settled?

I watched him drive away, I walked from window to window in the still house, and oh how I ached. Gina and Hugo and I clattered around for the next couple of years. We installed a gas fireplace, but somehow just flicking the switch never conjured the cosiness we craved. We freshened the rooms with coat after coat of *Illumination*, a soft white I chose as a gesture to the universe, but I remained unenlightened. We took up our old habits, shopping garage sales and thrift stores, Kijiji and Craigslist, looking for just the right classics, pieces that could be re-upholstered to fit the latest aesthetic.

Until Fiona set me on the pollen path.

33

THE LOSS OF THE BOYS set us seeking a challenge and that had brought us to Saskatchewan, where now Paul's offer seemed almost biblical, a chance to "restore the leaf that the locust hath eaten" (Joel 2:25). Hugo and I watched our days unfurl like apple blossoms, possibilities dancing bright with the promise of family again. As we readied ourselves for this next step, the move to the homestead, the spring breezed past. The annual June conference was over, and I was on my way back to Shangri-La.

It was nine o'clock when at last I hurtled the old Toyota up the driveway, dodging the potholes and straddling the ruts. Hugo came out onto the back porch to greet me. "How are you, *Käresta*? How did it go?"

I said, "I'm fine," though of course I didn't mean it. I hugged him briefly, and reached over to pat Lucky, who was trying to weave back and forth between our legs. "Where have you been, old timer?"

Hugo asked, "Did you eat?"

"One thing they don't scrimp on is food for the condemned. Jim made sure we had a hearty lunch before he grilled us," I said, rubbing the dog's ear.

"That sounds ominous. Should we go in? The sun may still be up but it's getting cool out here," Hugo said. "Supposed to freeze again tonight."

"Who could believe this weather at the beginning of June?" I asked. "Especially after such an early spring. I saw a lot of crop damage on the way home from Saskatoon."

As we walked in and slipped off our shoes, Hugo kept his arm around me. He seemed happy to have me lean on him, a rare moment for a husband with a fiercely independent wife. I'd been away for a week, and I wasn't an easy person to help, even at the best of times. When he flipped on the kitchen lights, for a second everything went black, great blobs of chartreuse and turquoise and white gliding by. But as the shapes cleared, I found a room lit by pot lights. A walnut-panelled island, its honed Carrera countertop cool and fresh. Five crossed-back bistro stools. On one side, a full pantry of walnut cabinets stretched from floor to ceiling. Across the room, in a row of glass-fronted white cupboards, Mom's china was on display, grey on white gleaming with silver. The kitchen window had been replaced, and beneath it acres of white counter held a huge sink with a sleek gooseneck faucet, and a marble herringbone backsplash extended all the way up to the ceiling, the variations echoing the slate grey floor. Stainless steel appliances gleamed bright.

Everything I'd ordered was there—and more. For once I was speechless, couldn't say a word. Hugo led me to the centre of the room. "So?" he beamed, "What do you think about the kitchen?"

He'd hit every note, found pieces I'd admired but had never asked for: a black Japanese cast-iron teapot with tiny cups, a square glass vase of apple-white hydrangeas just starting to blush. A linen tea towel, white with a block-printed indigo design. A domed cake-plate of European pastries. A pair of white and blue latte cups, waiting.

I surprised us both by starting to cry.

Hugo wrapped his arms around me. He reached up with one hand to brush my bangs from my eyes. I wanted to say something, show the gratitude I felt, act like a grownup. But when I looked up and saw his dear, worried face, I turned back to his shoulder to cry all the more. He just held me.

I knew I was being an idiot. I couldn't stop thinking of all of the time I'd spent longing for a new kitchen, and here it was, ours, finally.

"It must have been terrible," Hugo said, his hand still stroking my hair as he leaned down to look into my face. "What can I do? Do you want to talk about it?"

He thought I was upset about work. I couldn't bear to tell him what I was really thinking. I straightened up, pushed the hair away from my face, slipped my fingers under my glasses to work the tears away. Naturally, that smudged the lenses and I had to stop to wash them. How could I dry them on the brand new tea towel? I looked for some tissue.

At last I could speak.

"It couldn't have been much worse," I told him. That was the truth—though it wasn't why I was crying. I stopped talking and the tears almost started again, but I forced myself to stop. I continued. "I guess I shouldn't have tried to tell them at the conference. It was pretty dreadful. After all these years. Jim was furious when I asked him for a leave, said either I'm in or I'm out. I finally convinced him that that was unreasonable. He agreed to give me until the end of December to decide. If I'm not back then, he'll fill my position. In the meantime, he wants me off the project as soon as Marie can hire in help."

"But what difference does that make, Del?" Hugo looked puzzled. Gently, he led me to one of the bistro stools. "Suppose I fix something to eat. Maybe you're hungry? Your blood sugar must be low. What do you feel like? Cold cuts? Or would Madame prefer rollmops?"

I shook my head. He was teasing, I knew. "I'm not up to your Viking fare today, my love. Maybe we could just heat something up? There's some leek soup in the container with the red lid—it was in the freezer. I guess you moved everything over?" I was determined to gather my wits. "I can fix that while you make some coffee, and then we can talk. But really," I put my hand up, touched his cheek. "I'll be okay. I just need to think."

As I'd hoped, for at least a few minutes, there was no point in talking as the espresso machine hissed. Hugo frothed the milk and poured it into the coffee. There was no doubt but that I'd have to explain. I carried the bowls of hot soup to the island while Hugo delivered the lattes. He pulled out the bistro stools so we could sit, and as I glanced around the room again, I feared I would wake up from this lovely dream.

"So the most difficult thing for me, now," I said, trying to measure my words, to avoid hurting his feelings, "is that everything is so perfect."

"Of course!" Hugo said, looking confused. "Isn't that what we wanted?"

"Yes, we did. You're always so sweet, and it was very kind of you to surprise me, get all this done while I was gone, really it was." I took his hands in mine. "But to tell you the truth I'm completely in shock. I'd forgotten about the renovation until you turned on the lights. It's gorgeous, better than I would ever have dreamed." I lifted my hand, gestured around the room. "And I don't know what to do."

I took a breath to steel myself. No lies, not this time.

"To tell you the truth, I'm having doubts. It was hard enough to think about leaving here, where we've been so happy, when we had that ugly kitchen. I tried to tell myself the reno wouldn't matter because I was so looking forward to trying life on the homestead. I thought, what's the harm? We can always come back. But now, with Jim's ultimatum, we'll hardly be there long enough to make up our minds. Without a job here, we'll be stuck there for good, whether we like it or not. And we'll never have a space like this again—"

Hugo shook his head in that way he has when he's trying to figure things out. I could only guess how exhausted he must be. He ran his hand through his hair, looked at me sideways.

"Delphine, you're killing me. I thought you were looking forward to moving. You've never been one to cling; you've always looked to the next challenge. We can fix up our place at the homestead, too, of course. You know we will—

"But it will never look like this. Paul would hardly go for walnut or marble at the end of the world. I can't think he would let us waste our precious green electricity on espresso makers or potlights! I know, I know, it's stupid to second-guess a decision that seemed so right—but now I can't stop. I feel the promise of *this* life now more than ever, and to think we have to leave it. I thought I knew, but—"

Hugo spoke quietly, so quietly I had to hold my breath to hear his words. "I guess what Paul thinks about our décor choices won't affect what we do. And there must be a way to make lattes without electricity—what about a French press?" Squeezing my hands in his, he said, "Del—we don't HAVE to go."

"And when there's a pandemic, or terrorist attacks, or the glaciers dry up? Hordes of desperate city-dwellers roaming the countryside? I can't be the one who leaves us—the whole fam-damily—in harm's way, either! Maybe I need someone to order me to leave, make the rending and tearing not of my own making."

"Well, I could do *that*," Hugo smiled at last. "WOMAN! Pack your things! We head for the bush at dawn."

"And you know that much as I say I want that, I'd never budge if you did. No, we're going to have to think carefully about all of this," I said.

Hugo captured both my hands and held them gently. "Delphine, we did think carefully. And we can think it through again, if that will make you feel better. But staying here with the potlights and the stainless steel is not going to protect us when there's a pandemic, or pogroms—or any of the scenarios we've talked about that really might happen. Paul is giving us this chance to set up for a new future."

I stopped trying to free my hands, and looked up at his face. I had never felt more torn; he had to be the kindest man in the world. Life in the countryside had never been his cup of tea, not really, and he hated guns, the very idea of guns. And if what had happened to Anders wasn't bad enough, Hugo had also told me, back when he started watching prepper shows on TV, that trying to survive the end of civilization was hardly a task for middle-aged people. He was going through the motions for me, for all of us. I saw the worry dark in his eyes.

What the hell—it was only a kitchen.

As if he sensed the change in me, Hugo rose to get the plates and forks for dessert. He'd bought a real selection of our favourites from the new artisanal bakery, pieces of hazelnut torte and chocolate cake and raspberry-marzipan flan, but he could have been offering soda crackers or celery sticks for all the enthusiasm I felt. Out of politeness and habit I decided on the flan, and we settled back to eat our desserts and sip our lattes. I told him about the trip until finally the hurt and shock were all talked out. I wanted to hear all about the renovation and Hugo's own work.

As the clock chimed midnight, he led me off to bed.

34

HUGO HAD BEEN GONE FOR MORE THAN A WEEK up north, helping Paul on the homestead, and I saw no reason not to savour my time alone in the kitchen. I spent most of the day trying to finish my last work on the project; I had the final piles of surveys stacked neatly on the island beside my laptop so that when I needed a rest, I could sip my coffee, look around the room, settle into the luxury of it all over again, and just let my fears all float away.

I was having trouble concentrating. I found myself taking more and more frequent breaks as the afternoon wore on. By 3:30 p.m. I had spied the handprint smudged on the fridge, and, by the time I'd finished cleaning it, I wondered why people liked stainless at all. Still, it had only taken twenty minutes to achieve that streak-free finish this time. I was getting better at it; soon I'd be a pro. I sat back down, traced the veins on the marble counter with my index finger, rearranged the pears in the wooden bowl, turned them to ensure they were best sides up, and then I went to the cupboard, pulled out an indigo vase. Last week Hugo had pointed out the blush on the pale-green hydrangeas in their planter on the back porch. I stepped outside and clipped three large blossom heads, carefully carried them inside and cross-cut the woody stems to be sure they'd stay fresh in water. Once I had arranged them and set them on the counter, the room seemed as perfect as a feature in a magazine.

I wondered if I should go back outside and cut a bouquet of delphiniums. I'd never had them flower twice in one summer before. Marie had told me to cut back the dying blooms, to cut them ruthlessly in late July before the seeds could set, and sure enough, les voilà! Two weeks later, there they were, a second crop of blue and purple blooms, shorter, yes, but still swaying three feet tall beside the little house. I went outside again, but when I looked at them, they seemed so graceful in their natural state that I didn't have the heart to bring them in; I just left them be. After all, I had everything I wanted, everything I needed to relax in my elegant country retreat.

But I didn't feel relaxed. Something felt off, something, somehow, was wrong. When I went back inside, I tried to see if straightening up a little would soothe me. I smoothed the folds of the patterned indigo roman shade over the kitchen window. It had looked a bit rumpled when I'd seen it from outside. I twitched the fabric over a little, adjusted the way it draped. It was flawless. I knew I was procrastinating; I knew because I caught myself doing that more and more these days. I had to get back to work.

Certainly the room was bright enough, airy. Light flooded the kitchen, and the three pendants hung right above me at the island. Maybe I was a bit peckish. Hugo had been diligent about keeping the freezer—and thus the cake plate—full with the treats he'd bought at the trendy new café in Humboldt. As I looked at the selection of seed-encrusted organic muffins, suddenly I realized I was tired of all that healthy stuff. What I wanted was a nice fresh scone like Mom used to make, rich and hot, right from the oven. That would do it.

To keep me going, I whipped up a fresh cup of coffee, stirred in cream and sugar. I reached up and took down my mother's recipe book. It was dog-eared at the page I needed, the surface a little dusty with flour. I knew I could make her scones in my sleep; the book was a prop, something to steady me, and at first it seemed to do the trick. I even hummed a little as I measured the flour, the baking powder, and the salt. I cut in the cold butter, cracked an egg, beat it, and added the milk. But when I poured the wet ingredients into the dry, something was wrong. The mixture was sticky, much too sticky, and when I turned it out onto the floured marble, it just clung to my fingers. Such a mess—and suddenly I was furious. Could I not do a single thing right? I made a fist and tried to shake the thick stuff off—and as I did, I heard a voice intone, *Just what you always wanted, Del. A great big handful of dough.*

If only it were, I thought grimly, still shaking and peeling the goo off my fingers. *If I had that kind of money, we could keep this place, and still follow Paul.* Frustrated, I checked the recipe, and saw the problem straight away. I'd added *two*-thirds of a cup of milk instead of one. Honestly, what was the matter with me these days? I was going to have to double the other ingredients now, and if I didn't hurry up, the whole batch would be ruined. Maybe that would be a lesson to me. What did I want, anyway? I shoved that thought away. And in no time I had the dough fixed and kneaded and cut, right and ready for the oven.

When at last everything was baked, I seated myself at the island. I broke open the warm scone, slathered it with butter and some of the sour cherry jam I'd made last week, right from our very own orchard. I reminded myself as sternly as I could that things were about to change. I knew that, I did, yet the only way I'd been able to cope since I'd returned home to find the new kitchen in all its glory had been to coast along without dwelling on our departure. All the tweaking and styling and cooking were just ways of distracting myself from what I couldn't bear to contemplate.

Still, the rest of the house looked grand, too. Hugo and I had spent the summer fixing and de-cluttering, upgrading and staging to bring the whole house up to the level of the kitchen. We'd painted every room on the main floor a dreamy new white called *Bliss*. Hugo hadn't protested when I pointed out the places where Dandelion, the cat, had sharpened his claws on the corner of this wall and that, the long thick ditch in the plaster left by Lucky's boisterous leaps onto the couch. The urgency for the improvements, at least in his mind, was that buyers or renters would pay top dollar for a fresh, beautiful space. He suggested we paint the far side of the living room a colour he'd seen in one of my magazines, *Evening Sonata*. We arranged our collection of landscapes and portraits and line drawings in a gallery wall there, the wood and gilt frames shone so beautifully against the moody indigo paint. We used the remainder in the back foyer, where the contrast added formality and made the fresh white and rich walnut of the new kitchen seem even more bright and inviting.

I started to wander again, moving from room to room. The place seemed reborn. Even Aunt Francie would have approved of the white tone-on-tone damask wallpaper that framed the doorway, the bright hatchway accented by the white trim as we gazed into the living room. Strangely enough, painting the window wall dark had made the room itself seem brighter; it must have been the way the light played and glowed in the full white drapes at the two west windows. The now-elegant dining room opened onto the brilliant kitchen, so the three living spaces flowed as a grand suite, fit for the most privileged inhabitants. Us.

We no longer abandoned papers or cups on the tables and counters. It hardly felt like work to leave each room as perfect as could be. We both took more time, not just for cleaning, but for plumping cushions and arranging throws, creating vignettes with books and fresh flower arrangements. Hugo was working to entice the tenants that we were seeking. I never let myself think about that.

Later that afternoon, I had at last settled deeply into my work when Hugo texted that he was about to drive home. "What's for supper?" he wrote.

"Nothing yet. Working." Annoyed at the interruption, I thought for a moment, then relented. We had to eat, even if I didn't feel like cooking. "What do u have in mind?"

"Steak, medium rare," he shot back. I was sure he was teasing; he knew that frying up some thick slab of fat-laced meat would splatter more than anything, and the ceramic cooktop was a nuisance to clean. But the phone showed that he was still writing. "Would u like 2 eat in town?"

That was more like it. "Sure. ETA?" I wanted to make sure to be finished and I'd need time to change my clothes. My new white voile tulip top would look stylish over slim jeans, yet not too dressy. When Hugo drove into the yard at 5:30, I picked up my windbreaker from its hook near the door and took one last look up at the kitchen. I went back and pulled the window closed, then turned the lights on again as I walked to the door. I wanted to give the impression that we were there, though it wouldn't be dark until long after we were home.

35

THE NEXT DAY WAS SATURDAY, but there would be no rest for the weary. Hugo had promised Paul that we'd drive back up to the homestead together.

"Paul told me to tell you to pack some warm things along with the usual t-shirts and shorts. It's been near freezing more than once this month up there."

"Marie tells me that in some parts of the province the summer has been humid, downright wet, but here it's been a dry, cloudy month, so cold for August, no light or heat to break through those thick clouds of smoke."

"Yeah, it's drifting up from Washington. The whole summer, the whole year has been off-normal."

I agreed. "I thought it was bad in May and June when we couldn't see the trees on the south edge of the property, with all the smoke from northern Saskatchewan and BC, but it's worse now. The sun just peers down, even at midday, like some red ghost, an evil eye."

Hugo looked at the clock, which always runs four minutes fast, and switched the news on. That was a mistake. Boatloads of migrants dispossessed from Syria and Iraq, environmental refugees from small islands, thousands of adults and children drowning off the coasts of Europe as flimsy boats swamped. Attempts to transport survivors to Germany were underway, where they said they'd welcome one million. Meanwhile, Hungary's government was constructing a fence and threatening any migrant who breached it with imprisonment.

As the broadcast ended, Hugo reminded me to keep an eye out, to watch the ditches for moose and deer; they'd be coming into rut soon and would lose all sense of danger. Moose, particularly, were indifferent; they liked to amble onto the road, even charge a vehicle just for the fun of it. Sure enough, not far out from Humboldt, I spied the ghost of a dark cow moose, but she stayed away, haunting the verge of the trees, and it wasn't until much later, when we turned north at the junction, that we spied a pair of whitetails wandering off into the bush. When we turned off the highway and onto the grid, Hugo alerted me to a fox he'd caught sight of in the mirror, floating across behind us. Along the way, I was astonished by the number of trees sporting patches of leaves that were already unmistakeably yellow.

"It's not even September," I groaned.

At that point, as if he'd heard me, the radio announcer said, "There's a good chance of frost tonight. Cover those tomatoes, folks. So this is global warming!"

"Climate change brings climate weirding, bozo," Hugo muttered grimly as we pulled into the driveway at Paul's place. "Learn the terminology."

As we got out of the truck, I was surprised by the rush I felt when I saw the two new houses all set up and the compound nearly finished. Hugo told me that Paul had connected the solar/wind setup so he'd be able to work in the evenings. As if to complete the scene of country grandeur, the promised squirrels were darting from tree to tree, chattering and chasing one another as they stored spruce cones, and high overhead, geese and ducks were honking and quacking as they practised their routines, ready to fly south.

"Go on in, take a look. " Paul urged. "Your new palace'll have everything you'll need—"

But not everything you'll want, I heard a voice taunt. The words seemed to come from somewhere else, though no one else noticed.

I ran my hand along the new cedar railing as I climbed the stairs to the front deck. Time stopped. When I entered the house, I felt as though I were gliding in on a wash of sunlight. All the features I'd loved the first time I'd seen them were there, the light rippling and dancing on the ceiling, the rooms bright and spacious, the orientation perfect.

As I looked around the living room, I was surprised to see that the bookshelves were empty, thick with dust. But Jack's collection was still there—just in stacks and stacks of boxes, waiting to be unpacked. I went over and peered out the large south window, used my sleeve to smudge the pane clear on the inside.

The view down the hill to the creek promised to be breathtaking, though at that moment it was like peering through the trails of dust that hang in the air at harvest. I could see that Paul's crew had cut the trees nearest the house—we couldn't risk a fire—but the mixed-growth forest was still close enough to promise fine walks with Lucky and Hugo on peaceful mornings after chores.

I wandered from room to room, looking and listening. In the main floor bathroom I tugged open one of the windows and heard sandpipers peeping down by the water, then a red-winged blackbird shrilling nearby. As I looked into the distance, I saw him, Fr. Lewis, down near the trees, his stance angled, a chickadee lifting what had to be a crumbled peanut or a sunflower seed from his palm. He turned his head to look over his shoulder at me, lifted his eyes to meet mine in a long look, steady. I felt confused, guilty, ashamed.

It wasn't as though I'd tried to commune with him or seek his counsel lately. I knew he would never approve of my addiction to home decorating, either here or in the luxurious new kitchen. He had foreseen this. He'd warned me. Told me to *just stop looking at the pictures.* All at once a squirrel was chattering at me from the eaves above the window and I glanced up. When I looked back, the trees were empty.

This visit, if you could call it that, after so many months, left me anxious, awkward, yet his appearance was a comfort, too. At least he hadn't abandoned me. But that look, the distance between us, was he welcoming me here or chiding me for chasing this house-dream? I ached to talk with him, or Mom. He'd always assured me he'd be more use to me dead than alive. There had to be a reason for his appearance.

When last I'd seen him, we were under attack—unlike now, when everything seemed to be going so well. I shook my head, wandered back to the living room. The sun had disappeared. How had I not seen the ominous low front of dark clouds moving in from the southwest? Heavy shadows lay where light had warmed the air ten minutes before. As I retraced my way through the darkened rooms, everything seemed changed. It was going to take a lot of hard work to get the place set up. The walls, the floors, the counters, everything looked as if a giant hand had sifted thick layers of dust, coating every surface. The walls would need to be scrubbed, and we would have to repaint. We still hadn't even gone through our clothes or books, our pots and pans and dishes and valuables, so much *stuff* to finish packing and moving, food stores to be hauled in, cans and sacks, just for this coming winter. And next year and every year after that we'd have to garden, perform tricky canning rites on the woodstove—or dry and store produce enough to sustain the whole fam-damily. Imagine the wood we'd need to chop and split. And then there would be hay to haul, grain and feed to store, livestock to feed and care for.

Who was I kidding? When would there be time for walks, strolling about the property after chores, painting *en plein air*? The new reality would be relentless work, days of backbreaking labour, evenings spent huddled under heavy wool blankets near the woodstove, trying to absorb whatever warmth could we find, load after load of wood to be chopped for the fire. And when night came, we would ache our way upstairs to those icy bedrooms, dreaming of forced-air furnaces and electricity. The long winters, the terrible heat, the black flies and the deer ticks in the summers, the horse flies and wasps driving us crazy as we tried to pick the gallons of berries we'd need to survive.

And as for the family, what was there here for the kids, or even for Dad? How were we going to convince them to come? "Delphine," Dad had said the week before, in that tone he always used when I talked to him about coming to the homestead, even for a visit. "You abandoned me here, and now you want to inveigle me in your schemes," he'd said. "Christmas is such a long way away. I may well be on my cruise at Christmas. I'm earning no interest on my investments, anyway—and being of sound mind, I intend to spend it all."

When I reported this to Paul, he grimaced a bit, shook his head, and said that the work here was not going to wait, Dad or no Dad. We had to ready the place and pray that they would come, all of them.

If we really wanted to be ready for them, as he'd said, I should just grab the rags and bucket I'd seen by the back door and start washing—walls, windows, floors, anything—but I couldn't bear to stay here alone, in this dark place. Instead I walked out onto the front deck, took the stairs down and followed the path, right down to the creek, where I listened for a long time to the water burbling, the wind in the treetops, songbirds swooping and calling, geese squawking high overhead.

I could have sworn I smelled snow.

36

A S WE DROVE BACK TO HUMBOLDT, I reminded myself that there was no longer a decision to make. Nothing would change if the family wouldn't come up north with us. We were fully committed, despite not having found renters yet. All the people who'd come by had been looking for a larger place. I wasn't prepared to do anything so final as to sell either. But Hugo kept the faith; he had it in his mind that our Shangri-La was perfect for a couple with no children. He was certain that the viewing that night would be the one.

We stopped in town for hamburgers; this was swiftly becoming an expensive habit. If we didn't stop squandering our money, we'd have no choice but to move to Paul's place, whether it suited us or not. But the A&W was always the same, full of old-timers, and the food was as good as fast-food gets. At least, that's what we always told one another. I knew that wasn't the reason. As long as we didn't cook, we wouldn't have to clean, and the kitchen would remain in its state of pristine readiness.

Within ten minutes, we had finished our meal. No wonder they called it "Chubby Chicken," I thought, feeling my jeans bind at the waist. I wanted to get the evening over with. The drive home was uneventful, though I did admire the sunset. Right on cue, not ten minutes after we'd entered the house, a strange vehicle turned in, roared down the driveway, and parked right behind the old Toyota. Hugo came up behind me, and we watched the young man and woman as they looked around and made their way to the front door.

"They look perfect," Hugo said. "Don't say a thing to put them off, Delphine. Promise me that. The woman told me they want to get away from the bustle of Humboldt, experience acreage life. It sounds as though they've sipped the Kool-Aid of Country Living. He's a junior manager at the potash mine in Lanigan, and she's a public health nurse in Humboldt, so the location is perfect. They'll even take the horses. They want to ride every day."

When they reached the door, Hugo was all smiles, and I did my best. The young people introduced themselves as Jessica and Logan, and Hugo invited them in, gallantly showed them through the house while I followed. They seemed happy enough, praising the cleanliness, the good room sizes, and the updated kitchen. By the time they'd seen both floors, I started to relax—they didn't seem so bad, for renters—and then Jessica asked crisply whether they'd be able to redecorate. "We've had plenty of experience. We both worked our way through college as house painters."

Hugo stared me down. Against every instinct, I forced myself to keep quiet. Hugo simply said, "Go ahead, so long as you don't mark up the floors. We want you to feel right at home here—but leave the kitchen alone, too, of course. I think you'll agree it's perfect as it is."

The pair nodded and stepped away to walk through the rooms again, this time by themselves, opening and closing cupboards and windows and taps. I stood looking outside through the window over the kitchen sink, made myself watch as orioles darted by like flying dandelions through the dusk of the back yard. Within fifteen minutes the young couple returned.

"I think it will totally work for us," Logan informed Hugo. "We'd like to come back and look things over again by daylight, take some measurements, say Saturday morning? We can sign the lease then if you have it ready."

Hugo shook their hands and walked the young couple back to the front door. It was almost dark. He followed them outside and watched as they climbed into their SUV. The lights blazed on, and Hugo's silhouette waved cheerfully while they pulled out of the yard and turned onto the grid in a whoosh of loose gravel.

But when they vanished, I was waiting inside. I couldn't stop myself.

"Really, Hugo?? Really? They're going to undo all those weeks of work, ruin every blessed single thing we've tried so hard to fix up. And you're going to let them?" I stabbed his chest with my index finger so hard it pushed me back a pace.

Hugo said nothing at first, just seized my hand and held it tightly. I wrenched it free and pushed him away, stalked into the kitchen, looked desperately for something to purge their presence. Everything was perfect. At last I spied a tea towel hanging awkwardly on the stove handle. I twitched it straight just as Hugo entered the room.

I could hear him sigh behind me, imagined him steeling himself for the fight. "Delphine," he said, and just wrapped his arms around me, stood there, resting his chin on top of my head. After a minute, he turned me to face him. "You know this is our only chance. We've shown the house seven times in two months, and no one else has even seemed interested. Let them make it their own. You of all people should know how important that is. We'll be far away and you won't have to look at it."

He brushed my bangs back from my forehead. "Let's have a latte before we hit the hay, yes?" He glanced around the kitchen, snapped his fingers. *"Garçon? Servitör?* Where are the damned servants when you want them, anyway?" He smiled. "We should get more boxes tomorrow and then you can start realizing *the Importance of Being Earnest* about this move."

I wanted to joke, "This decision is too Wilde for me," but instead I snapped, "Won't that be counting your chickens? What if they change their minds? We can't leave without someone to watch the place."

Hugo dipped me back in a Hollywood kiss. Even though I was determined to stay angry, I shrieked a little. As he pulled me to stand again, he said, "The only chickens we have are on the homestead, *min älskling*, and Paul is going to need our help to take care of them soon. Whether these people move in or not, we're going to be in our new place by the beginning of November. Let's pray that they do take it."

37

AS HE HAD PREDICTED, I felt a bit of a relief when Saturday arrived at last and we closed the deal. I had no rational choice then but to accept my fate. Would the universe, against all the signs to the contrary, have finally sent us people who wanted the place if we weren't meant to move up north? Yet knowing what the cosmos had in mind didn't make it easy: a small part of me still ached to stay. I fretted about leaving the kitchen, and even my job seemed more attractive than it had months ago—Marie and I were almost ready to wrap up our project, against all odds.

True, we had so few friends, yet the ones we had—Marie and her husband Joe, Nadine, Stan, our neighbours Helen and Albert—all seemed more precious in the light of our coming seclusion. We wouldn't be able to stay in touch. All along, Paul had made us swear that we wouldn't tell anyone where we were going.

"Got to keep the location a secret," he'd wag his finger as he warned us time after time, as if we were in danger of telling the world how absolutely insane we were.

We endured his "reminders" for a while, but one day, Hugo had had enough. He said, "Yes, Paul. We get it. Loose lips sink ships. But in the long run, some diversity would be a good thing, even a necessity, if you mean this community to last."

Paul dug his heels in. "Hold on, Hugo. We'll need to be sure, talk it through before we even think about bringing people in. Plenty of details to consider. Leland made it a point to warn me about that type of trouble. Can't be too careful." His tanned forehead creased as he spoke.

"Of course," Hugo said. "Relax. New members by group invitation only. It's a moot point, in any case, since we only have room for family right now, even with that house you've brought in for your dad and all of Emma's happy campers. But I want you to get used to the idea that we might need to add others in the future. We can't expect the kids to be monks. No survival in that—"

"Time enough to recruit later, after we've tried out how things will work on a small scale. We can spend the winter sussing things out, maybe researching, drawing up a list of handy folk, people with skills and resources to approach."

As I listened to them map it out like some exercise in selecting stock, I felt more isolated than ever before. Choosing community members for the nuts and bolts of their aptitudes, what they would bring to the table, might be all very well for Paul and Hugo—but what about friendship? I couldn't bear the thought of abandoning our little circle without at least a proper goodbye. No matter how much I had always joked about our reclusive loner-status, how could we just vanish? People would send out the RCMP. And they always got their man. Or woman. What would Paul make of that?

In the end I talked Hugo into holding a party at our house, an early Thanksgiving Day meal, nothing ambitious.

I promised I'd just roast a prime rib or barbecue some chickens, serve some basic side dishes. If it turned out to be nice we could eat outside, sort of a last supper to share with our friends. We would tell them we were going away to travel, follow our feet, wander where the stars took us. And that would be true, at least in a way—the stars did seem to be leading us forward. Once we were safe at the homestead, we would stay hidden, and our secret would be the last thing anyone would ever guess.

As I prepared, everything conspired to foil my plans. I couldn't find a nice roast, the chicken was outrageously expensive, and the weather was clear but oh so cold, with a high of only 9 degrees the day of our party. Marie and Joe arrived late, 45 minutes after Hugo and I had settled everyone else in the living room with drinks and platters of tasty things to nibble on. I'd kept the food warm, but it was drying out. I tried to hustle the latecomers into the living room so I could set out the meal, but Marie ducked back as I led her past the kitchen, saying, "So this is the glorious reno-volution, in all its sparkle and flash! You've outdone yourself, Delphine. Is it everything you've dreamed of all these years, this transformation? The planning, the negotiations you went through with the warehouse…"

My mouth went dust-dry, I felt as if I had gagged on chalk. I couldn't move, couldn't speak. Marie was still talking, but the words were so slow I could hardly understand them. My own thoughts flew by so quickly I couldn't keep up.

I cleared my throat as softly as I could.

"Uhmm…Not sure what…you mean…you know, Marie, I told you how when you…we …were at the conference, Hugo did all the installation…such a beautiful surprise." Good. It was easier to talk once I started. I pulled the pot of fingerling potatoes off the stove and drained it, grateful for the cloud of steam that masked my face. I couldn't think who could have told her. I had been so careful, so care-full, to make sure sharp-eared, sharp-eyed Marie was nowhere around when I called the warehouse from work.

She just wouldn't let go. "Nadine said she had to wait forever to talk to you one afternoon. Said you were on the phone for what seemed like eternity; it was Holy Thursday, and she was trying to finish up before the artists' tour on Good Friday. There was quite the drama, she told me, you were all worked up, something about restocking an order at Bright Ideas?"

Marie winked at Hugo mischievously. I swallowed again. Hugo looked at me questioningly, and I was sure that my crime was writ large across my face. He turned to Marie and shook his head, saying, "She must have been mistaken. We couldn't order the kitchen until the middle of April. We had a family emergency on Easter weekend—Del's brother was ill and we had to take him to the hospital."

I wanted desperately to change the subject, but an inner voice warned me we couldn't talk about Paul, either, not without trouble. Best to get out of the kitchen, move on to supper. I asked Hugo to call everyone to the table if he was finished carving. "And could you carry in the turkey? It looks juicy, the brining seems to have worked better than ever, and I'll have this gravy there in a minute—" I *had* to create a diversion, and how. "I'll bring the candied sweet potatoes and the baby spuds when I come—and Marie, the red cabbage and this bowl of Brussels sprouts—could you carry them in for me, please? Should be very colourful all together. I think that's it—we're ready for launch—"

I was waiting for Hugo to joke that it was dinner, not launch, but I could see that he was still trying to figure out what was up. He wouldn't stop looking at me. "You all right, Delphine?"

"Just fine, Sweetheart! But no one likes cold turkey!" I forced a laugh, I felt transparent, every sin revealed, my thoughts sheer and thin and tangled as plastic wrap. I tried another joke. "Like us, quitting cold turkey?"

Hugo's eyebrows lifted high. He was behind Marie now, she couldn't see him put his finger to his lips, shake his head to silence me. He thought I was about to spill the secret about the homestead. Good! I was relieved when he walked briskly away, called into the living room, "Come on, everyone, come and join us at the table. And here we have a most succulent bird. Delphine's recipe is famous in no fewer than four counties." He placed the steaming platter in front of Helen.

Soon we were all seated and the meal was in progress. Marie had moved on, thank goodness, to talking about the changes to arts funding across Canada. My mind wouldn't rest. I'd almost forgotten about the budget cuts. But I couldn't care less about art or artists or the great dominion of Canada, not at that moment. What was Hugo thinking? Was he piecing the timeline together? I had worked so hard to be sure he was on board by the time I'd given the go-ahead to the warehouse.

I was desperate to think, to stop this crazy train of thought, to stop punning, for God's sake, but my thoughts were starting to blur together, a rolling ball of confusion. Time flowed like rhyme. What if he remembered the day I had tried so hard to say, what if he put together two and two?

Something flipped. I felt sudden, complete release. Ecstasy. I was euphoric. Everything I said was hilarious. I was clever, I was witty, I was the star of the party. My thoughts breezed by like banners, waving and rippling. I was on fire, cracking joke after joke, elaborate puns and bon mots, though the others did seem almost too dull to understand the humour of what I was saying. I couldn't believe they were so slow. But it didn't matter. Everything connected in the most intricate ways. The food was fantastic, the colours divine, the party delightful. I was on top and this was my world.

I had every single thing I had ever wanted.

38

I WAS LYING ON MY SIDE UNDER THE WINDOW. The light was diffuse, bouncing off the snow and clouds without a direction. I was in class, clicker and laser pointer in hand as I identified Doric, Ionic, and Corinthian columns. No, I was kneeling by the carrots in the garden Hugo built all those Septembers ago, the black earth clinging to the thick roots as I wiggled them free of their brethren. No, I was standing on Paul's veranda, gazing down the hill sloping to the creek, the fall leaves floating in shades of ochre— amidst this scatter of slow confetti in the slight breeze, geese wheeled overhead, soft honks and squawks mingled with the rustling branches, waving with the brave happy confusion of travelers who know their way home, wherever they land.

The mattress was hard and the plastic cover beneath the thin sheet felt cold and crackly. Where was Hugo? Why did he leave me here, abandoning me to strange thoughts and stranger people, nurses who came by at odd times to check the IV, security guards patrolling the halls, herds of young people in lab coats who appeared with insane theories, wanting to take my history. I teach art history, I am an historian, what was I thinking when it happened, when what happened, what had happened to make those visions kick in every time I tried to go to sleep, first the nostrils, then a face as close to mine as if we were touching noses, details of skin and hair emerging, a photographic print in a bath of developer. No, that was years ago, so long ago, in art school. Everything was digital these days. The lion face evolved into a horse's, nose first, gigantic paisley nostrils flared, the texture of fine grey moleskin. Lashes long and dark, eyes, deep sienna, patient, focused on something behind me, I was layered in light and shadow, and then the other eyes, human, such presence, milky thick rippling conjunctivas, faint grey-blue irises, almost animated, but hopeless, gazed obliquely past my ear, melted and reappeared at different angles. The silent advice of the dead.

Eventually the night came when one of them looked back, the iris flooding with color so true, so real, the teal splashing in beautiful strokes of yellow light as the pupil narrowed and widened with recognition. It was no one I knew, I was sure of that, but I felt so invited. I was so frightened. I tried to turn it off, and all at once all of the eyes receded into the thick black, indescribable, and I knew I had disappointed, refused a gift, ungraciously. I felt curious again, tried to will the looks back to me, but there was only disenchantment, refusal, absence.

I didn't sleep much anymore, the worry of what it all meant, the fright of being found absolutely inconsequential. Voices started. I slipped into an easy habit of pacing the room in the middle of the night when first they brought me here. I knew it was dangerous and I was determined to quit, but that night, the night after the night after the eye saw me, I saw the clock strike two, only four hours until they would force me to get up. I needed to console myself, the hell with it, I had to sleep, and just as I made up my mind to sneak onto the floor, a man's voice shouted, "Don't!" and a weightless hand restrained my shoulder. The rest of the night was worse, with shouts of "Over here!" and "Can you not understand?" echoing so loudly I was sure Hugo would hear and be frightened, the words slicing the slumbering room, as he lay in our bed, snoring like Dandelion, rattling gently in rhythm from her velvet chair.

39

M ORNING AGAIN. This time Hugo was there, and he
and Paul were sitting with a woman at a plain wooden
table at the other end of the room. I was lying on a bunk
near the woodstove, careful to make sure they thought I was
sleeping, my ears open and my eyes quite shut.

A tinkly voice asked, "Have the highways been cleared
yet, Paul? I must get back. My family will be worried. I have
patients to see."

I heard something in the way Paul paused. "You gotta
understand—this place is secret. Can't have you going back
and telling the world. Would be handy to have a doctor on
board—"

Quickly, the woman, a voice I recognized, said, "Of
course I will keep your secret."

A new voice spoke. It was Hugo, at last. He said, "Paul,
stop it. Nasrin doesn't know your sense of humour. If you

really think it's necessary, she can wear a blindfold."

"Yeah, yeah, I thought you'd know I was joking—"

By the smile on my face. I knew that old family joke. I could almost remember. Nasrin was in the ditch the night the storm first hit. But what was secret? Why would she wear a blindfold?

She said, "You can trust me. You know that you can."

I did, I trusted her, I always had. But suddenly I was furious. I felt myself split. I almost sat up and called out but had to stop myself.

I forced my eyes shut, unclenched my hands.

There was a thumping noise when one of them shoved a chair back. I heard Paul say, "I'll go get the tractor. Give me, say, fifteen minutes. Bet you're glad we got the machinery so early now, eh Hugo? Should be able to pull the doc's car out of the ditch if the highway crews haven't done that yet."

And then all the chairs were dancing on the floorboards. I peeked over at the group, saw Paul go outside while Nasrin gathered her parka and looped her pashmina about her graceful neck. When she looked over at me, I pretended to toss in my sleep, just rolled over so that my back was facing her. I heard the heavy wooden door open again, and then shut, and all at once I was alone. But no, there was a sound, maybe Hugo was still in the kitchen, watching me, as I lay on the daybed across from the woodstove. I could feel my hair fray about my damp face. As part of my performance, I'd dashed my legs free of the covers. I had goose flesh on my thighs and upper arms.

Hugo drew the blankets over me again just as the door slammed shut. I felt a whoosh of cold air, heard the clatter of feet stomping snow off. "Tractor's warming up," I heard Paul say. "We can go in ten minutes or so. But what about D.E.L.?" he spelled.

"It's been days. Shouldn't she have come out of it?" Hugo sounded worried.

"Hugo? Could you come and join us?" Nasrin asked, her musical voice low, guarded. I rolled over again, this time not so noisily, and faced the room, peered through my closed lashes. No one was looking at me. I could see she still had her coat on. She was holding the back of an old wooden chair, all wired together, like the ones we'd had at the lake when we were kids. Hugo nodded, went to the table, sat. He looked weary. As he ran his right hand through his hair, I squinted. I could just see his red sweater, the brightness against his pale hands and face. Nasrin leaned over, put her hand on his arm, and said quietly, "I'm wondering if you should return Delphine to Prince Albert. As her physician, I could write a letter, ask them to re-admit her."

I could feel Hugo thinking.

Paul chimed in, "If it was just the Haldol, sure as shootin' she'd have come out of it by now. What do you think?"

"You were the one who thought she'd be better off here!" Hugo said, and I heard him turn quickly to Paul. "I took her to the hospital! Coming here was all your idea. Frankly, I'm at a loss. I don't know anything about mental illness— Delphine always dealt with the lunacy in your family—no offence, Paul."

Paul murmured, "None taken."

"Nasrin? What do you think?"

It was all coming back. Nasrin was there at the hospital.

Her voice was soft. "The main question is whether you and Paul have the stamina to sit with her until she recovers. She must be watched whenever she's awake, possibly for months. I could prescribe a different medication, perhaps. But if it has the same effect? If she has another crisis, will you be able to handle her? You can hardly call the paramedics or the RCMP from here. They would have no reason to keep your secret."

Paul jostled in his chair, looked my way, and I squeezed my eyes shut. I imagined him turning towards Hugo as I heard him say, "Maybe the kids would come out and help? Wouldn't hurt to get the whole family established out here sooner rather than later. Hate to scare them, but they're adults now. They'll want to help their mother, I know they will."

The last thing I wanted was for them to know that I was listening, so I moaned a bit and rolled over to face the window. At least with my back turned to the traitors, I could open my eyes a bit. Outside everything was white, blobs of snow felted the screens. I heard someone rise and cross the room. I knew that step; it was Hugo. I closed my eyes as he squatted easily beside the bed. His long legs fold so gracefully. He smoothed my hair, stiff with sweat and spit, away from my cheeks, it felt so good when he put his cool hand on my forehead, but I couldn't let him know that. I couldn't let him know that I knew they were plotting to take me back. I needed to think.

I grunted, tried to push him away, clenched my teeth, forced tears—that wasn't hard. "When is Hugo coming for me?" I made myself rant. "I hate this hospital! I want Hugo!"

I pretended to thrash, worked myself around to face the table again. I could see the whole room. Hugo had vanished. But he was just here. Why would he leave? Was I imagining things? Was I really still sick?

"He'll be back soon, Delphine," Paul called over to me, rising to make his way to my side. "You're safe. Just try to rest." He offered me some juice—I think it was apple—from a light mug on the window ledge by my bed, adjusting the straw so I could take a sip. "Better?" he asked.

"So tired. Cold. Cold. Cold," I shivered.

Paul straightened the sheets for me, batted my pillow into shape, turned it over to avoid the wet place where I'd been drooling, and pulled the heavy old patchwork quilt up to my chin. I remembered helping when Mom had patched those pieces together. The ones with stems of bright cherries were from a dress I'd outgrown beside the patches from her own blue and white stripe. I thought we had abandoned all our housewares when Dad sold the cabin at the lake. Paul draped the heavy wool blanket over the top, tucked me in tight and opened the woodstove to add another log to the fire. Sparks flew as he poked at it.

Nasrin called to Paul then, told him she'd written the letter. "Never mind if you don't want to use it today; I've

194

suggested that you may bring her back if she isn't better in a week or two. And you really need to take her back if that's the case. It won't be easy, but you must think about yourself and Hugo. What will happen if you break down, too?"

"In the meantime," she continued, "Here's a prescription for the mood stabilizer that you're on. Sometimes family members respond well to the same medication. She should start slowly, two pills twice a day at first. But if she gets worse—"

Paul said softly as he stood over me, "We'll watch her like a hawk, like two hawks. She gets worse, we'll take her back, pronto. No shilly-shallying. Meantime, I'd better get you to the highway and pull your car out of the ditch. If we can locate it—"

Hugo came in from the back room, pulled a chair to the woodstove and sat beside me. I watched as the low clouds hurried across the treetops. I was almost warm, the blankets felt heavy and I had to fight the urge to let go, drift back to sleep. Nothing would feel more natural than to have Hugo climb into bed and hold me while I slept—but I couldn't let him know that I'd been listening, or that I knew their plan. They were going to take me away when they got tired, and that was inevitable. Just living on the ranch was so tiring. Moving snow, hauling wood, cooking, doing chores, the work was endless.

Hugo reached for the windowsill, picked up a book with a horse on the cover, stared far away. He thumbed through it, read a page or two, but then he rested the book face down on his thigh. His cell phone pinged. He looked at his phone. Paul and Nasrin had just stepped out on the porch. Hugo went out after them, calling, "Paul! It's Gina texting me. She asks: 'where are you guys?' What on earth can I say?"

The cold air swirled around my head. I shivered, but no one noticed.

"Tell her you're with me at the homestead," I heard Paul boom as he came back inside. They shut the door. "Find out what's up."

After a moment, Hugo said, "She says she needs to see us. She's bringing Lacey. They want directions."

"Ask for an ETA," Paul answered, sounding calm, confident. "Snowplough must have been through by now, but with this wind still driving hard, bound to be finger drifts. Pretty rough for her little car. I'll take Nasrin out with the tractor now. When someone's asleep," he paused, waving his hand at my bed, "think you could feed the animals quickly before she wakes up?"

40

THE MORNING AFTER THE PARTY, I was awake and my spirit singing. Such a wonderful evening, followed by Hugo and I making love like teenagers all night long. What could we have for breakfast? I was starving. Hugo was looking at me—did he want to go again? I reached for him, but he was already jumping out of bed, pulling on his shorts. He rustled in the wardrobe and held out a grey turtleneck for me. Why did he think I needed him to help with my clothes? He was throwing my socks and underwear, long and short, and a pair of pyjamas into the backpack—were we heading for the bush?

I wondered for a second, then I glanced out the window and noticed. "Look, honey, the moon is still in the sky. So beautiful!" I stood for a moment and watched, revelling in the magic, and when I turned around, he was already dressed.

"Yeah, right, it's gorgeous," he said. "Come with me. Let's get something nice to eat in the little bistro."

I was dizzy, even before I tried to walk. Hugo was holding my hand and talking, but I wasn't listening. What a glorious day it was. I was so hungry, I could eat a horse. But not our horses, not Misty and Commander. What would Mom say if I ate the leftover pumpkin pie for breakfast? Was there a bistro in Humboldt? Why would we go into town? Oh, that's what he meant—the little bistro, our bistro. The gravy was perfect. What was he saying now? Hugo was talking but oh so slowly, the words far away, just when I wanted so much to connect.

I couldn't seem to stop talking, even when Hugo asked for a moment of quiet to let him think. The muffins were so delicious, I had all three, right after my pie, piled high with whipped cream. I had cup after cup of coffee. It was all so grand, the room, the food, our night of love, a beautiful dance of ideas that pliéd and splashed in my mind. Before I was finished, Hugo told me we were going to visit a friend, and he took me by the elbow to guide me to the truck. I didn't know why he was moving so slow and acting so hurried. I wanted to go say good morning to all the animals, but Hugo said there was no time. "But our horses?" I pleaded. "What about their oats?"

"They don't want any this morning," he said firmly. "We're going to see our town friends this time."

Which town friends? Stan? We don't have any other friends in town, all our friends live in Bruno and Quill Lake.

I can't remember the rest of what we said, but by the time he told me we were going to see Nasrin, we were turning into the parking lot. "Why the hospital?" I asked. "Is Nasrin sick?"

Nasrin was not sick, she wasn't even *on*, whatever that meant. Hugo seemed dismayed to learn that they wouldn't call her "unless the emergency doctor deems it necessary," as the girl at the desk said. His voice gruff, Hugo told her that there was a family history, his wife had been under a great deal of stress, and she was clearly not herself.

But I was his wife. I was more than myself. I'd never felt better.

"Just how do you mean, not herself?" asked the girl.

"Altered since last evening," Hugo said. My eyes fell on a magazine, sitting at the bottom of the stack. It was *Homeward*. I flipped through the gorgeous photos, almost as nice as the kitchens I'd planned. One had a new type of tile that I couldn't recall ever seeing before. But I read the magazine cover to cover every month, and this one was—yes, it was September. But I didn't remember.

"How do you mean, altered?" the girl asked.

Hugo hesitated, then talked quickly, almost whispering. Was he ill? He said, "She's had an enormous appetite, been speaking too fast, not making sense, and, well, she…she wanted sex over and over again last night."

The girl turned to her computer screen. "And I take it that's unusual?"

"Could we just see the doctor?" he said. "I need to talk to Dr. Salari, Nasrin Salari."

The girl put a wristband on me and sent us to sit in the waiting room. There was almost no one ahead of us, just a four-year-old with a broken arm and an old woman with chest pains. Still, the people working there seemed busy, and no one had time for us. Hugo was anxious; I could see that.

I watched the clock. Hours later, we still hadn't been called. I looked through every magazine in the room, even *Field and Stream* and *Parenting* and *Popular Mechanics*. Normally I don't touch reading material in hospitals. I worry about germs, but I decided that the other people's problems that day—broken bones and chest pains—weren't contagious. I was so bored. I had so much energy. I got up to go explore, but I had to sit back down again because Hugo asked me to stay with him.

I sat, but my legs wouldn't stay still, they just swung back and forth. What was taking so long?

When at last we were called, Hugo told the young doctor quite the story. I tried to straighten him out when he said silly things—I was not manic, why would he say I was? Paul is manic, that I'd heard Hugo say many times.

The doctor asked who Paul was. I cut Hugo off, told young Dr. Fischer, that's what his nametag said, that Paul was my brother. He turned to Hugo and said, "You can't argue with genetics, though certainly not every person in a family with mental illness will become ill."

The next thing I know they were talking about Prince Albert. "And Queen Victoria?" I added. "Or are we going to visit Paul?" I asked Hugo. Hugo looked alarmed, as if he were afraid I'd spill the beans. I'd never do that, was he crazy? The doctor wanted us to see other doctors in Prince Albert, the hospital there, just for a week or two, no more than a few months at the most. Hugo asked if I could have a change in medication, perhaps like Paul had, without hospitalization. "Surely rest is all she needs?" he said.

Dr. Fischer said, "It's not that simple. Her chart shows she's been on antidepressants of one kind or another since she was a young woman, and now that she's swung the other way, changing her prescription won't be enough. The medication will be in her system for weeks, driving the mania higher. It will take time to see what will be necessary."

I was dying to go home then, but Hugo told me we would have to wait a little longer. We stayed in the waiting room, that was the perfect name for it, I thought; so much time wasted waiting while the doctor was away, making his call. It took forever for him to come back, but, when he did, he said there was a bed for me in P.A. I didn't understand. Why would I need a bed in P.A.? I heard someone screaming, "I want to go home. I have to go home. Let me go—" and then a nurse came out of nowhere with two men in uniforms. They grabbed my arms. I couldn't get away, I couldn't, and the screaming wouldn't stop. The nurse had a syringe and Hugo just stood there—

41

I WAS IN A BLUE ROOM, PERIWINKLE, I might have said, if anyone had asked, but they did not. I knew we were not at home, of that I was sure. There were heavy rails on the bed and I was so tired, I couldn't even lift my hands. I could feel them, just not move them. My feet felt strange, too. I tried to swing myself up to sit, over and over. But I was so tired. Who were these people, and where was I? Hugo? Someone in green and white was talking, but I couldn't follow the drift, I got lost, each word just lifted me like I was poplar fluff floating on a breeze. I must have the flu, I was woozy and lonely and scared, I was trying *so hard* to ask, but I couldn't make the connection. There was such loud screaming, "LET ME GO! LET ME GO LET ME GO LET ME—" One of the strangers fiddled with a tube in my arm.

When I woke up, there was a stranger talking to Hugo. They were beside me, I could hear that, but I couldn't see them, everything was out of focus. "Mr. Almquist—we've had a brief time without the sedation, and unfortunately, your wife was not able to make the adjustment. It's best now to let her rest. We'll see if we can try again tomorrow."

Hugo didn't look at him, he was watching me, his face was turned my way. He asked, "Was she in restraints when she woke? No wonder she was 'unable to make the adjustment'!"

I needed to tell him how frightened I was.

"Now, now, Mr. Almquist. These are very early days. It will take time and lots of care to bring her back to herself, if—" Hugo turned to stare at him. The stranger flipped open the cover and looked at the tablet he was holding and started again. "We'll need to establish a new plan, set some new goals. Why don't we sit down in my office and we can go through the options more comfortably?"

I WOKE TO SEE PEOPLE standing in the doorway, two men I almost recognized, talking to a young man in a white coat. Where was I? What was that ringing? Had we had an accident, or was there a shooting? Food poisoning? Maybe the turkey was bad. Why was I here? When I tried to get out of bed, my arms and legs seemed stuck. Oh my God. Maybe a war had started? Was I a prisoner? I called out, and someone came over, a woman, but she was moving so slowly. The men at the door turned to look, I could have sworn I knew them, but from where?

The men were walking across the room towards me. I could hear every word now, though I had no idea what they were talking about. "Thank you for letting us know, Paul, about your experience with Haldol. While family members sometimes share a reaction to medications, that is not always the case. We'll taper it off and monitor her over the next few days."

The older man wouldn't give in. "She needs to come off it now, she'll settle right down. Had me higher than a kite, was 200% better, not cured, mind you, but so much better once they took me off the stuff."

The other man said, "Please listen to him. She wasn't anything like this when I brought her to the hospital. That was four weeks ago tomorrow."

The one in the white coat was looking at some papers. "The ambulance brought her here, but this report says that she had to be chemically restrained. That's why the Haldol was given."

"I mean when I took her to the hospital in Humboldt, she was still well enough to read, she was just too fast at everything. Then they gave her that shot of Haldol, and—"

"Sometimes mania escalates quickly. Her behaviour may not be due to the medication. I'd hate to take her off it and have her become violent again."

Violent? Who was violent?

The three men were standing beside me now. The two looked at each other, and back at the one in the green clothes and white coat. "Do you have something else you could try? Just to see if Paul's right? Before things get worse?"

"Zyprexa's what my doctor ordered," the one with the grizzled chin said. "Works like a charm. Even on a low dose now, for maintenance."

"We'll certainly keep that in mind, Mr. Boudreau. I am concerned that if we take away the medication that's sedating her, she might try to harm herself—or others. Now I have to finish my rounds. Visiting hours don't start until 1:00 p.m., so if you could come back then—"

After that one left, I heard the one in the hat say, "Might just want to get that second opinion after all. Maybe we could call Nasrin, see what she can do?"

"How do you know Nasrin?" the other asked.

"Del took me to her in April. Saw her again in June for follow up. Sure set me right."

"Right. I remember."

"Lady has a world of sense. Why didn't you see her in the first place?"

"That was the plan, but she wasn't on call—and the doctor who was admitted Delphine for observation in P.A.—I had no idea. She was high when I brought her in, but just fast, nothing like now. God, Paul," the man said, "Did the

203

doctor mean to imply that she might not recover?"

"One thing at a time, Hugo. One thing at a time."

"If only I'd talked to you. But I was so worried, the hospital seemed like the safest place—"

"Hang in there, Hugo. Let's see what Nasrin says. One thing at a time."

42

A S SOON AS THE CABIN DOOR CLOSED behind Hugo, I lifted myself on my elbows, warily. I felt like a crocodile as I watched him walk away from the porch. He turned around when he was halfway to the barn, but something made me duck just in time, before he could see me in the window. My instincts were working, at least. After I'd waited a few more minutes, I sat up, swung my legs over the side of the bed, and set my bare feet to the cold floorboards. There was a mirror across the room, and I saw myself, really saw myself for the first time in weeks. I looked awful, no, worse than that. Terrifying, with a capital T. I couldn't let Gina see me like that. The backpack was on the floor by the foot of the bed, and I dug quickly through it, pulled out a pair of jeans, a clean shirt, some fresh underwear. Long johns. I took the heavy socks, too. I dashed the comb through my hair. It wouldn't matter how stringy it was, I tried to convince myself. I'd keep my toque on.

Within minutes, I was dressed. I went to the table, grabbed biscuits, cheese, the last bottle of mango passion juice—and the irony hit me, it was passion that got me into this mess. No, it was joking.

So how to slow the search party down? It was an old trick, even hobbity: I rolled some pillows with towels and shaped a body, drew the blankets high up to cover the head. I saw my cell phone in my purse but the battery was dead. I grabbed Hugo's instead, picked up his keys and a handful of bills from the wallet on the table. I took the flashlight and stashed everything in the backpack, pulled on a pair of men's winter boots and grabbed the sheepskin mittens from the basket by the door. There was a warm grey scarf there, too, the one Gina knit me last Christmas, and with that wrapped close about my face, I took one last look to make sure Hugo was nowhere in sight. He wasn't. I opened the door, and I was off.

I zipped up a little higher. Man, was it colder than I expected, flakes still falling in flurries, but I was so glad to think that the drifting would help cover my tracks. The sun shone brightly now and then, clouds flying over its face and showering me with snow. I knew they'd try to follow me, surely they'd have to, so I walked carefully, paced my steps to match Hugo's long strides on the trail halfway to the barn. When I reached the band of brush near the driveway, I hopped over the snowpile with both feet and slipped out to the bushes on the far side of the fence. I had to get away, right away from the cabin, before Hugo or Paul got back. In my white down-filled jacket, if I had to hide, I'd look like a snowdrift.

Maybe.

I followed a deer trail through the trees for about half an hour. Before I reached the edge of the bush that lined the grid road, I heard what I guessed must be Gina's little car turn in and bounce towards me. I decided to stay off the road, hide, take my own chances. Out here, away from the wi-fi in the cabin, I had no reception. At least I had Hugo's phone, even if I couldn't see if she'd texted him. She must have slipped by

Paul, or maybe he'd spotted her and told her the way.

But as the vehicle came into sight, I could see that it wasn't Gina at all, but a truck, looked like a 4 x 4. It never occurred to me that Hugo might call for help. There was never any traffic out here, Paul made sure of that. I crouched down in the bush, trying to blend into the snowy trees. My legs were in knots, and I fought the urge to stand up. The vehicle seemed to take forever to cover the length of road I could see, even at the speed it was going, but then the big black beast faded from hearing, and I was all alone again, all alone except for the coyotes, starting to yip near the highway.

It was getting late. An hour had passed since I'd sneaked away, and the brilliant red glow that had been the sun was sinking below the horizon, or what I could see of it in the bush. I knew I was hardly prepared to spend a long winter's night out there, but at least the roaring and swaying in the treetops had stopped. Some faint memory told me the wind always dies at sundown, it always had at the lake.

I pulled my mitten off, shoved my hand in my jacket pocket.

There was a book of matches, a souvenir from last New Year's Eve, when I set the fireworks off at the acreage. The cardboard flap was loose, but when I pulled out the pack, the stems were firm and the tips looked smooth and fresh, and for a few long moments I held the cover open. At last I gave in, struck one match and held it before me, shielding the flare from the road, just for seconds. When the skin started to prickle, cold as I was, I knew I had to blow it out. A fire was too big a risk: even if I could gather enough wood, there was the danger of setting the whole forest ablaze. And even a small fire would make it too easy for them to spot me. I knew then that even lighting the match was a risk I shouldn't have taken. I dropped the charred match, rubbed my palms together and massaged my fingers quickly and pulled my mittens back on.

The deepest blue stretched over the black branches above me, and it took longer than I expected for the fading yellow light at the southwest horizon to thin under and vanish. For a moment I leaned my face against the rough bark of a white poplar, afraid. The cold scorched my forehead as my breath caught in my throat. I heard a distinctive sound, whoo-whoooo—whhooooo. I straightened, scanned in all directions. Above me, a heavy white body, the perfectly round head of a snowy owl, its yellow eyes watching me.

Lights zoomed from side to side far away, up ahead, running at right angles to the grid. The road crews must have opened the highway, pulled all the vehicles out of the ditches. At least with the flashlight I could see the edge of the brush, but I had to save the batteries—I hadn't any extras—so off it went. It was best to stand in the dark and see what was out there, what might come for me. As I'd thought that, something so loud, maybe a tractor, turned onto the road, headed for the homestead. Paul. I hunkered down on my haunches behind some shrubs, knew the flare on the nylon of my white jacket would glare at him if he caught it in his lights. He didn't seem to be in a rush; he had the tractor bucket down and was scraping finger drifts. Good old Paul. He didn't carry a cell phone, he wouldn't even know he was supposed to look for me.

I was safe, I could breathe again. But I was impatient, wanted him to hurry and move past me, I had to make it to the highway before he got back home. Once he'd spoken to Hugo, once they knew I wasn't with either of them, then the hunt would be on, that much was certain.

I couldn't bear the thought of being locked up again. I had to get away. Yet how I ached to think of the fear I was causing them. Surely they would forgive me. Once I explained, once they saw how well I was, what a terrible mistake they'd made, they'd have to understand.

As I set off, the owl flew, too, leading the way, the great wings faintly thrumming above me. The bird perched when I paused, its enormous wings folding flat, effortlessly, as it settled in the poplar branches. I was grateful I was not alone, after all.

43

I MADE IT HOME, though it was after 9:00 by the time I arrived. The strangers let me off at the winding driveway, and I trudged in through those last hundred yards of drifts. The tall grass we always left at the side of the road so that we could find the track in winter served its purpose well; even with the flashlight on its last legs, so to speak, it was easy to plod my way towards the house. I was a little surprised, but so relieved, that the place was deserted. There wasn't a vehicle in sight.

Low clouds dodged the moon, and as I made my way up the long driveway, my path was lit as if by some slow-blinking lantern. It felt like the cosmos was swaying with the rhythm of my steps. When I climbed the back porch, I half-expected the tenants' dog to run up behind me, rip me to pieces. But when I turned the key, the door swung open to silence.

The strong odour of fresh paint is not something you forget, not when you've suffered a lifelong addiction to the stuff. All the same, I entered cautiously and promptly tripped, snagged my foot on something flimsy on the floor as I entered the kitchen. When I flicked on the light, pizza boxes and greasy paper plates and empty beer bottles appeared, crowding the island. A spray of dark paint speckled the clear glass globes and the marble counter beneath. All the walls and all the trim—even in the kitchen—were the colour of mud, something I might have called a mid-range taupe if I were so inclined, which I was not. And worse, so much worse, the floors were splotched with paint where the thin plastic drop cloths had wrinkled and bunched.

As frightened as I'd been, as angry as I felt, as desperate as things looked, all I could feel was a sudden enormous surge of relief. The only good thing about this entire adventure, the whole bloody back-to-the-homestead experiment, was that, of all things, my intuition—my sanity—I had been undeniably right. I was vindicated. I'd warned Hugo about those frauds.

I felt clearer in that moment than ever I had.

I savoured that feeling as I stepped slowly through the still rooms. But I knew I had to explain myself, call off the hunt, rescue the hunters. I had to phone Hugo, tell him what had happened. As I worked out what I would say, I could almost imagine him standing behind me, his head resting on mine, his arms around me. He'd have to understand. Of all the colours I hated—where was the music, the vibrations, in taupe? *If I had to pick a colour for the zombie apocalypse*—I thought grimly. Of course all of our things had been moved out, I had expected that, but it was still a shock to see the little bistro staged with garbage. On the other hand, I realized that if they hadn't made such a mess of the painting, the new tenants probably would have moved in already. And with the way they had botched the job, the damage they had done to the floors alone, we would have ample grounds to cancel the lease. I'd have the locks changed in the morning. And thank

God we found out now, when it wasn't too late to talk to Jim, and take back my job.

All the way home I had been working it out. The real madness lay in following Paul's plan, fleeing shadows, seeing disaster looming at every turn. No wonder I had been so stressed: that *was* the definition of insanity. No wonder I let myself crack. Not that I would ever forgive Paul for wanting to send me back to the hospital. The real world, our beautiful world, was still here for me, for Hugo and me.

At the nudge of his name I remembered again and reached for the phone to tell him to call off the search. By now they could have tracked me to the highway, figured out my destination. The last thing I needed would be to have to explain myself to a mob of concerned neighbours, fend off a rescue operation for an escaped mental patient. I took a breath and started to dial—but I had Hugo's cell, and I could hardly phone him with his own phone. Gina answered her phone on the second ring. She was crying. "MOM? Are you all right? WHERE ARE YOU?"

"You mean you haven't checked your app to find Dad's phone yet?" I had to let them know how together I was, still more than a step ahead, not crazy at all.

But apparently I *had* forgotten a few things. "What? Oh—he wouldn't let us set that up, don't you remember? Big Brother, surveillance by CSIS, the NSA, and all that? Where are you? We've all been so worried!"

"I'm fine, honey, just fine. Ask Uncle Paul. He-of-little-faith, he knew—well, at least at first. It must have been the medication that caused me to become so ill. Don't blame your dad. I'm so sorry for worrying you, but when I woke up at Uncle Paul's and they were talking about putting me back in the hospital, I couldn't risk it. I had to sneak away, I had to. And now I've seen the light, you could say. It's time to get back to work, help Marie finish our project. I have new insight into the nature of contemporary global insanity."

Suddenly I heard the owl, not far off, a white blur whoooooshing by the window, like the night I'd ordered the kitchen. The surreal image of Hugo at the window, everything distorted and glowing. The attack.

"Mom, are you sure you're making sense now?"

"Could you put your father on, Sweetie?"

"Sure, Mom. But don't go anywhere, okay?"

There was barely a pause and Hugo said, "Delphine? Are you crazy, running away? We've been frantic, worried to death. Why didn't you tell us? And where in God's name are you now?"

I knew he wouldn't understand, not at first, so I saved my strength. I made myself speak slowly, simply. "I had to go home."

"But *this* is home now, you haven't even seen the house the way Paul fixed it—"

"No, I mean our home, back in civilization, where I still have a job."

"What are you talking about? All of our things are up here. We're here, the boys are on the way, Marc is picking Erik up at the airport in Saskatoon. The plane lands at 2:00 p.m. tomorrow."

"Now *that's* insanity. Are you crazy? For heaven's sake, call them off. You shouldn't have worried them. I'm fine, just fine—I never felt better."

Hugo paused, seemed to consider this. After a moment he said, "You do sound better, more like yourself. So, what happened? The tenants took you in?"

"Not exactly. I'd say they took us both in."

"What do you mean? You're not making sense—"

"I mean they fooled us. They've trashed the main floor, especially the new kitchen, spilled paint everywhere—on the counters, the floors, even dappled those pricey pendant lights. There's no way we could rent to them now."

"But what does it matter? If we're up here—"

"*If* is not an option anymore. Why in the world would you trust them now? You think they'll keep their word, keep up the payments, on a place they've ruined? And speaking of trust, after what you did, after Nasrin and Paul were going to send me back—"

There was silence. Then Hugo said, slowly, "Delphine, listen. You were so ill. We had to do what the doctors recommended. I was terrified, believe you me. But there was no other way."

"Well, imagine it from my perspective." I was suddenly angry, furious. "Really, Hugo, I'm fine. Really I am. I only called so that you'd know I'm safe."

After a few more minutes, I said my goodbyes and set the phone down on the island.

I looked around the house, found blankets in the living room and a pair of clean towels folded on the bathroom shelf. *They must shower after they paint*, I thought wryly. I was glad they were keeping something clean. I fetched my backpack, took the liquid soap from the vanity, and ran myself a nice long hot shower. It felt amazing. The release, the liberation I felt, the sense of being at home in the world—all of that showed me how terrified I'd been, and for such a long time.

Of course I knew that my problems were far from at an end. I would have to face the tenants, if they arrived, and Hugo would likely be at the door before dawn. I towelled off as briskly as I could, ran my fingers through my hair. I always kept it short, but now—well, it was badly in need of a trim. Maybe in the morning I could make an appointment. It was time to re-enter civilization.

Though the warmth and steam followed me from the bathroom, the contrast made the rest of the house seem chilly as I looked for my knapsack. There was an electrician's light hanging from a hook, but I left it off, decided to dress in the dark. I reached into my backpack and pulled out clean panties and jeans and a sweater and pulled them on as quickly as I could. My stomach growled, and I realized with no small surprise that I couldn't remember when I had last eaten.

I was starving.

As I went to the kitchen, before I could look in the cupboards, my mission evaporated: I had to look at my baby, conduct one last inspection. It was all still there, the beautiful bones. I could see the room as it had been and would be again, the warmth of the walnut, the cool of the marble, the elegant countertops, spacious and glowing, everything in its place. Including me.

Surely the forces that had protected me wanted me to see the lesson in everything that had happened. When we'd abandoned this home, it was because IT had called us, I knew IT had. The trickster, the shadow side of spirit. We'd never been frightened away by an attack before; why had I let it happen this time?

Wait—I hadn't let it happen. I had been overcome. Fr. Lewis had had a physical attack of a spiritual nature. Wouldn't an emotional attack be that much more likely? In any case, after I munched down the food from my backpack, I curled up with a blanket on the floor, lulled myself to sleep thinking, *this is where we're meant to be, this work, this place.* The owl had guided me.

As I felt myself drift off, something deep inside said, *But the first owl—the one on the power pole—appeared the night of the attack, the night of the kitchen order—*

I squashed that thought and drifted off to sleep.

44

AS I EXPECTED, Hugo arrived before the low clouds had even thinned to acknowledge the start of a new day. We talked and argued almost until noon, but, in the end, he relented. You couldn't argue with a sign like that, and no matter how many times Paul told us money didn't matter, I'd found the ticket. The winning ticket. I had pulled it from the backpack when I went to pull out my food last night. I must have left it there the day we stopped for gas when we were on the road to the homestead that first time in April. There had been something in the air that day, I'd felt it. But I had completely forgotten; I hadn't even wondered. We were so deep in preparations for our life at the end of the world, it hadn't seemed relevant. When it appeared last night, I checked it on Hugo's phone, just for a lark, and—miracle of miracles—there it was. We had the won the lottery. Not millions, but enough to leave us comfortable for the rest of our lives.

And now we could afford to stay here and figure out a way to rebuild. Travel a bit. Settle the kids. We would buy gifts for Dad, Emma and Geoff and the kids, and Hugo's mother. We couldn't forget the aunts, and Fiona, Marie, Nadine and Stan. Even Paul, if he'd accept. We could invest in good causes, the new green energy, micro-loans for people in far-off countries. We had freedom at last.

"Happy wife, happy life," I heard Hugo tell Paul when he phoned to break the news of our decision, letting him know about our fabulous windfall. I gathered that Paul didn't have much to say, for once, and I could understand this; I was keeping my thoughts to myself, too. I didn't know if I could bring myself to talk to Paul, to tell him how hurt I was that he, of all people, could have tried to send me back to the hospital. I'm sure he sensed the coolness in my words when Hugo relinquished the phone and it was my turn. I decided to keep it simple, just thanked him for all he'd done.

The tenants were out-of-their minds furious, but our lawyer was steadfast, and at last they had no choice but to concede. Our move back to the little acreage left us with plenty to do. Hugo drove around to let the neighbours know we were back. He laid in sacks of steam-rolled oats and alfalfa pellets for the horses, and worked for two days to stack four cords of split birch firewood to season in the shed beside the garage. There was no question that we needed to reclaim our sense of the home place, make it ours again. Even Hugo's mother, a woman known for her staunch kindness, was dumbfounded when we Skyped to show her the damage the tenants had done. She simply said, "At least you like to paint."

Paint we did, and pronto. Now that I knew that it was our forever home, I needed more than ever to perfect it. Gina had finished her exams, and she was so pleased to see me acting like myself, so relieved to find out that all Paul had told her that night had been a mistake, so happy that Hugo and I were speaking again, that she was eager to help me re-feather our little nest. We scoured Humboldt for the latest magazines, haunted the paint departments of Home Hardware and the Timber Mart and Canadian Tire, assembled a nuanced collection of paint chips in inspiring colours. We savoured names like *Deep Lagoon, Country Charm,* and *Spun Silk,* taped the swatches up at strategic points, consulted them in all lights—day and night and in between—considered the effect of sun and moon, lamplight and shadow. When we'd narrowed our choices, we primed the living room walls white, blocked in large squares of sample colours, left generous spaces between. Hugo asked if it would take *forever* to decide, but, for Gina and I, this luxurious deliberation was pure delight, a precious time to reconnect. We knew we wanted to get it right: money or no money, this we meant to last. We wouldn't make a mistake, not this time.

IMPERIAL BLUE HAD THE DEEP DARK BLOOM of a ripe plum. It would be a stunning contrast in the dining room, but such a risk—the small house might feel smaller. *Celtic Sea* was a lively true turquoise, and Hugo's favourite was *Norwegian Fjord,* a complex blue, a hue that somehow read as ultramarine or cerulean, depending on the time of day and the angle of the light.

"Third time's a charm," Gina said, as we readied ourselves to buy the paint.

In the end, we just dove in, embraced our new approach to the old situation. We ordered new metal windows with frames in *Grand Piano,* a glamorous black. All the holes in our salon wall had disappeared under filler and paint, thank-you untenable tenants, so we repainted it *Norwegian Fjord* for Hugo, remapped our artwork on brown paper, painstakingly transferred the markings to the wall. After a two-day session of steaming and removing the damaged wallpaper, soon *Celtic Sea* defined the dining room above freshly painted wainscoting, and a new cream called *Aerial* brought subtle warmth to the walnut in the north-facing kitchen. I selected a faint blush, *Parisian Kiss,* for our south-facing bedroom, while Gina chose *Morning in Rome,* a tint like first light for the loft that would revert to her.

We taped and cut in and rolled for days, just as Mom and I had all those years ago. And Gina and I had all the fun of joking and teasing—even the occasional spat, but we never stayed cross, not for long. When we were done at last, when the brushes had been cleaned, the paint bucket lids hammered on and the pails stored away in the basement, and the canvas drop cloths folded and put away, when the couch and chairs and bookcases had all been set in their new places, the new gallery hung, we backed up, and walked through.

Silence. We were breathless—with dissatisfaction.

The new colours should have looked fresh and hip, though I would have settled for exotic, bohemian. As we gazed around the house, room by room, we had to admit that the effect verged on odd, and not in a good way. Things felt awkward. Our magazines had been full of images of bold contemporary character homes in Toronto and Vancouver and Calgary. We had tried to imitate the look so carefully. In the end, Gina and I agreed on why we failed: we lacked access to the flea markets and second-hand stores that graced even Saskatoon or Edmonton. There were no expensive fabric outlets, no places to buy large rugs at a discount, no textured collectable balls of rattan or sunburst mirrors or Chinese ginger jars in Humboldt, and the second-hand treasures at the Good Neighbour Store had simply failed to meet the bar.

The colours were stunning. That was the problem. Against those strong walls, as never before, our books looked like a scatter of random sizes and mismatched colours. Our faithful furniture looked out of place. And there was interference. While we had been busy prepping, Dandelion had been quietly shredding the corners of the velvet armchairs. Even the tried and true linen sofa looked wretched and lumpy.

How had we not anticipated this?

In the end, Gina and I decided that the familiar universe of things in their previous stations must have drawn the eye away from any one area of distress. After our ruthless editing, the decisive de-cluttering, what should have seemed up-to-the-minute stood not edgy but soulless, all charm or grace fled.

No matter, we told ourselves. It would take time to get

the bespoke look right, that was what all the magazines said. We would restage the rooms, learn to layer beauty on beauty. Gina and I reminded ourselves that we could shop online, and though we gasped at the terrible weakness of the Canadian dollar, we overcame it. We could afford to now.

The kitchen, at least, well, that was magnificent. As I stood there, surrounded by the freshly restored walnut, the lightly veined marble, the gleaming stainless steel, I could hardly believe our luck.

Every time I entered the room, I pinched myself and said, with a little pirouette, "I live here."

45

A WEEK BEFORE CHRISTMAS, Gina was in town visiting friends, and Hugo and I were relaxing, propped up with an army of cushions on the brand new sofa, taking in the sun that streamed through the south living room window. Hugo was, as always, gentle. He stroked my cheek and said, "You'll have to forgive Paul, sooner or later. I bet one day you'll find you want to. It wasn't his fault we were going to take you back to the hospital. He was just trying to do what was right for you. He was the one who made me take you out of the hospital, against doctor's orders. Of course, you won't remember much. The resident insisted that they had to keep you on the meds; he wouldn't budge, even for Nasrin. He told us we could discuss your treatment with the staff doctor at rounds on Monday morning. Paul knew it was making you worse."

I felt wary. The sun was so nice. I'd rather not have talked about any of it, but Hugo was insistent, said I had to hear the story some time. I confessed, "I recall bits and pieces, but so much is scrambled, I can't find a through line."

Hugo smiled. "Well, it was quite the dilemma for us. When Nasrin came back from her holiday in Iran, you had been in the hospital for more than three weeks. And you weren't any better. She finally agreed to drive up and see you, give a second opinion, though she was reluctant to intervene because she wasn't the admitting physician. When she saw you, she asked, 'How are you, my dear? We'll soon have everything fixed for you,' and you almost gave the secret away." He pinched me lightly, and continued, "You just looked up and said, 'Oh, yes, the place will be glorious. Don't worry. Gorgeous house. The butler will ring the dressing gong soon. Windmills and solar panels. Views of the creek and everything—' before we could cut you off. The resident seemed to think you were just rambling, but Paul tensed up and was trying to figure out a way to stop you before you revealed anything else about the homestead. I hadn't even considered that when I agreed to admit you."

"So what did you do?" I asked, sipping my latte.

Hugo was careful. "When we stepped out in the hall-way, Nasrin told me you were not well at all, and that we would have to wait and see what the staff psychiatrist said on Monday. I was disappointed, of course, but deep down I was—at least in part—relieved to think you were in a place where you'd be safe, where you would get the help you so clearly needed. It was terrifying to see you manic. After they admitted you, you seemed so sick, so muddled and confused, and all I could think about was how to help you, how to make you *you* again. It was such a relief to finally talk to Nasrin, someone who knew you, to have her confirm that what I had done was actually for the best."

I felt angry all over again. "For whose best? I would never have done that to you." I sat quietly for a moment, and Hugo just hugged me more tightly; the last thing either of us wanted was another argument. "So what happened?"

"I walked Nasrin to the security gate, and by the time I

got back to your room, whatever relief I felt had disappeared completely. You were struggling to keep your mouth closed as the nurse tried to feed you, and you were working yourself into a fury. I can't tell you how scared I was, but Paul was a rock—he wasn't put off at all, just offered to try. She was more than happy to let him take over." Hugo paused. He shifted as he confessed, "I was desperate. I told Paul I couldn't watch you like that anymore. I said I'd go get the truck, brush it off and warm it up—"

"I remember that, or I think I do. Paul just said, 'Now Del. Looks like the chef has sent up chicken and taters and gravy. I'll have a bite, and then you can have one.' He was so calm, let me eat at my own pace. And then, after I was full, he helped me out of bed, led me to the bathroom, and gave me a moment. Then he led me back, drew the curtains, and helped me on with the things he must have liberated from my locker."

Hugo said, "Yes, when I came back to tell him that the weather was really ramping up, the drapes around the bed were already drawn. I thought the nurses must be doing something to you. I waited a few minutes, and then—"

"I remember how angry you looked! I'd never seen you like that."

Hugo said, "Yes, you were dressed, and Paul was combing your hair. He had the nerve to shush me. I was livid. I tried to stop him, telling him what Nasrin had said, but he just got you up, kept you walking. He told me, 'I've seen this before, from the other side. They're not going to change her meds. Nasrin can see it—and so can I.'

"I told him Nasrin wouldn't sign you out, that we had to defer to her experience. You needed real help, I told him, and it wasn't as if we could call 911 from the homestead, not if we didn't want to blow our cover." Hugo shook his head.

I asked how Paul had finally convinced him to sign me out.

"He told me he'd had lots of time to get to know the little crew on the ward that afternoon while I was talking to the doctors. One patient's husband told him about her electroconvulsive therapy. Said his wife had had it before, but always lost her memory, didn't know who her own kids were, had to relearn her own family. He said it had saved her, she'd stopped trying to kill herself, didn't get so depressed. But what if they tried it on you? Your memory is your life. You weren't suicidal—at least, you hadn't been. Sure enough there was another woman over in the second bed who had tried to kill herself three times since she'd been admitted. The nurses took everything away, every shoelace and compact mirror, for heaven's sake, but somehow she'd always find something. She was put in that room of four—well, of three—so the others would watch her. The last bed was empty because the patient had just been moved to solitary for trying to stab a nurse with a shiv made from a toothbrush."

Hugo stroked my face, turned it up to his. "That was terrifying enough, but still I wasn't convinced. But Paul said if it was stress that caused your breakdown, how would you get better in a place like that? And after I thought about that, it didn't take long. I had to agree."

He paused.

"By the time we reached the parking lot, all of the cars were covered in inches of fluffy, fairy-tale snow. You laughed and played as it fell on your mittens, but Paul was worried about the roads. I sat on the passenger side, holding you as you chatted about the pretty flakes hitting the windshield. 'Ballet weather,' you called it. 'Swan Lake.' Paul somehow found the turn to the homestead from the highway through all the snow. But right at the turn he spotted a car in the ditch, flashers blinking, the driver still in the car."

Hugo continued, "All I could say was, 'Christ—what now! How can we stop?' but Paul had already slowed down and was squinting at the car. 'Should make sure she's okay,' he said. He pulled over, set the flashers blinking. Then he looked again and said, 'Hold on. That's Nasrin.'"

"I don't remember that. I must have zonked out again."

Hugo nodded and told me the rest. While Paul got out of the truck to check on Nasrin and her car, Hugo hoped that the darkness would conceal me. He was so relieved that I was peaceful at last, it was hard to believe I was ill at all, except that I had no idea what was going on. While we waited, we listened to soft music on the radio, and Hugo listened for the weather report. Sure enough, the announcer said there was a storm coming up out of Montana and the highway south of Wakaw was closed. There'd be no getting back to Humboldt that night. Nasrin was lucky that Paul had seen her, but how would we get her to keep the secret?

Paul had opened the door to the truck and said, "Prepare yourself, Hugo. The highway is closed. Have to bring her home with us. Can't hurt to have her there when Delphine comes around, in any case."

I shuddered, remembering—those were the very words I'd heard that first day at the homestead. They'd seemed so odd then.

Hugo didn't seem to notice my distraction. "In minutes he was helping Nasrin inside, and she was exclaiming, 'Oh, no! What are you thinking? Do they know you've taken her?'

"'Well, yes ma'am, they know. Quite the squabble,' Paul told her. 'But in the end they agreed we could sign her out against medical advice, since Hugo was the one who sent her.'

"Nasrin said, 'But they won't help you if she does not recover and needs to be admitted again. And what about her medication? She's still feeling the effects of the sedation, but when she wakes up—?'" Hugo fell silent.

We both knew the answer to Nasrin's question.

46

THROUGHOUT DECEMBER, Hugo tried not to fuss, but I could see that he was worried that I might relapse. One of the articles he found online said that playing the memory game could help patients find their feet again, make sense of a breakdown, weave it into the narrative of their lives. He chose his moments when he could. One afternoon Gina was in town Christmas shopping so we settled in, watching Lucky doze in the oh-so-glorious sun. I wanted to talk about anything but mental illness. "We used to reminisce about my co-op year in Sweden, the lovely times we flirted our way through all those museums and cafés—the Blå Porten's famous spread of desserts—that medieval table—"

"The bracing walks by the sea," he said wistfully.

I was sorry to make him homesick, sorry to cause him any kind of distress, so I changed the subject. "Remember our first house, that summer in Edmonton? Remember?

Now that was memorable weather. I was rolling a soothing shade of pale peach in the kitchen."

"To match the vinyl paper we were going to put up that evening. The family that can wallpaper together...."

We fell into an old pattern, talking over top of one another. "Erik and Marc were playing with baby Gina in the living room, turning huge appliance boxes from the store into submarines, decorating them with giant blue wax crayon octopuses and tiny pink whales and lime green starfish."

Hugo corrected me. "Well, the boys were drawing and Gina was crawling around with a plastic pail and a shovel. As I recall, I was to make sure she didn't EAT the crayons."

"Sounds about right. Lost in the land of domestic bliss, tracking the price of paint and pickled herring. You and Dad kept track of all global uncertainties."

"We were almost finished working our way through grad school," Hugo said. "Now that was some weather."

Black Friday, July 31. Who could forget? I had been painting and he was on the sofa, half watching the kids, half reading the newspaper, from time to time calling out details about the perils of foreign investment. We had no reason to be afraid of the weather, not in Edmonton. Not in Canada. Well, we had no *idea*. Oh, there'd been fierce storms every night for a week, each day hotter than the last and all so incredibly humid. Then the lightning started to flash non-stop and the wind drove rain in every direction. We had every one of the windows open to help clear the heat. The thick black belly of the sky was so low I couldn't see anything out to the east but clouds rolling and rolling, illuminated as if by some giant strobe light. We weren't worried, of course. We loved it. Then the neighbour phoned to tell us to turn on the radio, and the tornado warning came on. I just tossed my painting tools into plastic bags and we headed to the basement. When the "all clear" was given an hour later and we returned upstairs, it was to find shreds of plastic bags and torn paper and tangles of shredded pink insulation all through the yard, festooning our prize vegetable patch—even then we didn't get it.

"Twenty-seven people dead," Hugo said, shaking his head.

"Most of them just three miles from our house as the crow flew, if a crow could fly in a tornado, which, of course, it could not."

"And even after that, people still wouldn't believe in climate change."

I admitted, "Life in general always seemed a bit surreal in the 90s." We had tap-danced pretty fast as sessionals, teaching as many sections as we could find, rarely pondered the secrets of the universe in those days. There was simply no energy to do so.

Hugo smiled. "We translated all our free time into buying good-enough houses. What did we call it? 'Reimagining them.'"

"That was the euphemism I used to keep you on board, keep you from thinking about how hard it all was." How many times had we shampooed rugs or ripped them out entirely to sand and stain old maple floors, apply paint and wallpaper in pleasing tints, plant perennials and shrubs, fix the dog-patches in lawns?

"Ah, but we always made money. We were good at it. And I made sure that Erik and Marc and Gina helped, knew the satisfaction of all that hard work," Hugo said, smiling.

"Yes, you taskmaster!" I swatted at him. "But they're pretty great kids, even if they do come from a house of child exploitation."

"Remember that avocado bathroom in the Woodcroft house? The price rose by $20,000.00, the agent told us, just because we installed new white fixtures and tile."

"But we never did a kitchen." I shook my head.

"No, we never did a kitchen—not until now. No matter how you badgered me." He gave me a little shove.

I shoved back. "And when the kids started spending all their time with their friends, that's when you finally got bored with fixing up forty-year old split-levels or semi-bungalows."

"What we needed was a challenge. And then Fiona told you about Saskatchewan—"

"And the rest, as they say, is history."

"Or herstory."

Hugo patted my hand, and Lucky, ever the opportunist, heard the sound and stood up, coming over to be petted.

The sun had slipped away, and the light was low in the west instead. We didn't even notice that the sofa where we sat had grown cold in the shadows.

47

CHRISTMAS EVE.

Erik stomped his boots on the mat at the back door, his arms full of split birch logs, the papery bark as bright against his black wool coat as the snowflakes were in his dark hair. His eyes relaxed when he saw me watching him from the corner of the kitchen. I smiled. "That'll make for a nice fire. Thank you, Erik. You look so rustic—it suits you!"

"Well," he smiled, hoisting the load with his left arm, freeing his right hand to brush the snow away, "the pace out here is nice. Relaxing. Perhaps all my schooling has been for nought. Can't see much of a need for an architect out here."

"Honey! You know that I meant it—"

"As a compliment. I know. And all the best people take to the hills when the going gets easy." He grinned as he climbed the stairs towards me.

"Don't forget that I brought everybody back to civilization."

"If you call this civilization," he smiled. "Yes, you did. I'm proud of you. The Pied Piper."

"And the rats…?"

"The rats placed the midnight call to Montreal saying you'd disappeared, the RCMP couldn't be told, all hands needed on deck…Seriously, it was pretty frightening, Mom. You terrified us, all of us. That was quite the risk you took." He was standing beside me, and I had to glance up to try to read his expression. I hadn't had a chance to discuss my illness with either of the boys, not yet. They'd only arrived a half-hour before and I wanted to wait until just the right time. Hugo and Gina would need to be part of the discussion, of course.

For the moment, I hurried on. "It was all a misunderstanding, Honey. I'm sure they've told you I had a bad reaction to the medicine."

Erik frowned and opened his mouth, but I cut back in. "I was incredibly stressed. Your father couldn't know." I had to change the subject. "And Stan said the other day that within fifty years, people will have medications tailored to their genetic makeup. No more trial and error. Or maybe we'll consult mystics when we have a crisis, not exhausted first-year residents."

To my surprise, Erik took the bait, switched the topic. "Fifty years…does he really think that?"

"What?"

"Does he think we still have fifty years?"

"Well, not Dad and I, of course, but you, your children—"

"Mom, some scientists are predicting that climate change will be severe in twenty years, with devastation in thirty. You know it's bad when the International Monetary Fund is calling for action," he said wryly.

What could I say to that? We just looked at one another. But we didn't have time to get into that discussion, either, as Marc and Gina were calling up from the back door.

"Who's having children? Something you've been keeping from us, Brother?" Marc teased as he hung his jacket up on a hook. "Devastation in thirty minutes?"

And it was amazing to watch how Erik handled his stress, like our moment had never happened. He just said, "Mom, hide the cookies. The monsters are here," and he grabbed the plate of *pepparkakor* from the island, dodged behind it, balanced the plate high in the air on one hand like some waiter in a fancy restaurant. The others rushed up the stairs and chased after him, but he had no trouble evading them. He had plenty of practice with this kind of battle.

"Hey! Who said you could start without us?" Gina laughed. "Seriously, aren't they delicious? I helped Dad make them."

"They're GRRREAT," Marc said, his "r" a-rolling. He helped himself after Erik had lowered the plate and passed it around. "SEEERRRIOUSLY great. We should get this party started. Where's the nog? And the rum? Or did Dad really make *glögg* this year?"

Before long, we were all gathered in the living room around the cosy fire in the old woodstove. The boys had brought some stylishly wrapped big-city gifts, and Gina and I had kept Canada Post and UPS busy with our online purchases. With the arrival of the money, my need for solitude, my drive for simplicity, had almost completely evaporated, and we had refurbished the entire house. The forlorn old sofa was gone, as were the tattered chairs, and in their place the clean lines of mid-century pieces gave the space a chic Scandi vibe. Hugo arrived back from town just as we were passing the photo album around, looking at pictures of all the years back in Edmonton, neighbourhood after neighbourhood of friends, house after house, the five of us in our signature poses: for every *before* photo we brandished hammers and crowbars, and in every *after* we were dressed to the nines, artfully arranged like glamorous models, in every impeccable room.

"And there's Aunt Emma," Gina exclaimed. "And Grandpa Boudreau."

"Where?" I asked, puzzled. "I don't recall any pictures of them in the reveals."

"No, not in the album. They're here. At the back door!"

Janey and Ewan stepped inside and Lucky went wild; he couldn't stop barking and wagging. He was so excited, licking their faces. It seemed like years since we had seen them. I couldn't believe how grown up they were, and there was Dad, seemingly no older, still spry as he had been a full twenty years ago. As I hugged him tightly, I teased, "Where's the painting, Dorian Gray?" and then I saw Geoff still standing on the porch, looking as jolly as if he were Santa Claus himself, his arms full of bags and presents. I squeezed my way through to the door, ushered him in, and, for a moment, we all crowded around, hugging and greeting one another. Hugo took an armload of coats and tossed them onto our bed, emptying the hooks for the newcomers. Erik and Marc helped the guests off with their outdoor clothing and Gina led them to the living room.

Soon we were all seated by the fire, drinks in hand, laughing and talking. I hadn't expected them to arrive for another half-hour, but the food was almost ready. The new double ovens had made cooking a delight. Gina and Hugo and I had chopped and stirred and whisked our way through all of the Boudreau family favourites and an impressive array of the Almquist specialties, too: juicy roast goose and tender venison, spiced ham and rollmops and gravad lox, potatoes dauphinoise, candied yams, and our own home-grown slow-roasted root vegetables, beets and turnips, carrots and ruta-bagas. Thanks to Emma and Gina, we even had a decadent display of thirteen desserts. It was French tradition, they assured me, and who was I to argue? The island and counters overflowed with treats. We had eggnog or wassail for the children, and spiced *glögg*, cognac, aquavit, and elderberry liqueur for the adults. Geoff smiled when Hugo drew the bottle of Crown Royal from the deep purple bag he handed him.

"Now this will go nicely in the dining room," he said, lining up the glasses.

Laughing and joking, we filled our plates and glasses,

and settled around the low table in the living room to toast
the miracle of family.

48

WE HAD CLEARED MOST OF THE DISHES AWAY and were in the thick of the 1998 edition of *Trivial Pursuit* when the lamps went black and the Vienna Boys' Choir ceased in mid-carol. It was a bit of a surprise, especially for the city slickers. Hugo and I were used to brownouts on the acreage. The power went off once or twice a month, sometimes for minutes, other times for hours, but it was rarely a bother. That night it meant that the kids wouldn't be able to use their cell phones, no more googling those tricky questions, but we knew we could make do, go old school, pull out the print dictionary or the encyclopedia or rescue the stacks of *National Geographic* from under the bed. It was still early in the evening—plenty of time for a repair.

The clouds had cleared off after sunset, and we knew that meant the house might get chilly by the time the power stuttered on again. Hugo had made sure we had plenty of birch split for the occasion, and really there was no heat like a wood fire to keep the living room and the master bedroom cosy. At least we hadn't lapsed into darkness. The little house was alight with the soft glow of red and white candles, not to mention the flickering flames in the woodstove. The gentle light and crackling fire made things more intimate, Christmasier, if there was such a word. It was perfect.

I said my thank-you to the universe that the power hadn't failed before the food was cooked. Hugo, always calm, hauled out the old enamel coffeepot and set to work, joining in as we laughed and joked and finished our meal. For the rest of the evening, we grazed our way through the desserts and set up games of *Yahtzee* and *Risk* and *Stock Ticker*. I looked over at Emma's bright red hair and remembered the times that she and Paul and I had put puzzles together by kerosene lamplight at the lake, or played crib or hearts or crazy eights with our friends from the other cottages. Mom would sip her coffee and visit with the mothers while we joked and teased and laughed with one another, game after game. The hurt feelings that arose from time to time were swiftly settled with Girl Guide cookies and cocoa, or a trip outdoors to light a fire, roast marshmallows, and sing camp songs. When Paul was there, he teased Dad to break out the violin and he joined him on the harmonica he'd learned to play God-Knows-Where.

At the thought of Paul, I suddenly wished he had come after all. He shouldn't be alone, not at Christmas. When he said he needed to stay on the homestead, tend to the animals, I didn't try to change his mind. He must have known I hadn't found a way to forgive him yet. I found hardest to accept that he, of all people, with his experience, his first-hand knowledge of what I was going through, for God's sake, could have been so ready to send me back to the hospital that day when Nasrin had proposed it.

I knew, because Hugo had reminded me, that Paul was the one who talked him into having me released, and that he had been willing to act against medical advice. How quickly he'd lost faith after that though. He just gave up, even when Hugo wasn't ready to. How much of that fine brotherly instinct was designed to protect his precious secret instead of me?

"Mom, it's your turn. Roll!" Erik and Gina were always the most ferocious combatants. Marc was rarely competitive, like Hugo, but the other two were sharks, calculating the odds for every single throw. I blew into the cup, shook it as hard as I could, and the dice sprayed across the table. Three fives, a two and a three. I ignored the cries for "small straight, small straight" and tossed the two and the three back in the cup. The next toss was disappointing, a one and a two. I took a swig of my *glögg*; this was my last throw. I shook as hard as I could while the other players chanted, "Five, Five, FIVE!" and the dice tumbled free.

We were all screaming "YAHTZEE!" when Marc cocked his head and said, "Hey! I think someone's at the door." Lucky started barking and running in circles, nearly thrashing the cups off the coffee table with his tail.

I pulled myself up to standing, threaded through the living room and down to the back door, but there was no one there. I saw fresh large footprints in the snow. I jumped into Hugo's big boots and ran down the porch steps. As I cornered the house, I saw Stan, getting back into his truck. I yelled for him to come back while Hugo pulled down the heavy rug that hung over the inside of the front door to preserve the warmth. Soon the rest of the party was calling out the front to Stan, and he shyly trudged back again. He waved to the group as he took the path around the house. "Tradesman's entrance," he called. Everyone else went back to the games and I went to the porch to let him in.

"When I saw the yardlight off," he said, as I took his coat and hung it up. "I thought you might have gone to your brother's, or to Edmonton." He handed me a bottle of wine and a present, both wrapped in cloth and festooned with twists of white ribbon.

"We're so pleased you stopped by, Stan. The power went out not too long ago, but we've lots to eat and drink, and the kids are doing their best to whip us at the traditional Christmas *Yahtzee*. You'll be able to meet everyone. I'm always telling them you're a prophet."

He frowned as we walked into the living room. "There's a risk of losing your head that comes with that job description. I don't know if I'm up for that." Soon he was surrounded by the family as Hugo introduced him to the rest of the crowd. I poured him a drink and got out a plate, heaped it high with anything I thought he might like. After he finished his meal, he and Geoff and Dad stowed themselves safely away from the game, on the soft new sofa, to discuss politics.

All through the evening, Hugo had been quietly excusing himself now and then to feed the fire, but by ten o'clock, he decided it needed to burn down. With so many people, the room was actually becoming too warm. Despite the full moon, the clear sky was lit far and wide by a stupendous display of northern lights. When I glanced out the window at the thermometer, it read -31, five degrees colder than the hour before. I wanted to show Janey and Ewan the miracle of high pressure out here, away from the city lights, and I took them over to the north window. The moon on the soft snow looked for all the world like some museum diorama, each flake glittering, so perfectly fluffed and sparkly, while the aurora borealis flowed and rippled in greens and crimson above.

All the kids wanted to go outside for a better look, and before long, most of us had donned coats and boots and traipsed outside to lie on our backs in the snow and take in the full view, if only for a few minutes. The coyotes obliged, and soon we were all silent, the eerie trills racketing around us.

The sound made me nervous, though it never had before, and I took my flock back inside. But Hugo had no idea I was thinking of the attack. He set his telescope for Dad and Stan and Geoff. With all the traffic in and out of the house, the room had cooled off quite a bit, so I tossed some thin shreds of bark onto the embers to draw back the flames. Emma and

I decided to get everyone singing Christmas carols. Erik and Marc grinned, looked at one another, and started off together with Weird Al Yankovic's "Christmas at Ground Zero."

I was horrified, even more so that Janey and Ewan knew the words. What hope was there when the end of the world seemed funny to children? I tried to shush them but Dad pointed out that Emma and Paul and I always sang "We Have Seen the Glory of the Burning of the School" whenever Mom set off a box of fireworks. As a teacher, even a former one, he hadn't been too thrilled about that.

"Kids will be kids," he told me. So, reluctantly, I let them have their fun—and sure enough, as soon as I stopped protesting, they switched to "Douglas Mountain," and we were back thinking about happy times.

As much fun as we were having, it was late, and I started to feel weary. Emma looked worn out, too. She and I quietly cleaned up. We stacked the dessert plates and gathered the empty glasses, and navigated by flashlight as we made our way back to the kitchen. When we'd filled the dishwasher, we set the remainder in the sink and thanked God for the acres of new countertop.

Erik and Gina and Marc helped Hugo figure out the sleeping arrangements. The original plan had been to let the young people sleep in the basement bedrooms, and to put Emma and Geoff in Gina's loft room. Since the power was still out, we settled everyone in sleeping bags and quilts throughout the living room, except Dad, who was to sleep in the master bedroom with the door open to draw the heat from the woodstove. Stan decided to go home, but as he stood by the back door, pulling on his boots, he said, "Maybe you should open that gift I brought you, Delphine. It might want a bit of explanation."

49

I UNTIED THE RIBBON to reveal a gorgeous cover, a charming photo of the young Walter Benjamin. *Selected Writings*, Volume 1. I had read it long ago, at the library in Edmonton. I knew it included *Einbahnstraßße*, my first word of German, *One-Way Street*, Benjamin's prescient warning written in 1923, that "the only limit beyond which things cannot progress is annihilation." Stan had never seemed to understand me the way Fr. Lewis did but the book was perfect for me. I loved mystics and Benjamin in particular.

I was stunned.

The volume fell open at the bookmark, a fierce photo of a dark violet sky split by forks of lightning, bearing a saying about Kafka, of all people, another of my favourites: "Once he was certain of eventual failure, everything worked out for him *en route* as in a dream."

What failure? Kafka's name reminded me of how Nasrin had warned me that I seemed to be undergoing a metamorphosis. Reading it, I felt absolutely bewildered. Yes, things had seemed dreamy—but failure?

"Fr. Lewis asked me to give this to you when you were most in need," Stan said. "That time is now."

I was baffled and desperate to avoid becoming embroiled in one of our lengthy metaphysical discussions, no matter how much I enjoyed them. Honestly, the man must be out of his mind. I tried not to hurry him away, so I simply thanked him.

He continued, "Ask yourself why the attack would end when you still have all the same wants. Nothing has changed, except now you're separated from your vision—and your visionary."

"What attack? You told me all our bad luck was coincidence."

"And all the time I was praying, *let it go easy on her.*" He looked away then back at me wryly, changed somehow, as if he were suddenly channelling Fr. Lewis.

"I couldn't tell you what was happening. As the prophet said, if you had known the peril that was inside you, the fear would have killed you. But all the time I was herding you, trying to make you see the source of the danger.

"It's always been so simple, as Fr. Lewis told you: *just stop looking at the pictures.* That story you told me about the lake, the one that took possession of you when we were talking about spiritual attacks. You told me you *felt* comfortable when the wasp nest was inches from your knees."

I was trying to digest what he was saying. "Remember what it means to want, to be found wanting." He went to shake my hand but I pulled him in close for a quick hug. There was nothing left to say. I opened the door, and he set off into the moonlit yard, crisscrossed as it was with all our tracks, our snow angels, our endless to*ing* and fro-*ing*. I watched him, wondering why I suddenly felt calm. His truck's engine turned over after a little protest, and he revved it for a few minutes. Soon he was down the driveway and out on the grid. I stood there, trying to digest what he'd said. He really was so strange.

I watched him turn onto the highway and then he was lost in the traffic, dissolved in the rush of people travelling for Christmas. I closed the door and rejoined my family.

50

WHEN HUGO AND I AWOKE the next morning, every muscle was stiff and sore, even the ones we had forgotten we had. "Some homesteaders," I whispered, as we raised ourselves up on our elbows and glanced around the room at our guests. They looked so uncomfortable, Emma and Geoff draped with quilts and stretched out in easy chairs and footstools, the kids in sleeping bags on the floor. The living room had stayed pleasantly warm all night, but once we left the living room, when we stepped out beyond the reach of the woodstove, the house was freezing cold.

The power was still off?

I heard a rustle and glanced behind me. Emma, tousle-headed and rumpled, had joined us. "Merry Christmas!" she whispered, and the three of us huddled together in a group hug. It was so good to be together.

Something was nagging at me.

I tried to reason it away. We had plenty of 5-gallon jugs of drinking water set by; for nature's needs, there were the chamber pots and the outhouse, and though it would be bitterly cold, that set-up would do; we had plenty of food, and even though the refrigerator was off, everything would be well-chilled, to put it mildly. Hugo had drained the pipes in the kitchen. Yes, we could make do, we had made do, and surely this was not a serious disruption. It was Christmas, after all. The crews would be making mountains of overtime.

I was thinking of Paul. We couldn't even phone to tell him why we hadn't phoned.

And then it came to me: I *could* embrace my failure. "What do you think, Em? After all the fun we're having, just thinking about him all alone up there makes me feel guilty. Having the whole fam-dam-ily for Christmas *was* his idea."

Hugo and Emma exchanged glances, but I couldn't read them. Hugo looked away, then his eyes met mine, and he asked, "How do you feel about going back up there? You're not scared?"

Emma was watching me. I wondered what the problem was. At last I got it, and said, "Scared? It's not him that frightens me. As long as you two promise not to pack me off to the psych ward, everything will be hunky-dory, just copasetic."

"The kids would love it," Emma said. She turned to Geoff, who was quietly standing by the kitchen sink. "What say you, husband?"

"Another roadtrip? Works for me. Maybe Paul has electricity."

Hugo paused, then nodded and smiled with something that could have been relief.

I leaned through into the hallway and called, "Hello! Dessert for breakfast!" In minutes we had the platters of food spread out on the kitchen island. I pulled out the paper plates—there was no point in saving them for the end of the world. The one thing we wouldn't have to do today was wash dishes. And after we'd all feasted on leftovers, Hugo helped me pack the rest of the food to take with us.

Hugo still seemed a little nervous. "I did feel guilty thinking about him, all alone, but won't it be unfair to descend on him like this, en masse? And won't we look like fools?"

I smiled. "*I* will, but I've earned my discomfort. And all will proceed as if in a dream."

HE WAS STANDING ON THE NEW VERANDA, leaning against the railing, watching the road south when our little convoy pulled in. The whole journey, our entrance, had felt surreal. The radio had been dead all morning, even Sirius, but we hadn't panicked. The cell phones were useless, stoplights were off, traffic was heavy. There was nowhere to gas up, no electricity meant the gas wouldn't pump, but we'd filled up on Christmas Eve. There was no way to warn Paul of our intentions, so we were especially relieved to locate the homestead. And him looking as pleased as ever we'd seen him, though not one smidgen surprised. He knew we would come.

The young people made sure there was ample hooting of horns and waving of arms out vehicle windows, and before long we had all spilled out. It was still definitely on the cold side, and Hugo hurried us to get Dad inside, unload our things and settle everyone. The young folk joked and teased and they carried in most of the luggage and the food. Emma and Geoff went to Paul first. They chatted, and he waved at the new home next door to ours. Janey and Ewan ran ahead while Geoff and Emma made their way to see what Paul had readied for them.

At last I walked over to where Paul was still standing, on the wraparound porch, and gave him an enormous hug. When we tried to speak, it turned out that there were no words to say. We were at peace.

He just led the way inside. It was the first time I'd seen the house from Watson since before I was ill. Fear flooded back as I entered the porch, the expectation of darkness and chill. But this time, despite the best efforts of the Artic vortex, the little room was warm. The separator and the cream cans were still there, but the space was transformed, the floorboards bright with trapezoids of sun.

Inside the house proper, too, everything was clean and tidy. Paul had dressed the rooms with the relics from the cottage, and when I took this in, suddenly, inconceivably, at last I felt perfect ease. My eyes, always so obsessed with colour and line and texture, rested with pure pleasure on the stiff old wooden chairs, their worn leather seats padded, held on with ancient upholstery tacks, the thick wire twisted to reinforce the frames. I spied the old vinyl couch, the one you had to prop up with books to keep level when it folded out to make an extra bed. The spring-frame bunks. The old-fashioned easy chairs from Mom and Dad's first home. I walked into the living room, my thoughts singing.

Out the south window, Marc and Gina and Erik stood backlit on the deck, their hair suffused with light, palms held high. The sun was overhead. As I looked around, I realized that there must have been incredible fog to create this effect. What had Fiona said about Fr. Lewis, what he had said the fog meant? Each nub and twig stood articulated against a piercing blue sky, so thickly bristled in white, some careful hand might have set each crystal in place *as a sign of victory*, I thought I heard Fr. Lewis say. I felt more relaxed than ever I could remember. Hugo came up behind me, rested one hand on my waist, pointed the other over my shoulder.

The first chickadee found them, flitted lightly from one offering to the other. I could see my children's faces bright with pleasure. In the distance, down near the creek, my father was walking with Paul, in a pair of his boots, two sizes too big.

This time the voice was unmistakable. I could hear my mother say,

All dreams have but a single destination.
Home.

ACKNOWLEDGEMENTS

My thinking in *Want* has been influenced by several mystics, most directly Fr. James Gray, OSB; Teresa of Avila; and Rumi. My character Fr. Lewis says, "what we seek seeks us" (43), reworking the Rumi commonplace, "What you seek is seeking you." I drew specifically on *The Essential Rumi*, translated by Coleman Barks, for Stan's treatment of Delphine: when she wants to know if she is under spiritual attack (*Want* 21-24), Stan knows the story of the holy man who sees a snake enter a sleeping man's mouth (Rumi 202-03). Instead of telling the victim what has happened, the holy man chases him and forces him to eat rotten apples so that he vomits up the snake. This is what Stan does for Delphine: he is rough on her but doesn't tell her of her initial danger, yet later, when she is within reach of safety, he does what the holy man does: he admits that she has been under attack, and tells her that if she had known the danger she faced, she would have died of fear, and all the time he has been praying, "let it go easy on her" (*Want* 240).

Enormous thanks go to the Saskatchewan Arts Board, who funded that formative experience with Sandra Birdsell, fabulous mentor, when I wrote the first draft of *Want* through the Humber School for Writers. Tremendous thanks, too, go to Palimpsest Press for their unwavering vision and generosity: especially Aimee Parent Dunn, editor and publisher, and Ginger Pharand, copy editor. I am so grateful to Kate Hargreaves for the stunning design, and to Abigail Roelens for the fine publicity.

I can never repay the kindness of all those who gave me courage: Al and Elizabeth Harms, Shawna Lemay, Anne McDonald, Tracy Hamon, Jeanette Lynes, Elizabeth Greene, dennis cooley, Annemarie Buchmann-Gerber, David Carpenter, Dave Margoshes, Elaine Hulse, Val Koroluk, Sylvia Legris, Guy Vanderhaeghe, Joanna Lilley, and Br. Kurt Van Kuren, OSB. Last but never least, my deepest thanks go to my family: Maureen and Reno; Hildi and Fred; Matthew, Angela, Beth, and Owen; Rosie and Rudy; Michael and all the crew. You are my home.

Born and educated in Edmonton, AB, BARBARA LANGHORST teaches writing and literature at St. Peter's College in Muenster, SK. Her first book, *Restless White Fields* (NeWest 2012), won Poetry Book of the Year Awards in Alberta and Saskatchewan. *Want* is her debut novel. She lives in Humboldt, SK.